I0819409

Mouthwatering Praise for Nancy Coco's Mysteries

THREE FUDGES AND A BABY

"Suspects are ultimately uncovered and problems solved in a delightful cozy larded with appetizing fudge recipes."

—***Kirkus Reviews***

"Readers will be carried along with Allie and her investigations by the swift plot that leads to a reveal sure to surprise even the most experienced puzzle-solving mystery expert."

—***Kings River Life***

GIVE FUDGE A CHANCE

"An enjoyable character-driven whodunit that mixes murder with a touch of romance and the requisite sweet treats."

—***Kirkus Reviews***

A MIDSUMMER NIGHT'S FUDGE

"Charming characters and settings make for a pleasant stop before trying your hand at the fudge recipes."

—***Kirkus Reviews***

HAVE YOURSELF A FUDGY LITTLE CHRISTMAS

"Two nasty murders, charming surviving characters, plenty of Christmas cheer, and enough fudge recipes for a major sugar rush."

—***Kirkus Reviews***

DEATH BEE COMES HER

"Personable characters and lots of honey lore."

—***Kirkus Reviews***

"Sprinkled with delightful notes on honey and its various uses, this debut novel in the Oregon Honeycomb Mystery series is a fun introduction to a new cozy series. Everett, the Havana Brown cat, is an animal delight, often proving to be smarter than the humans around him."

—***Criminal Element***

"The author writes a captivating story with interesting characters. Naturally, Everett [the cat] contributes to the solution. A charming read."

—Reviewingtheevidence.com

"This warmhearted book is fast paced, with realistic dialogue and a captivating plot."

—Mystery and Suspense Magazine

FUDGE BITES

"An easy romantic read complete with fudge recipes that make it even sweeter."

—Kirkus Reviews

FOREVER FUDGE

"Nancy Coco paints us a pretty picture of this charming island setting where the main mode of transportation is a horse-drawn vehicle. She also gives us a delicious mystery complete with doses of her homemade fudge . . . a perfect read!"

—Wonder Women Sixty

OH, FUDGE!

"*Oh, Fudge!* is a charming cozy, the sixth in the Candy-Coated Mystery series. But be warned: There's a candy recipe at the end of each chapter, so don't read this one when you're hungry!"

—Suspense Magazine

OH SAY CAN YOU FUDGE

"Beautiful Mackinac Island provides the setting for a puzzling series of crimes. Now that Allie McMurphy has taken over her grandparents' hotel and fudge shop, life on Mackinac is good, although her little dog, Mal, does tend to nose out trouble. . . . Allie's third offers plenty of plausible suspects and mouthwatering fudge recipes."

—Kirkus Reviews

TO FUDGE OR NOT TO FUDGE

"*To Fudge or Not to Fudge* is a superbly crafted, classic, culinary cozy mystery. If you enjoy them as much as I do, you are in for a real treat."

—**Examiner.com (5 stars)**

"A five-star delicious mystery that has great characters, a good plot, and a surprise ending. If you like a good mystery with more than one suspect and a surprise ending, then rush out to get this book and read it, but be sure you have the time, since once you start, you won't want to put it down."

—***Mystery Reading Nook***

"A charming and funny culinary mystery that parodies reality-show competitions and is led by a sweet heroine, eccentric but likable characters, and a skillfully crafted plot that speeds toward an unpredictable conclusion. Allie stands out as a likable and engaging character. Delectable fudge recipes are interspersed throughout the novel."

—***Kings River Life***

ALL FUDGED UP

"A sweet treat with memorable characters, a charming locale, and satisfying mystery."

—**Barbara Allan,** author of the Trash 'n' Treasures Mystery Series

"A fun book with a lively plot, and it's set in one of America's most interesting resorts. All this plus fudge!"

—**JoAnna Carl,** author of the Chocoholic Mystery Series

"A sweet confection of a book. Charming setting, clever protagonist, and creamy fudge—a yummy recipe for a great read."

—**Joanna Campbell Slan,** author of the Scrap-N-Craft Mystery Series and the Jane Eyre Chronicles

"Nancy Coco's *All Fudged Up* is a delightful mystery delivering suspense and surprise in equal measure. Add that to the charm of the setting, Michigan's famed Mackinac Island, and you have a recipe for enjoyment. Mouthwatering fudge recipes are included. A must-read for all lovers of amateur sleuth classic mysteries."

—**Carole Bugge (Elizabeth Blake),** author of the Jane Austen Society Mystery Series

"You won't have to 'fudge' your enthusiasm for Nancy Coco's first Mackinac Island Fudge Shop Mystery. Indulge your sweet tooth as you settle in and meet Allie McMurphy, Mal the bichon/poodle mix, and the rest of the motley crew in this entertaining series debut."

—**Miranda James,** author of the Cat in the Stacks Mystery Series

"Enjoyable . . . *All Fudged Up* is littered with delicious fudge recipes, including alcohol-infused ones. I really enjoyed this cozy mystery and look forward to reading more in this series."

—**Fresh Fiction**

"Cozy mystery lovers who enjoy quirky characters, a great setting, and fantastic recipes will love this debut."

—***The Lima News***

"The first Candy-Coated Mystery is a fun cozy due to the wonderful location filled with eccentric characters."

—***Midwest Book Review***

Books by Nancy Coco

The Oregon Honeycomb Mystery Series

Death Bee Comes Her

A Matter of Hive and Death

The Candy-Coated Mystery Series

All Fudged Up

To Fudge or Not to Fudge

Oh Say Can You Fudge

All I Want for Christmas Is Fudge

All You Need Is Fudge

Oh, Fudge!

Deck the Halls with Fudge

Forever Fudge

Fudge Bites

Have Yourself a Fudgy Little Christmas

Here Comes the Fudge

A Midsummer Night's Fudge

Give Fudge a Chance

Having a Fudgy Christmas Time

Three Fudges and a Baby

Fudge and Marriage

Some Like It Fudgy

Some Like It Fudgy

A Candy-Coated Mystery

Nancy Coco

Kensington Publishing Corp.
kensingtonbooks.com

KENSINGTON BOOKS are published by

Kensington Publishing Corp.
900 Third Avenue
New York, NY 10022

First Printing: May 2026

ISBN: 978-1-4967-5697-8

ISBN: 978-1-4967-5698-5 (ebook)

10 9 8 7 6 5 4 3 2 1

Printed in the United States of America

The authorized representative in the EU for product safety and compliance
is eucomply OU, Parnu mnt 139b-14, Apt 123
Tallinn, Berlin 11317, hello@eucompliancepartner.com.

This one is for Thomas and Diana:

Thank you for always being there,
no matter how many times I get into trouble
and have to go to the emergency room.

Chapter 1

"Bearding the lion in her den, I see," Frances Devaney, my hotel manager, said. Frances had her brown hair cut short. Her wide-set brown eyes seemed to be able to see into the hearts of others. Today she wore a turquoise-blue T-shirt and a white flowy skirt with a turquoise pattern, along with her usual tennis shoes.

"That's a very weird saying," I answered. "I'm only going to try to be nice to a neighbor." As a newlywed, things were so rosy that I thought it might be a good thing to make nice with Melonie, my husband's ex-wife. After all, she'd become the new manager of the Old Tyme Photo Shoppe, right next door to the McMurphy Hotel and Fudge Shop. The McMurphy had been owned and run by my family since it was built in the 1870s. Now it was my turn, and I loved nothing more than making fudge and giving fudge demonstrations while telling my Papa Liam's stories to the crowds.

After my ten o'clock demonstration, I gathered up a five-slice box of fragrant fudges, from Traverse City

Dark Chocolate Cherry to Melonie's favorite, Rocky Road. At least, that's what I'd been told by the seniors I hung out with. They should know. They knew everything.

I didn't expect a warm welcome and even braced myself for her to knock the box out of my hands. It's why I went close to lunchtime, when her shop was full and she couldn't really make a scene.

"As long as she lives next to us, we should at least be civil."

"Good luck with that," Frances said, without ever looking up.

I sighed, knowing she was probably right. But I had to try. I hung up my chef's coat, then ran a hand over my hair, which I'd pulled up into a high bun, hoping the natural waves stayed in place this time. Then I waved to my assistant, Roxanne Jones. With her intelligent brown eyes and silver-streaked brown hair that she wore in a bun, the older woman proved invaluable to the fudge shop. She was an avid baker and had been quick to learn my fudge-making techniques. Now she was able to help on her own when I needed a day off. She took care of everything the week I got married, and for that I would be forever grateful.

Taking a deep breath, I pasted on a smile and walked out the door of the McMurphy.

The Old Tyme Photo Shoppe specialized in portraits of people dressed in Victorian costumes. The costumes were provided in the back, along with two dressing rooms. The front of the shop looked like an old apothecary shop as an acknowledgment to the fact that film and cameras were generally sold in pharmacies. The studios were behind the window display and discreet. If I remembered right, once you went inside, you saw a modern camera set up with various scenic backgrounds rolled up or down, depending on the costumes the customers picked. Behind the screens were the costumes and the dressing rooms.

I walked in to the sound of tinny, old-time music. Swallowing my trepidation, I stepped into the small studio waiting room only to hear the camera *click*ing and *click*ing. I waited for the shoot to be over. It was the polite thing to do, but after five minutes, I got worried. No one ever took so many photos in a row. I stepped around the corner. No one was getting their picture taken. Confused, I looked at the camera—and then to the floor.

There was Melonie. She wore one of her costumes and stared straight up. I put the fudge on the cash-register counter and hurried to her side. Carefully, I shook her, but she didn't respond. Checking for a pulse, I put my ear near her mouth to see if she was breathing.

No pulse. No breath.

"Is she okay? Because she looks dead," a woman's voice said over my shoulder.

I nearly jumped out of my skin. I'd been concentrating so hard on Melonie that all I'd heard was the *click* and the sound of the flash. The killer could have come out of nowhere and killed me, too. "She's dead," I replied, then stared at the surprising woman and the beautiful Great Dane sitting beside her with no leash on.

We studied each other for a minute or two until the other woman said, “Oh! Oh, no, I wasn’t here when it happened. The door was open, and Finn uncharacteristically came in.”

“Who’s Finn?” I asked, waiting for another person to pop in.

“Oh, um, Finn’s my dog. He’s very well trained and, you know, loves kids and pets and wildlife. He basically loves anybody. And when I heard the constant pop of the lights and clicking of the shutter button, I thought someone might need help.” She paused and stared at the body. “Not, you know, first-aid kind of help”—she stumbled for her words—“I’m a photographer.” She lifted the expensive camera around her neck. “Semi-professional. My degree is in culinary arts, but I also studied photography at NYU in my spare time. I enjoy taking pictures, of pets and wildlife mainly.” She took a deep breath before continuing. “Newbies often have equipment problems, but she’s beyond help. Isn’t she? Wait, is that Melonie Strausberg? I guess she has a different last name now. She’s been married at least twice. Anyway, I didn’t realize this was her shop. Last I heard she was in Texas or some other warm place. Oh, my goodness, I’m rambling. To be fair, I’ve never seen a dead body before, except, you know, when my great-great-grandma died. Oh, and my great-aunt Helen, my great-uncle Harry, on my mom’s side. Then there’s my great-great-grandpa on my dad’s side, my Aunt Mary, and my mom, of course. But never up close and, you know, dead. It's weird, I can almost see the little x's on her eyes like in the cartoons. Only her eyes are open." She took a deep breath and gave me a half smile. "See, I ramble."

It took longer than I hoped to sort out the important information from her babbling. "It's okay," I said. "I passed out when I found my first body. We all react differently." I stood, watching her every move. "Did you know Melonie?"

She moved her head from side to side as if she was going to say, "*sort of.*" "We went to school together for a while. But usually, Aunt Annie and Auntie Charlene kept me up-to-date with my old classmates. Auntie Charlene told me that Melonie's first husband was a horrible man, and Melonie came back home to be safe after the divorce. Then, within a year, Aunt Annie said that Melonie had married again, this time to a guy with a movie character name." The woman looked up at the ceiling, tapping her chin in thought. "Some movie, some movie, some— Oh! I have it. *Empire Records*! Anyway, Aunt Annie said Melonie had married a Rex Manning—like the character in the movie, and now the movie's this kind-of cult thing, and some people even have a Rex Manning Day. Have you ever heard of that?"

"No," I said, half-curious about the movie, half-horrified that people actually celebrated Rex Manning Day. "I'm going to call nine-one-one now."

"Okay," she said, then nodded and glanced around, her dog sitting quietly beside her. Then it was as if she'd remembered something. "Oh, I have a camera. Is it okay if I take some, you know, crime-scene photos for Shane?"

I looked at her, surprised and concerned. First, she knew Melonie, now she knew Shane. Was this going to be one of those situations where everyone knew her except me? "You know Shane?"

She seemed to calm down while she snapped photos in a careful, thoughtful way, from one side of the room, clockwise to the other, along with the floor and the ceiling. The beautiful dog remained at her side. "We went to school together," she said between snapping pictures, then paused, looking around to see if she'd missed anything. "After graduation, I got into New York Culinary Institute, while Shane went to Michigan State. We haven't really kept in touch, but Aunt Annie tells me he got married to a lovely transplant from Chicago, I think, and now has a baby boy."

"Gotcha," I said wondering if she was nervous-babbling because she had something to do with the murder and was inserting herself into the investigation. None of this was helping Melonie, so I dialed 911.

"Nine-one-one, what's your emergency?"

"Hi, Charlene," I said.

"Oh, for goodness' sake, who is it this time?" Charlene asked. "I'm keeping a tally."

"Charlene!" I chided her. "What if I just wanted to see if you want to get a coffee sometime? It would be nice to meet you in person. Also, Melonie Manning is on the floor in the Old Tyme Photo Shoppe. I'm pretty sure she's dead."

"I would love to get a coffee with you soon, but seriously? Rex's ex-wife number two?"

"Yes, that Melonie Manning," I said calmly. "Charlene, please send Rex and the usual crew and let them know to hurry. People are gathering at the door. Also, get Shane here ASAP. There's a woman here—"

"Rowan. Rowan Giles," the woman said loudly as if I were deaf.

"Rowan Giles," I repeated. "She's taking photos of the crime scene."

"Rowan? Really? Goodness, I haven't seen her for close to ten years," Charlene said. "What's she doing at Melonie's? Everyone knows they've been ignoring each other after that thing in fifth grade." I gave Rowan a curious look and couldn't help but wonder what had happened to keep two people apart in such a small school. "Can you put her on?" Charlene asked.

"Charlene wants to talk to you." I handed her my cell phone. It seemed odd that she had appeared right when I found Melonie dead and then took pictures of everything. Were the pictures meant to distract Shane from other evidence?

"Auntie Charlene, hi," Rowan said with a smile, letting her camera fall against her as it hung from its thick strap. "I'm good. How have you been? Really? Yup, I did work in New York, but I met someone, and now I'm back. No, I didn't know Melonie worked at the Old Tyme Photo Shoppe. Who am I dating?" I watched her flawless, cream-colored skin with a touch of freckles across her cheekbones blush from the neck up. "Lochlan Forester—yes, I know." Her blush grew deeper, and her eyes avoided me. "Oh, yes, we should catch up, but right now probably isn't the best time."

Rowan handed me the phone, but Charlene had already hung up.

"'Auntie Charlene'?" I asked.

"My mom's best friend," Rowan replied, still blushing. "I call her Auntie, but we're not related."

"Charlene told me you went to school with Melonie, too. I didn't know she lived up here. I thought she moved here later," I said.

"She did live here for a while, but she moved away our junior year. I don't know where." She shrugged. "We weren't the best of friends."

Someone popped their head in, and Rowan snapped her fingers and pointed at the door. Her beautiful, merle, gray-blue dog went straight to the door and blocked anyone from coming in before I could even open my mouth. I love my sweet little bichonpoo, Mal, but she wasn't quite so obedient. She was, however, very friendly and treated everyone like they were part of the family. Everyone except for killers. Somehow she always knew whom not to trust.

"I'm so sorry," Rowan said. "I didn't catch your name."

"Allie McMurphy . . . er Manning," I said, and she stuck out her hand, so I shook it.

"Manning *and* McMurphy? What a coincidence," Rowan said. "You and Melonie have the same last name. You must have married someone in the same family as Melonie's second husband. Small islands are like that, I guess—only so many people to marry and all that. And McMurphy? Why, Finn and I are staying at the McMurphy Hotel and Fudge Shop next door for the next week. Is that, like, a family place?"

"Yes, it's been in my family since it was built. I'm the current owner."

"That's so amazing," She couldn't seem to stop herself from babbling. "Wow, I mean, I was so happy to find your hotel. Most hotels won't take Finn, even though he's well trained." She brushed her curly red hair out of her face. I was strangely envious of her hair. It wasn't an orange red, but instead a deep reddish-brown with highlights of lighter red that shone in the light. Then there were those curls—real curls. While mine was simply wavy, not straight or curly, and mostly frizzy. That's why I tended to keep it in either a bun or a ponytail.

"I have a little bichonpoo who has free range of the hotel," I said. "I don't believe the size of the dog matters as much as the dog's behavior," I added. "Just out of curiosity, did you see anyone when you entered? Besides Melonie and me, of course."

"I saw five people," Rowan answered. "In the back room. I assumed they were dressing for the next picture, but then they stepped out in street clothes. One left out the back, but all I saw was dark hair and a blue T-shirt. The other four seemed to have come together. One of the other men headed for the front door, saw Finn, and turned around. They all took the back door out. Which is odd. I mean, I have to assume they paid, because she didn't have the back door locked or alarmed. Which she should have done, anyway. You never know who could slip in while you're working. It's not safe." Rowan glanced at Melonie. "I guess she found that out the hard way, didn't she?"

I cleared my throat. "Would you know them if you saw them again?"

"The four of them? Maybe. Finn will help, of course. He's got a keener sense of sight and scent."

There was activity outside the shop. "Brown, get these people back, and Davis, set up a perimeter," I heard my new husband, Rex, say. "Hello, dog. I'm going in. Good dog." Rex walked around the corner and looked at Rowan with his policeman eye for detail. "That your dog?"

"Yes, that's Finn. Isn't he so smart?" she said with the love of her dog clearly showing on her face. "I told him to guard the door so that no one would get in."

"He let me in," Rex said and glanced over his shoulder.

"Oh, of course, he does know the difference between a civilian and a policeman. He was rescued from a horrible situation as a pup by two policemen," she explained. "He's loved them ever since. He can even tell a law enforcement person in civilian clothes. There's something about them that he can sense."

"Smart dog," Rex said, then turned back to us, his expression fierce when he saw his ex-wife lying there. "Melonie?" he asked as he looked at her body with sadness. The camera still *click*ed, and the lights still popped.

"Yes," I said. "Are you okay?" When he didn't answer, I pushed a little further. "Maybe you should sit down until the shock wears off." I grabbed a stool and brought it to him, then gently pressed him down until he sat. "Um, maybe you should let someone else be in charge of the case. She was an important part of your life."

He didn't stop staring at Melonie. "Brown!"

"Yes?" Charles stepped into the scene. "Is that . . ."

"Melonie," Rex said. "Have Davis keep the crowd back, and for goodness' sake, turn the darn camera off."

"She's probably lying on the remote switch and has to be turned over," Rowan said, with Finn now at her side. "You should wait. Oh, are you Melonie's ex-husband, Rex Manning? I heard you two divorced over Melonie's hatred of cold and snow because you love it here, and you refused to be a snowbird. Which makes sense, if you're a police officer and work here year-round. I bet it's hard for police officers to be snowbirds. So, I totally understand."

Rex turned toward her. His jaw was tight, and a muscle at the bottom twitched. His beautiful dark blue eyes narrowed, and his mouth formed a firm line. I took a step and put my hand on his shoulder. "This is her first murder scene, and she tends to babble," I told him.

"Oh, yes, sorry, I do tend to babble when I'm faced with surprises. And let me tell you, this was a surprise, since I've never seen a dead body in real life before. Except for, you know, relatives who've died—"

"Let's not get into that right now," I said gently. I kept a light touch on his shoulder, reminding him that, while he was torn up and angry, I wasn't going to let him take it out on the woman. He relaxed a bit at my touch, and his jaw loosened. It was barely noticeable. So subtle that only his wife would know.

The most interesting part of the whole interaction was that Rowan wasn't even the least little bit intimidated by him. And trust me, my husband could be intimidating. He looked like an action hero, from his bald head to his wide shoulders and well-muscled arms and chest. Put that together with his well-pressed, perfectly tailored police uniform and add the gun on his belt; it rarely got more intimidating than that. He turned slightly to Officer Brown. "Where is Marron?"

"On his way," Charles answered. Charles was around six feet tall, with broad shoulders. He was big-boned, with light brown hair and dark brown, hooded eyes. Even though he was popular with the young women on the island, he tended to date off the island and was very private about his life. I always wondered if he simply hadn't found the love of his life and didn't want to hurt anyone he'd have to see every day he did his rounds.

Most of the time, the police stuck to the crowded tourist areas to ensure people didn't walk in front of a horse-drawn vehicle, and the pedestrians and bicyclists gave the carriages and wagons plenty of room to get their work done.

"You need to take the case," Rex said.

I knew it was hard for him to give a case over to a junior police officer, but Charles was very capable, and Rex knew he was too biased to do a good job.

George Marron walked in, pulling a stretcher with his new EMT, Henny Pilgrim, pushing the back end.

George had copper skin, high cheekbones, and a strong jaw that made all the women stare. He was an excellent teacher, and the county always sent him the new EMTs to train and then switch out. George didn't seem to mind. When he saw who was on the floor, he said, "Well, that's not good."

"No," I answered. "It's not."

At that moment, we heard heavy footsteps coming down the stairs from the apartment above. Finn moved in front of Rowan and growled softly, letting us know he wasn't happy about this situation.

A man with a plumber's tool kit around his hips and a red toolbox filled with plumbing supplies in his right hand hit the bottom of the stairs. "What's going on? Did I miss something?"

Maybe he did, I thought. But most likely, he didn't. And if Finn's reaction was to be believed, this guy knew more than he let on.

The Perfect Mix Cookie Recipe

(Peanut Butter, Oatmeal, and Chocolate Chip)

Ingredients

2 teaspoons of cinnamon
¾ teaspoon of baking soda
½ teaspoon of baking powder
¼ teaspoon of salt
1¼ cups of flour
½ cup of white sugar
½ cup of brown sugar
½ cup of peanut butter
½ cup of butter (softened)
1 egg
1 teaspoon of vanilla
1 cup of oatmeal
2 cups of mini chocolate chips

Directions

Preheat oven to 350°F.

In a medium-size bowl, mix together the cinnamon, baking soda, baking powder, salt, and flour and set aside. In a large bowl, cream sugars, peanut butter, and butter. Add egg and vanilla. Mix until incorporated. Carefully mix in dry ingredients. Add oatmeal and chocolate chips. Stir by hand until incorporated. If it's sticky, refrigerate for 1 hour. Roll into balls.

(I prefer not to make all the cookies at once. After I roll the balls, I put them in the freezer for two hours, then place them in freezer bags and bake fresh cookies when I want them.)

Bake for 6 minutes. Pull out of oven and use a fork to flatten them. Bake another 10 minutes for a total of 16 to 18 minutes (12 to 15 if you prefer softer cookies) or until golden brown. Remove from cookie sheet while still warm, taking care not to crumble them. Place on baking rack until cool. Enjoy!

Makes two dozen cookies or less,
depending on what size you prefer.

Chapter 2

"Rex, honey, come home with me," I said and put my hand on his shoulder. "You've had a shock, and you should come lie down on the couch. I'll put a blanket over you and get you some tea. Mal and Mella will sit with you."

"No, I'm fine," he said without even glancing at me. "I need to watch and make sure the team does everything by the book. I want to catch whoever did this and see them go to jail for life."

I gave EMT George Marron a meaningful look. He whispered something to his assistant, who left and came back with a thick blanket.

"Thanks," I said as I draped the blanket around Rex, doing my best to keep him warm.

"You're welcome," Henny said. She was a short woman, nearly as wide as she was tall, but it was pure muscle. I think she could lift at least two human beings, maybe even a small horse. She went back to helping George examine Melonie to determine any exterior cause of death. The coroner's office was not on the island, and sometimes he came, but most of the time, he relied on George to help with the details of time of death and how the victim died.

Shane walked in, glanced at the scene, and went straight over to Rex. He set down his kit and squatted down to look Rex in the eyes. "How ya doing, buddy?"

Rex looked at him, his gaze still stunned. "I'm okay."

Shane stood and patted Rex's shoulder. "Sure, you are, buddy. Sure, you are." He looked around at everyone and spied Rowan. Shane's eyes widened along with his smile. "Rowan!" He stepped toward her.

"Hello, Shane," she said with a matching grin. They hugged hard.

I took note, cautious on the one hand and upset for Jenn on the other. "So, you do know each other."

"Oh, yeah," Shane said and stepped slightly to the side. "But we haven't seen each other in what? Eight years?"

"Ten," Rowan said. "I hear you're married to a beautiful woman now and have a sweet little two-year-old at home."

"I wouldn't call Benji 'sweet'," Shane said and adjusted his thick round tortoiseshell glasses. "He's in the terrible twos. It's not for the faint of heart. What brings you to the island?"

Finn stepped in, sat right beside Rowan, and studied Shane, as if judging whether he was safe or not.

"New York City didn't really work out, so I moved back in with my family. With any luck, I'll find a job and make enough to move out. It'll be nice to have a place of my own again."

"So, you're staying with your family?" Shane asked.

"It might as well be my whole family." Rowan winced. "My brother Colin owns the house now and all four of his kids plus his two grandkids move in and out as if it were their house. Since my brother Patrick's wife is in the coast guard and gone for weeks at a time, his two kids also live there. In fact, I'm rooming with my niece Chloe, who's thirteen. All and all, not a good look for me. But when the bakery I worked for in New York City went out of business, I didn't have much of a choice."

"I'm surprised. I remember when the last thing you wanted was to stay in the family home with so many people coming and going." Shane turned to me. "She has eight—"

"Ten," Rowan corrected him. "Eighteen if you count spouses. Will got married six months ago."

"Huh," Shane said. "I had no idea. Anyway, she has eighteen aunts and uncles. Everyone on her father's side lives so close you could throw a rock and hit one of their houses. Most of her mom's side also moved to Charlevoix and are always around. Plus her countless cousins."

"Oh, and Aunt Kathryn still lives there taking care of the place as if she were everyone's mom." Rowan looked at me. "It's a mess."

"Must be nice," I said, feeling a touch lonely. "I'm the only child of an only child. Well, on my dad's side at least. We won't talk about my mother's side."

"It's not as nice as you'd think," Rowan said.

"Is this beautiful fella your dog?" Shane asked and let Finn sniff him before slowly reaching over and curling his fingers into the dog's fur and scratching him. "You are a good boy, aren't you?"

"He's really well trained," I said, unable to keep the amazement out of my tone.

"She's good at training animals," Shane said.

Rowan laughed. "You should see Paddy, my big orange tabby. He does what he wants and rules the house."

"Well, ladies, and Finn, I've got to get to work."

"I saved you some time and took photos of the crime scene using a grid pattern like you taught me. Then I made a quick video so that you can hear the camera clicking." Rowan lifted her camera. "Where do you want me to send them?"

As Shane gave her his work email, I turned to see how Rex was doing. His expressions varied from cold anger to disbelief to grief. I could only imagine what it was like to lose someone you'd once loved—and still loved enough to help them out in their hour of need. Rex had let Melonie stay with him when she'd returned to the island, running from something she'd refused to talk about. Maybe whatever it was had finally caught up with her.

Chapter 3

Charles interviewed me last. He talked to the plumber first. Turns out his name was Stan Powell, and he lived in St. Ignace but had a small work shed on the island where he kept necessary tools. Stan was a handsome man with cream-colored skin, a wide face, short black hair, and dark brown, almond-shaped eyes. He said he was there at Melonie's request. She had a leak in the bathroom somewhere that was dripping into her costume room.

"It was a combination of the toilet and the shower," he said. "I had to call my partner, Teddy Schmidt, to bring me some things. I was too busy to go get them. After a while, Teddy came up, gave me the parts, then left. But he forgot a washer. Between you and me, Teddy's not the brightest. Nice guy, though. Hard worker. I went to the top of the stairs and hollered at him before he got too far. I could hear Melonie taking pictures, and I felt bad for hollering. I didn't think he heard me so I texted him and went back into the bathroom to do as much as I could without the washer. Teddy brought it up quick, and I told him that I'd gotten a call from the Smiths, and he needed to get his tail over there and help them. I finished up shortly after. That's when I came down and everyone was here, and Melonie was dead on the floor."

"And you didn't hear anything?" Charles asked.

"No," he said. "I had my earbuds in and was under the sink finishing the job. When I turned on the water to see if the patch worked, it did. Held nicely, too, if you want to go look at it."

"We'll be sure and do that," Charles said and let him go.

Rowan went over her story next, and I ended with what I'd seen. My box of fudge still rested on the countertop. That's when I noticed the register.

"The register is open," I pointed out. "Do you think it was a robbery gone wrong?"

Charles frowned at me.

"I know, I know," I said. "You're still in the preliminary phase." He looked at me blandly. "And you can't discuss the case," I finished.

"Thank you both for answering my questions. I would suggest, Ms. Giles, that you stick around a while." Charles handed her his card. "If you think of anything else, let me know."

"Sure," Rowan said. "I'm staying at the McMurphy."

Thank goodness Rowan had decided to stay at the McMurphy. It would be easier to keep an eye on her.

A glance out the window told me the front was filled with people wanting to know what was going on and that it was best to go out the back. "Rowan, would you and Finn want to leave with me since you're staying at the McMurphy?"

She looked out of the window. "Sure, if you're going out the back way," she agreed and followed me to the back, with Finn by her side. I opened the door to find Carol, Ida, the rest of the book club, and a pretty, dark-haired woman I didn't know. Beside them were pharmacist David Peele, Mr. Beecher, stable manager Ed Blanchard, and Officer Davis. Officer Davis was a lovely woman with short blond hair and light brown eyes. She'd worked on the island before. Charles had assigned her to keep watch over the back door, after Rex had told him to secure the perimeter. Leave it to the book club to sniff out a murder and show up as soon as possible. The rest were a surprise, though, especially Ed. He was pretty far away from his workplace.

"Allie, what's going on?" Carol asked. "Is Melonie dead?" Carol had recently decided that her short gray hair bored her, so she started adding a different-colored streak a week. This week it was purple.

"We don't know if she was murdered yet, ma'am," Officer Davis warned her.

"I found her dead," I admitted.

"Oh, my goodness, Rowan Giles," Mr. Beecher said. "It is still Giles, isn't it?"

"Hi, Mr. Beecher," she said and gave him a hug. This time, Finn stayed by my side as if he knew I was the one who needed to be kept safe. "Mrs. Tunisian, Mrs. Gooseman," She addressed everyone in the book club and hugged them. "Ed, it's nice to see you."

Ed blushed and took off his hat. "I can't believe it's you, Rowan," he said. "You turned out to be very pretty."

Rowan laughed. "I don't look any different than I did in high school. It's simply that the rest of you have finally caught up to me."

"So nice to see you back," Betty Olway said. "We thought you went to New York for good."

"You did shake the dust of this place off your feet," Laura Morgan said.

"I know, but then nothing ever works out quite the way you think it will," Rowan said and tucked a wave of curls behind her ear.

"Oh, I forgot my manners. Rowan, Allie, this is my cousin Merriam's daughter, Valentine Maas," Laura Morgan said. "She's looking to open a gourmet fast-food restaurant on the island. Isn't that wonderful?"

"Hi," I said. "Nice to meet you."

"All right," Officer Davis said. "I hate to break up this happy homecoming, but if people see you standing back here, they're going to come here, too."

"We're on our way," Mr. Beecher said.

Officer Davis was right. The last thing we wanted to do was contaminate the crime scene even more.

Chapter 4

"I think my pup, Mal, is going to love Finn, even if she's a small bichonpoo," I said as we reached the alley door to the hotel. I opened the door and ushered them in. "I've been dying to ask since I heard you have family in Charlevoix. Why stay the night at the McMurphy when you could simply stay with one of them?"

Mal heard the door and looked around the corner. As soon as she spotted me, she came running, slid under Finn, and hit my shins, as she loved to do when she wanted me to say hi and be picked up. I picked her up, and she licked my face, her little stump tail wagging as fast as it could.

"That was a neat trick," Rowan said. "Finn looks very confused. He's never had anyone slide under him before."

I chuckled. "Mal will do that when someone she loves comes into the lobby. 'Slide and shin bonk' is her favorite thing."

Mal looked at Rowan and Finn, her head tilted. "Mal, this is Rowan."

"Nice to meet you, Mal," Rowan said, giving Mal a

sniff of her hand and then a scratch behind her ears. Mal kissed her wrist.

"You are fully approved." I pointed to the Great Dane. "And this is Finn."

Mal tilted her head one way and then another. She'd never seen a dog so big. She scrambled to get down, so I let her. She approached Finn with a play bow, and they exchanged butt sniffs. Well, as best Mal could do, considering the size difference. After that Mal ran to the end of the hall, then looked back as if to say, "*Well, aren't you coming?*"

"Release, Finn." Rowan gave the command that let him go off. "Go play." The Dane loped behind and then beside Mal.

I heard a surprised gasp and chuckled. Finn must have startled Frances. After all, it wasn't every day that a Great Dane came scrambling around the back corner. "That gasp is from my general manager and all-around boss, Frances Devaney," I explained. "She's pretty unflappable, so it's nice to hear her surprised. I didn't give you a chance to finish. Why stay the night?"

She half smiled. "I need a vacation before I go back into the chaos."

We'd rounded the corner of the short hall to where Frances helped a couple check out.

"Mrs. Frances!"

When Frances heard Rowan, she finished the checkout, thanked the couple for their time, and stepped out from behind her desk. "Rowan Giles," she said and hugged her. "I suppose that monster belongs to you?" She pointed at Finn.

Finn found a large spot of sunshine coming through the window and lay down on the carpet. Mal still wanted to play and nudged him, but Finn closed his eyes and refused to budge. Mal stopped, looked at us, and came back for more scratches.

"Yes, ma'am," Rowan said. "Mrs. Frances, you still look the same."

"Thank you, and so do you. Call me Frances, I was your teacher ages ago." Frances squeezed her hands. "I wondered if that was you when the reservation came through online. Why are you staying here and not with your family?"

"That seems to be the question of the day," Rowan replied.

I waved at Roxanne and leaned against the desk to hear what Rowan had to say.

"You know we moved about an hour south of here near Charlevoix after Mom died," Rowan began, and Frances nodded. "Now that I'm home I have to room with Patrick's daughter, Chloe. I'd forgotten how crazy my dad's house was. When I was in New York and living on my own, I could just close my door and put my feet up." She took off her backpack. "But not anymore. I thought a nice little vacation would be good before I dove back into the family chaos. Mackinac Island seemed the perfect place."

"Did you have Finn in New York?" I asked, trying to imagine such a large dog in what would have had to have been a small space.

Rowan smiled. "Yes. Finn was rescued by police officers when he was a tiny puppy. I saw him in a shelter ad and adopted him right away. They told me he was a mix, most likely eight to ten months old, and wouldn't get any bigger than fifty pounds. Who knew he'd grow to be almost taller and longer than my tiny apartment in Brooklyn."

"Did you work as a pet photographer there?" I asked.

She laughed. "Oh, no, I worked as a pastry chef in a small gourmet bakery. In my free time, I enjoyed taking candid snapshots of pets and then finishing the photos with different clothes from different time periods." She unzipped the photography bag that was cross-shouldered and rested on her hip and showed us a wallet-sized portfolio of pictures. They were hilarious, with both serious and fun pictures of dogs, cats, a hamster, even lizards in costumes. One with a 1600s ruff. Another in a royal robe and crown. Another in a suit and tie from the fifties. And on and on it went.

"Those are so much fun!" I declared. "You are really talented."

"Thanks," she replied as she stuck the wallet back into her photographer's bag. "I'm much better at pastries though. I went to the New York Culinary Institute and even graduated with top honors. I'd rather work in photography, but jobs are few and far between and at least I had a job at the bakery."

"What happened to your bakery job?" Frances asked.

"The owners had to close it when the husband became very sick." She teared up. "New York City rents are so high, and I didn't have enough funds to purchase it. Now I'm home, trying to figure out the next part of my life. Since pet photography is what I really want to do. I'm hoping to find an affordable place to start a business of my own. I thought maybe I'd check out here first. A lot of people bring their pets with them to the island," Rowan said.

"Good luck," I said. "If you need sample pictures, Mal and my kitty, Mella, can be your first clients. Everyone here knows them. You could put copies of their pictures in your front window for display. That's Mella right there, lying on top of the chair in front of the window trying to take the sun away from Finn."

"Thanks!" she said excitedly.

Frances checked her in, and when Rowan went upstairs, she asked, "How'd it go with Melonie?"

"Oh, I figured you already knew, what with how fast the gossip spreads here. She was dead when I got there."

"Oh, dear! How's Rex taking it?"

"Not well," I replied. "Part of me is jealous of his reaction, but the rest is worried about him. He was in shock. Thank goodness he understood immediately that he couldn't lead this particular investigation. He called Charles in and put him in charge."

"Do you have any idea what killed her?"

"None," I replied. "There were no wounds that I could see, no blood, no foaming at the mouth, she didn't look strangled."

"Well, you would know." There was a *ding*, and Frances clicked on the notification and was done with a few taps of her fingers. "The Browns will be coming in late tonight."

"I don't like the fact that a murder happened so close

to the McMurphy again. For goodness' sake, we're going to be called the murder hotel pretty soon," I said with concern.

"We already are," Frances said, looking at her screen through the reading glasses that balanced on her nose.

"What? When? How long have you known this?"

She glanced at me. "I take the reservations, remember? I'd say it's been going on for a couple of years. At least once each season, a group calls and asks for the 'murder hotel.' It gives them a reason to stay here. They come, buy fudge, have a giggle, maybe scare themselves on the rooftop deck, and go home. What's the harm?"

"Papa would be rolling over in his grave."

"Your Papa Liam would be dancing in the halls. First of all, he loved mysteries as much as you do, and secondly, he would be excited to see all the new reservations."

"I suppose," I said. "Can you keep Mal from following me out again? I'm going out the back way. I need to see how Rex is holding up and drag him home, even if I have to carry him all the way."

"Now, that would be a sight to see," Rowan said as she finished bounding down the stairs.

"That was fast," I said.

"I'm only staying for the weekend so all I brought was my backpack. Most of the things inside are for Finn."

"Finn is very patient with Mal," I said, pointing at the Dane, whom Mal was currently trying to play-bite. He ignored her.

"He's always in a gentle mood," Rowan replied. "It keeps kids and other animals calm. Speaking of calm, I'm going to go visit an old friend of my mom's. Finn, come." The dog got up instantly and went to her side. Mal watched them go, and her little face looked so sad. It made me wonder if I should get a second dog.

"Give her an extra treat," I whispered. Mal heard me and came running.

"Now you've done it," Frances said with a straight face while she rearranged rooms on her computer. "Every time Finn leaves, she's going to think she gets a treat."

I laughed and picked Mal up. "I know," I said and kissed Mal. "But I can't help myself."

"Just like you can't keep yourself from investigating a murder?" Frances looked at me over the top of her reading glasses.

"I didn't say that—you did." I gave Mal her treat, handed her to Frances, then went out the back door.

Chapter 5

The back alley was empty except for Officer Davis. "How's it going? Any more lookie-loos?" I asked as I approached.

"One or two is all. They think they can slip by me," Officer Davis said.

"Is Rex still in there?" I didn't wait for a reply. Instead I poked my head in. Shane worked in the costume room, with a very angry Rex leaning against the wall, his arms crossed as if Shane didn't know how to do his job. He no longer had the blanket on and stood in full uniform and gear. I figured he'd most likely given the blanket back, grumbling that he didn't need it.

Shaking my head, I walked in, went straight to Rex, grabbed hold of his arm, and pulled as hard as I could. "Come on, let's go."

"They're not finished yet," he said, not budging no matter how hard I pulled.

"Trust me, they don't need you standing over them like some demon from hell," I said. "Now, don't make me do this the hard way."

He kept his gaze on Shane and made a noise like

there was nothing I could do to move him if he didn't want to be moved.

"Hard way it is, then." I grabbed the cuffs from his belt, and he turned, astonished. Taking advantage of his surprised reaction, I grasped him by the thumb, pulled it back, and twisted it just enough to get his attention and make him move from the pain. Just like I'd watched him do so many times over the years, I cuffed his free arm first and then the twisted arm. Grabbing him by his collar and arm, I perp-walked him out of the place.

"Thanks, Allie," Shane shouted when we got to the threshold.

"You're welcome," I called back. Officer Davis stepped aside and averted her gaze.

"Allie, so help me, I'm going to—"

"What?" I said sweetly, holding up the key to the cuffs. He kept walking without saying another word. We took the outdoor apartment stairs. "Open the door."

"It's locked, and you'll have to take off the cuffs if you want me to unlock it," he grumbled.

"I'm not falling for that," I said with a chuckle. "Besides, it's unlocked."

"What?" He turned his head as best he could to look at me. "How many times do I have to tell you not—" I raised the cuffs enough to make it uncomfortable and remind him who was in charge. "Okay, okay, okay. I'll open the door." I let him turn sideways to reach the knob while giving me a dirty look. I grinned at him. When he turned the knob, he suddenly understood that it was, indeed, locked and I'd been messing with him. "I am so going to—"

"What?" I asked. "What are you going to do to your wife, the woman you love, who is only doing this because you're too stubborn to do it yourself? Does that sound familiar?" I pulled out the apartment key and unlocked the door.

He went across the threshold muttering, and I laughed, then closed the door behind us. Mella greeted him with the curl of her tail around his legs. As soon as we were safely inside, I locked the door behind me, stood in front of it, and released his handcuffs.

He whipped around, anger boiling off him. I simply smiled. "We could have done this the easy way, you stubborn man."

He narrowed his eyes. "And I could pick you up, move you right out of my way, and go back down there to monitor the investigation."

"Of course you could," I replied blandly, swinging the cuffs. "I'm sure that storming back down there will look . . . less embarrassing?"

He glared as he rubbed his wrists and rolled his shoulders. Mella jumped up onto the counter, then executed a trust jump right into his arms, where she purred contentedly while he dug his fingers gently into her fur.

"Besides," I said as I sauntered past him and took two beers out of the fridge, "you're the one who taught me how to do that."

He grumbled some more as I opened the beverages

and put them on the coffee table, sat on the couch, and put my feet up.

"You're welcome," I said. "Now, come rub my feet and tell me how much you love me. And that if I were ever to be found dead, you would go mad and tear through the city stalking the killer instead of glowering over everyone else's shoulder."

He sighed and let Mella jump down out of his arms as he came over, sat, pulled my feet onto his lap, and firmly rubbed them. I handed him the beer in my hand and took the other. "I'd tell you not to ever do that to me again, but I doubt you'd listen." He took a long pull on the beer and set it down to continue rubbing. "You don't understand. It's Melonie. She's my wife."

"All righty then." I stood, went to our bedroom, then closed and locked the door. "Enjoy sleeping with your 'wife'."

I sat down hard in the chintz chair near the window in the sitting area of the room.

"Shit," I heard him say and could imagine him rubbing his right hand over his bald head. I heard a soft *thunk* as he rested his forehead against the door. "I'm sorry, Allie. It was a shock, that's all. I've never had someone kill my wife before."

I rolled my eyes, silently crossed my arms, and let him think about what he'd said—again.

There was a long pause before he continued, "That's not what I meant, and you know it."

I still didn't answer. Let him squirm. Okay, I was a bit jealous of how much he'd fallen apart after learning about Melonie's death. I mean, they'd only been married for a short time, and she was a terrible person who hated my guts. Why wouldn't he go bonkers over her murder? Okay, I had to admit it also made me angry.

"Allie . . ." he said softly. "Come on. You know I'm not handling anything right today."

That was when I decided neither of us was handling stuff well today. So, I threw some clothes in my overnight bag and gave Jenn a call.

"Allie," she said.

In the background, I could hear Benji running around screaming, "Dinner, dinner, dinner."

"Sorry, he is always hungry, and the worst part is, he's thin like his dad, while it takes me two years of dieting just to lose five pounds."

"You look beautiful," I replied.

"Oh, you're so sweet. By the way, I have some news." She sounded breathless.

"Can you hold that thought?" I asked.

"Oh, my goodness, I haven't even asked how you were doing," she said, contrite. "I heard about Melonie. How's Rex holding up?"

"Badly," I replied. "Can I come spend the night?"

"Of course!" she replied. "Stay as long as you need. And don't mind Benji, he'll stop sometime between dinner and his late-night snack."

We both laughed. "I'll be right there," I said. Then I grabbed my bag, took a deep breath, and opened the door. Rex stood there, looking one part angry and two parts contrite. "I'm going to Jenn's for the night. I think we both need a moment for you to grieve."

"Allie—"

"I'd advise you to stay away from the crime scene and trust your team to do their best for your *wife*." I walked out, Mella following me out the door. Mal was down in the lobby, keeping Frances company and greeting customers. I figured I'd call Frances before she went home and ask her to bring Mal by Jenn's place. Benji loved to play with my pets anyway.

Chapter 6

I knocked on Jenn's door, and she opened it with Benji on her hip, sucking on a frozen banana. "Hey," I said as Mella streaked inside.

"Kitty!" Benji gave his mom the slimy banana and demanded to be let down.

"Say hi to Auntie Allie first," Jenn said.

"Hi, Auntie Awie." Benji's toddler face turned away, too busy watching the cat to look at me. The second Jenn let him down, he went running off to play with Mella, who pretended not to like it.

"Come on in," Jenn said, holding the door open wide with one hand and the slimy treat in the other. "Welcome to the chaos."

"Thanks," I said. "I understand chaos."

She closed the door and gave me a one-arm hug. "How are you really?"

"Things are a little emotionally weird for me right now." I watched her put the banana in the composter and wash her hands.

"And?"

"And Rex keeps saying his 'wife' this and his 'wife'

that. I mean, I know exactly what he's talking about, but still. Get a clue, bud, your *actual* wife is standing right in front of you."

"That sucks." She dried her hands on a kitchen towel. "Men can be idiots."

"It doesn't help that he's looming over everyone at the scene, watching their every move."

"Oh, I bet Shane likes that." Jenn's sarcasm wasn't lost on me.

"I know, right? Suddenly all his trust in his team is gone when his"—I used air quotes—"'wife' has been murdered. I told him to come home and let them work or I'd have to. He refused. After my second time, he gave me a look like I was an annoying insect buzzing in his ear."

"Now, that's being an—"

"That's when I told him, 'or else'," I said as I put my bag down on the floor and sat on her kitchen chair.

"Oh, I bet that went over well," Jenn said with a grin as she reached up and gathered two wine glasses.

"I simply cuffed him before he realized what was going on and walked him out of the scene and up into the apartment." I grinned. "It felt good, and Shane actually thanked me."

"Good for you, and yay for my baby."

"That didn't stop Rex from fuming about his 'wife' being murdered." I sighed loudly. "Frankly, it didn't get any better the more he talked. I thought we needed time for both of us to cool down and use our heads and not our emotions. Mostly I mean him."

"Wow, yes." She hugged me. "Of course, come stay with us until he gets over his stupidity."

I got up and tossed my overnight bag on the extra couch for guests while Jenn placed two glasses of red wine on the table.

"It's five o'clock somewhere," she said, then glanced at her watch. "Look, it's five o'clock here!"

We laughed and clinked our glasses, then I took a sip as Benji came over with Mella hanging on his arm like a dish towel.

"What are you drinking, Auntie Awie? Can I have some?"

"It's wine, and no, little man, you can't," I said.

"Why?"

"You have to wait until you're really old—at least twenty-one—before you can drink it," I answered.

"Why?"

"It's made out of spoiled grape juice," Jenn replied. "Do you want spoiled grape juice?"

"Ewww." He shivered. "Yuck. Why you drink it?"

"Because when you're a grown-up, sometimes you like things you didn't like before." Jenn sent him a loving smile. He pulled his eyebrows together over his big brown eyes with the round eyeglasses strapped gently around his head. With an expression of confusion, Benji absent-mindedly petted a content Mella.

"Auntie Awie, what happens when you're really, really old, like you and Mommy? Do you like it even more? 'Cause Daddy doesn't like it, and he's really old."

"Everybody likes different things, even old people,"

I played along, with a wink at Jenn, who rolled her eyes. “You like orange juice over grape juice, right?”

“Yup,” he replied, and Mella purred from all his absent-minded attention.

“Well, your daddy likes his drink better than ours,” I said.

“My daddy’s smart.”

“Of course he is, honey,” I replied. “He works a very important job that takes a very smart person to do.”

“That’s why he doesn’t drink spoiled grapes,” Benji concluded and carried Mella away.

“So, we’re really, really old, and Shane’s only really old,” I teased. “You cradle robber.”

“I’ll have you know, he’s three whole years older than I am.” She took a drink and waggled her eyebrows at the thought of Shane. Then she put her glass down. “You’re investigating, of course, for Rex, and let me guess, because it happened right next to the McMurphy.”

“Yes, I’ve decided that since Rex is out, and I found Melonie’s body, Charles could use a little help.”

“Do you think Rex will investigate with you?”

“You know he’s very much by the book,” I told her, playing with the stem of my glass. “I highly doubt he’ll investigate with me. Anyway, first he needs some space to figure out the whole ‘my wife was murdered’ thing because I’m still here. Then I need to figure out how to deal with my jealousy before we can do anything else together.”

“So, you *are* jealous,” she teased me over the top of her glass.

"Yes, I am, and I'm not afraid to say it out loud. If I wasn't, then I shouldn't be married to the man."

"That's fair." She stood. "I'm making meat loaf and baked potatoes for dinner. Shall I put another potato on for you?"

"You don't have to go to any trouble for me. I'll go to Doud's and pick something up."

"Nonsense," was all Jenn said, and she put another potato in the oven, then sat back down.

"Doesn't it take time to bake a potato? It's five-thirty already."

"Whenever there's a murder, Shane works late, sometimes as late as midnight."

"I didn't realize that," I said, drawing my eyebrows together in concern, even though I knew my skin had begun to wrinkle in that particular spot.

"I'll feed Benji in about ten minutes, then it's bath and bed for him by seven."

"I can read him a book once he's in bed," I offered. "It'll give you more time to get things done."

"Thank you," Jenn said. "What do you know so far about the murder?"

"Please tell me you don't know Rowan Giles," I said with a wince.

"I haven't a clue who she is," Jenn said and watched my face. "Don't tell me she's Rex's first wife."

I felt my insides uncoil a little as I relaxed. "She's the woman who showed up at the scene and started taking pictures. And everyone who saw her knew her and seemed to be infatuated with her and her dog. Not that I mind that," I said quickly. "What I mind is that there's another local person I don't know that evidently everyone else knows except me. Like Shane, for example."

"Shane," Jenn repeated. "What's Shane got to do with this?"

"They acted like best friends who hadn't seen each other in years," I said and took another sip. "They even hugged, and he kissed her on the cheek."

"Oh, that's not going to fly in this house," Jenn said. "He's not kissing another woman—not even on the cheek—old friend or not. What does she look like? Tell me she's at least big in all the wrong places and that I'm more beautiful, baby or no baby."

"You're more beautiful," I said sincerely. "But she's tall, with long legs, thin, but not skinny, with long, curly red hair and blue eyes."

"Let me guess, she has a smattering of freckles across her nose and cheeks, like a darn love interest in a romance novel."

"I wouldn't say a smattering of freckles."

"Oh, good. Lots of freckles is even better." Jenn stood and refilled our glasses.

I took my glass out of her hands and winced again. "Nope."

She stood frozen to the spot. "Nope? What do you mean 'nope'?"

"She had very few freckles as far as I could tell." I suddenly became interested in the wine, and I noticed she drank from a different bottle than I did. Why hadn't I noticed that before? We usually liked the same thing.

"She's a gorgeous redhead with naturally curly hair,

smooth pale skin, and long legs, and he kissed her on the cheek." Jenn headed toward the table, her expression filled with growing anger.

"And hugged her," I added. The glint in Jenn's eyes had me realizing I wasn't the only one wanting to do battle.

"Sit," I said and patted the chair. "Come on, sit down."

"Rowan Giles, you said?" She paced absently, holding the glass of wine in her hand.

"I did." I stood and took her hand to stop her pacing. "Sit. It was probably just an old friend greeting another old friend."

"Have you ever had an old friend kiss you on the cheek?" she asked.

"Once," I reminded her.

"Oh, right—that guy your mom tried to set you up with because he was running for some political office."

"See, it's all nonsense. I felt nothing from his kiss. I'm sorry I worried you when you're pregnant."

"How did you know?" she asked me, her expression one of confusion.

"You're not drinking actual wine with me—and you told me you had news," I replied.

"How did you figure out I'm not drinking wine? I have two open bottles."

"We usually drink from the same bottle. Don't worry, it took me a while to notice." I got up and hugged her. "This is wonderful news! What does Shane think?"

"He's happy—or so I thought," she grumbled. "But

now he's out kissing beautiful women while I sit here getting fat again."

"You haven't gained an ounce, and you know it." I shook my head. "How's this one? Do you have terrible morning sickness?"

"Actually, it's better this time," she said.

"Must be a girl," I teased.

"Let's forget about me. How are you going to solve this case when there isn't any proof of murder? You don't even know how she died. It could have been a heart attack or an embolism."

"I can't explain it," I said, "but it feels like murder. You're right, though. I should wait for the autopsy."

"You know, you should forgive Rex," Jenn said. "In a couple of days."

"Only if you forgive Shane," I replied. We both laughed and she finally sat down. "Men can be idiots."

"Sometimes." Jenn shook her head. "Sometimes."

There was a knock at the door, and we looked at each other, surprised. "Are you expecting anyone?" she asked. "Because I'm not."

"Oh," I said. "It must be Frances with Mal. I asked her to bring Mal over on her way home."

At the sound of a second knock, Benji came running up. "Mommy, there's someone at the door." Benji abandoned Mella, who immediately climbed as high on the furniture as she could, having had enough of the kid. I laughed.

"Benji, wait!" Jenn said and stood but she wasn't fast enough. Benji already opened the door. "Doggie!"

I felt relief that Mal would be with me tonight.

"Hello," came a familiar woman's voice, and I stiffened. "Frances said to bring Mal over." Mal came running into the house and straight into my lap, but Benji didn't come over to Mal like he usually did. Instead, he stood near his mom, grasping Jenn's leg and staring at the woman who stood in the doorway.

This time I got up and flanked Jenn to let her know I was there for her no matter what she did. From the look on Jenn's face, she couldn't decide which of one hundred ways to kill Shane and then Frances.

"Hi, you must be Shane's wife, Jenn. How nice to meet you! I hope you don't mind if I come in. It's a little chilly out there." She stepped in, Finn at her side, and closed the door. "I wouldn't want to let in the cold air and give Benji a cold." Rowan stopped to smile at Jenn for a moment. "I've heard so many things about you, you know. Shane wasn't kidding when he said you're beautiful. Oh, I'm so sorry. How silly of me. Here I'm standing in your house and haven't even introduced myself yet. I'm Rowan Giles, an old friend of Shane's. He said I could come by for dinner. Unless you don't have enough. I could go grab something from Doud's. I really don't mean to intrude." She glanced at me. "Allie, how good to see you again. Are you staying for dinner?" She turned back to Jenn. "I understand Shane works late, and he thought it would be nice for you to have company with your dinner," Rowan said. "Sorry, I tend to talk a lot when I'm nervous. Meeting new people is hard. I mean, all I have is my family, and they're handful enough. They take up all my time. That means I don't often get to make friends. I think Shane knows it and thought I'd make some new friends if I came over here."

I knew it was too late when Benji ran over and put his little arms around what he could reach of Finn's neck. "Big doggie! I love him, Mommy. Can he stay?"

It was a long moment before Jenn answered him. "Yes, he can stay."

Mal jumped out of my arms and went to push Benji down and give him kisses. Finn wasn't sure he liked it until the little boy started to laugh.

"What a little sweetheart," Rowan said. "Shane tells me you have another bun in the oven. Congrats!"

Jenn stiffened. "He told you what?"

"Don't worry," Rowan said. "He told me not to say anything, and I promised."

"He told you?" Jenn couldn't seem to get over what she'd just heard.

"Yeah," Rowan said and turned to Jenn after watching Benji play with Finn and Mal while Mella looked bored on top of the bookshelf. It was then that she looked up and noticed Jenn's face. "I'm sorry, was I not supposed to know? It's just that we—Shane and I—were best friends up until we went to different colleges. We even wrote back and forth for a while, then it was email and text until we both got busy. You know—life is like that. Anyway, Auntie Charlene has been keeping me up-to-date on everything. Even you, Allie. She says every time you call, she knows that someone is dead, or badly hurt and then dies. She told me it's been that way since you came to the island. Funny, isn't it? I mean, before that we had a murder, like, once."

"Wait—" Jenn said. "Charlene is your aunt?"

"Sort of. She's my mom's best friend, so she's always been an aunt to me. In fact, my best friends, Amy Hanson and Marijo Rooney and I always hung around together pretending to be 'Charlene's Angels' and solving crimes. Auntie Charlene helped by leaving clues lying around. We were always so excited when we figured them out."

"You know a lot of people," I said with a frown.

"Oh, don't worry. Most of them are family. There are seven of us and then my parents, my grandparents, my eighteen aunts and uncles, if you count spouses. My great-grandparents came from Ireland, and as Catholics, they all believe in big families."

"You're Charlene's niece." Jenn couldn't seem to let it go. Not that I blamed her. Even though I knew, my own ego couldn't comprehend that Rowan knew Charlene. The woman I'd been talking to for years, yet hadn't met in person.

"Not technically," Rowan replied and sat down at the table, forcing us all to sit. "But she might as well be. She was a lifesaver after my mom died."

"You certainly do talk a lot," Jenn said as she gave up and poured Rowan a glass of wine, then pushed it toward her.

"Thanks," Rowan said. "Gramma has this thing that we're not supposed to drink because it's easy to become addicted. Let me tell you that as long as I'm careful, I haven't gotten addicted yet. Anyway, like I said, I do talk a lot when I'm nervous."

"You're nervous now?" Jenn asked with some satisfaction in her tone.

"Oh, yes," Rowan said and took a sip of her drink. "I mean, here I am sitting with Shane's beautiful wife, who's one of the best party planners in the country—and that's not Shane talking, either. Then there's Allie, who's not only beautiful, but as smart as a whip, and brave, catching killers over and over. Even Auntie Charlene admires you, Allie, and it takes a lot for her to do that," Rowan said. "Meanwhile, I'm an unemployed pastry chef and a wannabe pet photographer who's living with her family. But that's enough about me. So . . ." Rowan's eyes sparkled. "The coroner proclaimed it murder. It seems that she was shot in the heart with a nail gun—but not in an accidental kind of way. That leaves only one question. Allie, when do we start the investigation?"

Chapter 7

"The investigation?" I replied with a tilt of my head.

"Yes, of course, the investigation. Auntie Charlene says you usually start right away by going over the scene or talking to the book club or gathering your girlfriends." Rowan eyed Jenn with a grin. "You make a list of suspects, right?"

She wasn't wrong, but with both Jenn's and my own personal lives a bit of a mess right now, the investigation was the last thing on my mind. How did she even know the coroner's report or about the nail gun? A nail gun? Who uses a nail gun to kill someone? "Right, the investigation . . ." I said. "We're a little—"

"Allie and I were just talking about that," Jenn said, giving me the *not now* look.

I blinked while my mind went through what could happen if I answered the wrong way. "Melonie wasn't exactly liked on the island. Or maybe it was me she didn't like."

"Oh, no, she was pretty much disliked by the entire island," Rowan said. "My Auntie Charlene told me all about how glad everyone was that Rex divorced her.

And thrilled when she went away for a while. Who knows why she came back. She hates the winters here. Anyway, a lot of people aren't happy she's back. Or, I guess, weren't. She sure liked to stir up trouble, and she could split up even best friends. She was hateful to everyone. I mean, that's not a reason for murder, but . . ."

"But she's been back here for a while," I muttered. "Why kill her now?"

"Now, see, that's something for us to figure out." Rowan grinned with excitement in her eyes.

"'Us'?" I asked.

"Me, you, and the book club, of course," Rowan said.

"Of course," I said.

"So," Rowan said. "What's for dinner? Shane really did ask me to stay until he gets home."

"Great," Jenn muttered under her breath so only I could hear. "I'm going to kill him." Then she smiled at Rowan in her best hostess way. "We're having meat loaf and baked potatoes. I'll put a potato in for you right now."

"No, thanks," Rowan said. "I can't eat white potatoes. They're nightshades and not good for you. I'll go to Doud's and get you some sweet potatoes. They're full of vitamins. Very good for you. Even little Benji might like them." Rowan got up. "Finn, come." She snapped her fingers, and the big dog was immediately at her side. "Oh, my gosh, did I even mention that this is Finn? He's good with children, obviously, and other animals. He's pretty chill. Anyway, I'm going to Doud's. Do you need anything but sweet potatoes? More grape juice, perhaps?" she said with an eye on Jenn's bottle.

"Sweet potatoes are enough," Jenn said.

"I'll be right back." Rowan and Finn left, which gave Mal more time to Benji herself.

"I'm going to kill him," Jenn said.

"I wouldn't blame you," I agreed. "Maybe coming here tonight wasn't such a good idea." I got up, and Jenn grabbed my wrist.

"Oh, no, you don't," she said. "You're not leaving me alone with that woman."

"Okay, fine," I said. "I won't go." I moved to pick up Benji, who squirmed because Mal and Mella were there.

"But if you do happen to murder someone," I said with a grin, "I know how and where to get rid of the body."

"Bye, Rowan, talk soon." Shane waved after her at the end of the night, then turned to see Jenn and me both frowning at him. "What?" he asked, his eyebrows drawn together.

"Come on, Mal." I got up and put her halter on her. "Time to go for a walk." All I could say was that Shane was very lucky Jenn didn't chuck a pan at his head. No, even pregnant, Jenn was much more civil than I was.

The night was cool and quiet as we made our way around the neighborhoods. I could hear the lake lap lazily at the shore. A few tourists laughed as they came and went into their hotels or bed-and-breakfasts. There were several seasonal workers still downtown, talking and laughing about the best and worst parts of their days. Mal and I wandered a bit. I let my pup lead as I tried to piece together the puzzle of what had happened to Melonie and why. Could someone have killed her over their pictures? That seemed silly. It had to be something else.

"Allie, what are you doing out this way? Hi, little Mal, are you helping Mommy with the case?"

I turned to see Carol carrying grocery bags from Doud's. Even in the twilight, I recognized her purple-streaked gray hair, rounded face, and blue tracksuit. "Hi, Carol," I said. "No, we're not working the case, just out walking. It's a bit of a story, really, but I'm spending the night at Jenn's. And right now, she and Shane are having a little talk. I thought it was best to disappear for a little while."

"Ah, I bet it's because Rowan is back on the island," Carol said.

I laughed. "In part. Shane invited Rowan to dinner and didn't ask Jenn first. Then Rowan didn't like baked white potatoes. She said something about them being nightshades and bad for you. Then she ran to Doud's, picked up sweet potatoes, washed them, and baked them in Jenn's oven without so much as a 'may I?' She kept talking away while she did it."

It was Carol's turn to chuckle. "You have to understand, she comes from a big family, where everything belongs to everyone. She probably did it without a second thought. Habit, really."

"At least she brought back ingredients to make a dessert. A delicious cannoli pie. Even Jenn had to compliment it. But then she glared at Shane when he said it was the best dessert he'd ever had."

"That boy was painting himself into a corner, wasn't he?"

"Yup," I said. "Just like Rex's every other sentence earlier tonight, talking about his 'wife' being murdered."

"Ouch," Carol said. "Sounds like Melonie's death, along with Rowan's appearance, has stirred things up a bit. You look cold. Come with me." She tilted her head toward her house. "We can have a hot beverage, set up the murder board, and start adding subjects to eliminate."

"Thanks." I took a deep breath trying to calm my emotions, which were all over the place. "Rex can't work the case, which means he has more time to keep an eye on me, once he realizes *I'm* his wife and not Melonie.

"Or maybe he'll help us, if he's as mad about her killer as you said he is," Carol said as we walked up to her house.

"I suppose," I said, resigned. "Let me help you with your bags while you open the door."

"Oh, thanks." She handed me the bags.

Her home was warm compared to the cool of early June, and it was immaculate as always. I slipped off my shoes at the door. "Where do you want these?"

"Put them on the counter, please," she replied.

I placed the bags down and watched her put a kettle on, then put the food away. "Where's Barry now?" I picked up Mal so she could watch.

"He's in Belize, hunting whatever they hunt there," she said.

"Do you think he goes on all these trips to get away from you?" I had to ask. He was usually gone for months at a time, stopping at home to switch his gear out and hopefully spend time with Carol. She deserved it.

"Oh, we both prefer it this way," she said while pulling down some tea bags and displaying them for me to choose one.

"I'll take the orange spice," I said. "I don't understand. You're both retired, but you'd rather not spend time together?"

"We love each other very much, but we've found through the years that being apart for a little while brings the spark back in our marriage."

We moved to the living room with our tea, Mal following me with her leash in her mouth. I leaned down and snapped it off her halter, and she lay at my feet. She'd been at Carol's house often enough to know not to jump up on the furniture.

Carol took a sip of her tea. "Okay, out with it. There's something else bothering you besides stupid husbands."

"Why do these women keep popping up out of nowhere and everyone knows them?" I blurted out. "My cousin Victoria is a good example. I didn't even know she'd ever been on Mackinac Island, let alone know so many people here. Then Melonie came. Now there's Rowan. It makes me feel . . . like an outsider." I tried not to sound petulant, but I didn't do a very good job.

"You're not an outsider, and I wish you'd stop thinking about yourself that way." Carol patted my knee. "Just because we know them doesn't make them a townie."

"Thanks for the ego boost," I said with a half-smile. "I know I'm being silly. Rowan was the first person to be there after I found Melonie. She sort of snuck up on me. I don't know how she does it, but she does it a lot."

"That girl always seemed to find herself in the middle of things." Carol shook her head.

I sipped my tea. The aroma calmed me as much as Carol's words. "Do you know, she has a Great Dane named Finn? He's so calm and well trained, I'd say he was the best dog—next to Mal, of course."

"Oh, yes," she said. "Her Aunt Tonya told me."

Aunt Tonya. I inhaled and blew out a long sigh. Then tried to ignore how everyone not only knew Rowan, but her family as well. I changed the subject back to the murder. "I heard that Rowan and Melonie weren't on the best of terms. Do you think there's any chance that she—"

"Did it?" Carol finished my sentence. "Since, like you said, she was the first one on the scene, she could very well have done it. But it doesn't seem right that after all these years she'd come back only to kill Melonie. I mean, who would return all the way from New York City to bump off their childhood enemy?"

"True," I said with a quick tilt of my head to the side and shrugged. "But she took pictures of the crime scene for Shane, without even asking. Doesn't that seem odd to you? Personally, I find it creepy."

"It does seem suspicious," Carol said. "But it could

be just a coincidence that she was there. Was she there before or after you called Charlene?"

"Before," I replied, curious where she was going with the point.

"Maybe while you called Charlene, she texted Shane and learned what he needed."

"No," I countered. "When Shane got there, he seemed truly surprised to see her."

"Hmmm, we both know that killers often insert themselves into the investigations. What better way than to take photos for the CSI? We'll add her to the murder board and see where it goes," Carol said. "Do you think Rex will join us this time?"

"I doubt it. I called Charles, and he said they would put Rex on traffic duty. That way he can remain on the island. Otherwise, they'd loan him out to another department in the district.

"After today, it might not hurt to have him on temporary duty for a while," I muttered.

"Oh, you don't mean that," Carol said. "You're practically honeymooners still. It's only been a year."

I shook my head. "Watching Main Street to make sure fudgies don't walk out in the middle of the road when a taxi or wagon goes through is a far cry from his usual lead officer role," I said. *Fudgies* were the loving names we used for the tourists who came to enjoy the island and leave with at least one box of fudge. "I can't imagine what his mood will be. And I'm the one who's going to have to live with him through this."

"It's all going to be alright," Carol said. "So, any other suspects?"

"There was this plumber upstairs who said he'd been repairing her toilet and bathroom," I replied. "He could have slipped down, killed her, then gone back upstairs without anyone noticing. Also he said his assistant was coming and going at the time. Plus, there were five people in the costume room who had finished their photo shoot who could have done it. Finally, anyone on the island that Melonie pushed too far could have popped in and done it."

"Basically, the list is endless." Carol frowned "Any idea how she died?"

"Before Shane got home, Rowan said that Shane told her Melonie died from a nail gun shot straight into her heart."

Carol sat up. "That is odd. Are you sure? Who would have a nail gun?"

"I don't know. Plumbers, maybe? Don't they repair walls or flooring if they have to get into or under them?" I thought out loud. "That is, if Rowan wasn't lying about Shane telling her how Melonie died. He doesn't normally say anything to anyone about these things, not even Jenn."

"Maybe Rowan *is* the killer. If Shane never tells anyone, how else would she know?" Carol said. "But first, let's go back to the plumber. Did he have a plumber's tool bag? You know, where a nail gun might be kept?"

"Yes, he did." I frowned. "Come to think of it, though, he didn't have it when Charles questioned him. They must have taken it for evidence. I bet they took my fudge, too. You know, evidence." I laughed, and Carol joined me.

"What we really need to figure out is motive." Carol winced. "Never mind. Everyone has motive."

"But not everyone would kill Melonie just because they could," I said. "Rowan did say that whoever killed Melonie had to have placed the nail gun pretty close to her heart before they pressed the trigger. And not just that—the register was open."

"Robbery?" Carol sounded astonished. "Who would rob a portrait studio with a nail gun?"

"It doesn't fit, does it?" I said. "It also looked like all the money was still there."

"All of this is odd." Carol put her empty cup down, her expression one of deep thought. "You said there were those five people in the back room changing clothes. That means she'd taken their pictures not too long before she was murdered. Did that leave enough time for the killer to walk in, silently kill her, and leave?"

"Maybe." I shrugged. "For me, it's the silent part. How do you silence a nail gun?"

"The people in the back could have been laughing and talking and didn't notice a nail gun going off," Carol said as she got up and went to the murder board, which now seemed to be a permanent fixture in her living room. "Think of it. Nail guns are a regular part of home repair that we ignore. We hear them all the time when roofs are repaired or drywall is attached to studs. Plus, why would the people changing their costumes notice whoever was in the studio?"

"They wouldn't, especially if it was a repair person," I said. "Workers like plumbers, electricians, and construction guys coming and going in and out of another person's business or home aren't really noticed. For example, remember the last time you came into the McMurphy for a cup of coffee?"

"Sure," Carol said. "I grabbed coffee while you chatted up a guest. He went upstairs, and you came over to talk to me."

"Only he wasn't a guest," I said. "He was a painter in painter's overalls and shirt with a big logo on the back. He was carrying a white bucket with rollers and brushes in it. Some were even sticking out. We're painting some of the rooms on the third floor."

"No, it was a guest. He had on jeans and a baseball cap, and he held a fishing bucket and gear," Carol insisted.

I grinned. "Do you want to bet? Then, not fifteen minutes later, you faced the front when the rest of his team came in talking and laughing. They had painters' clothes on with paint splattered everywhere, and they carried paint gear. They went straight upstairs. I know you saw them because you made a comment about how noisy young men could be."

"No." She shook her head, confused. "Those were guests."

"See what I mean? If you want, come by tomorrow, and I'll take you up to the third floor and show you the team at work."

"Well, shoot," Carol said.

"We need to find those five people in the back room.

One or more of them could be the killer. They had opportunity. They could have had the means or a motive," I said.

"You're right. We won't know about means or motive until we do," Carol said. "Do you happen to have their names?"

"I'm hoping Melonie wrote them down in her client book," I said. "It's hard to do with walk-ins, though, when your schedule is already full."

"You went there to bring her fudge when you found her body," Carol stated.

"I did. I wanted to make some sort of a peace offering, or call a truce at the very least."

"Then you could be a suspect, too," Carol pointed out. "Did Charles interview you?"

"He did," I said, drawing my eyebrows together. "Huh."

"Don't be silly," Carol said. "Everyone knows you wouldn't murder anyone."

I chuckled. "Sometimes I wish I could."

"Oh, honey, sometimes we all wish we could murder someone. It's whether you actually do or not that makes a difference."

Shortbread Lemon Raspberry Bars

Ingredients

Shortbread Crust

1¾ cups + 3 tablespoons of flour
7 tablespoons of corn starch
7 tablespoons of sugar
⅛ teaspoon of salt
1 cup of melted butter

Toppings

¾ cup of seedless raspberry preserves
(if using preserves with seeds, run it through a sieve to remove most of the seeds)
2 cups of canned lemon pie filling
Optional: ¼ cup of powdered sugar and fresh raspberries for garnish

Directions

Preheat oven to 350°F.

Line 13x9-inch cake pan with parchment paper.

Sift dry ingredients into a medium-size bowl. Add melted butter. Use a rubber spatula to gently stir and press dough until no dry ingredients remain. Don't over-stir!

Use spatula to gently pat into a pie pan and create a smooth surface.

Bake for 35 to 40 minutes or until golden brown. Remove from oven. While warm, spread raspberry preserves, making sure to cover all the shortbread. Gently so as not to mix the two, spoon filling over the top. Place back in the oven for 20 minutes. While warm, use a hot knife to score the bars to keep from crumbling later. Cool. If desired, lightly dust bars with ¼ cup of powdered sugar and fresh raspberries. Refrigerate for 1 to 2 hours. Once set, carefully remove bars from the pan. Gently cut along scored lines and serve.

Makes 24 bars.

Chapter 8

"Have you started the infamous murder board yet?" Rowan asked. Mal and I were halfway to Jenn's house when we ran into Rowan.

"I thought you were going back to the McMurphy."

"Oh, yes, I intended to, but then I thought I'd take a walk around and see how the island has changed since I was last here," she said.

"Has it?"

"Oh, no, it's pretty much the same, except for that new 'Grander Hotel.' Don't you think it's sad that they felt they had to use The Grand Hotel's name to get noticed?" Rowan asked.

"Personally, I thought it was funny," I said, doing my best not to take her words as an insult. "Have you seen their ads? They claim to have the smallest porch in the United States. It's a tiny doll porch off the front door."

"Oh, I didn't see that," she said, and glanced my way. "But I can see how that would be funny."

"I have a friend who works there," I said. "She's a gifted chocolatier. She can re-create anything in chocolate.

You're a trained pastry chef. You should go in and check out their menu."

"She can re-create anything in chocolate? That *is* gifted. I took a semester in candy making but I was never any good at creating large or complex chocolate replicas." Rowan said as we walked side by side. Finn pranced along with us, his gaze lovingly on her, while Mal sniffed the walkway. "It takes a real artist to sculpt like that. The best I can do is create small standard pieces for accents and plating. Now I have to go in and check out their dessert menu." She looked down. "Are you really staying with Jenn now?"

I had a bit of whiplash at how quickly she changed the subject. "Staying with Jenn?" I repeated.

"Yes," she replied. "I noticed you brought both of your pets, and an overnight case was on the couch. . . . Also, I believe you mentioned something about it at dinner."

"Right," I said. "I'm only staying tonight. Then I need to get back to fudge making."

"Good," she said. "Jenn seemed upset and looked like she could use the company."

"I think we could both use the company tonight," I said.

I thought about how Jenn could be a force to be reckoned with when she was upset. When I left, I'd caught a glance at Shane's face. He'd wanted to leave with me.

"I do want to apologize," Rowan said sincerely. "I had no idea you were Rex's new wife. I can't believe I said all those things. But I'm Catholic, and I can't understand having so many different wives. I mean, unless the others died . . ." She clasped her hand over her mouth. "Oh."

"Only one more wife to die, and I'm golden, right?"

"Oh, oh, no. That's not what I meant at all. I wouldn't wish death on anyone. Poor Melonie."

"I thought you hated her," I said.

"*Hate* is a harsh word for something that happened a long time ago. Dislike, maybe, but not hate. And it definitely doesn't mean you want them dead."

"Of course," I said.

"Wait! Am *I* a person of interest?" Her eyes lit up.

"You and me both," I said. "Since neither of us was on the best of terms with Melonie."

"That's so cool," Rowan said. "Don't you think that's cool? Can I come to the next book club meeting and see my picture on the murder board?"

"You do realize the book club will look at you suspiciously," I said. "Since murderers tend to poke their noses into the investigations."

She laughed. "I am nosy. I learned it to get the skinny on my sisters. Otherwise, I never would have learned anything about them. Trust me, I now know too much."

I laughed. "I'm an only child, so if I was going to snoop, I'd have had to snoop on myself."

"But you're so good at it, according to my Auntie Charlene, of course."

"Of course." Even after she told me she was nosy, I started to like Rowan. I definitely was in love with Finn. "Look, the McMurphy's doors close at nine. But you can use your key card afterward."

"That's good to know," Rowan said. "Safety first.

Of course, Finn is my first line of defense, but not everyone has a Finn."

"Didn't you say you also had a cat?" I asked as we walked.

"He's the family cat. Just showed up one day and took over the household."

I laughed. "Sounds like Mella. What kind of cat is he?"

"He's a tabby cat. Mostly orange with black stripes and spots of white on his chest and his feet. He has big murder-mittens, chubby cheeks, and smallish ears. His name is Paddy. I adore him. He tolerates me."

I laughed. "You met Mella. She adopted me. Then, a year later, I learned she already had an owner. I took her back. But the owner told me that it sounded like Mella had left home and adopted me and the McMurphy instead. And, as long as she was happy at my place, I could keep her. I've since learned she'll go back every now and then looking for treats."

Rowan laughed. "Seriously, it sounds like Paddy. He goes into the back of one of the bars in town. Pretty much everyone there knows him and gives him something to eat, until the bartender or the bar owner kicks him out, which he thinks is quite rude. And one of us has to go get him because our family's name is on his collar. He's been doing it so long they know him by name. He's considered the mascot of the bar."

I couldn't help but laugh out loud. I took a deep breath after. "Thanks for the dose of reality," I said. "This is where we split. You turn left toward the lake for the McMurphy, and I go right."

"Gotcha," she said. "So, murder board?"

"Ask Carol," I said. "But you do realize it'll be a couple of days. And your stay on the island is only three nights."

"Don't worry," she said. "The trip up from Charlevoix doesn't take that long."

I walked to Jenn's house, and there on the steps of the porch was Rex. He looked so dang mouthwatering in jeans and a tight, dark blue T-shirt. His shaved head, blue eyes, and stupidly long black lashes had me falling for him every time I saw him. But I wasn't going to budge on this one. It was a matter of honor, at the very least.

Mal, the traitor, pulled her leash out of my hand and ran straight to him. He reached down and picked her up, gave her a kiss, and stroked her soft curls. "Hi."

"Hi," I repeated and kept three feet between us, or I'd throw myself at him. "How'd you find me?"

"You always go to Jenn's," he replied, and I made a note to go to either Frances's or Carol's place next time.

"Hmph," I replied.

"Look, I'm sorry," he said. "I was wrong all the way around. *You* are my wife and the love of my life. Seeing Melonie dead on the floor like that made me crazy. All I could think about was that it could have been you lying there and there would be nothing I could do about it. I was out of my head. All I saw was you on the floor. Now I realize how it must have sounded to you and everyone else who was there. And I understand why you dragged me out of there."

I didn't answer. No matter how ready I was to take him back.

"Just so you know, I've already apologized to Shane and Charles and the crew for badgering them."

"What did they say?" I had to ask.

"That if anything ever happened to you, they'd have a team of bouncers ready to take my bum to jail until after the investigation. They said it would make the investigation better without badgering or distractions."

"I see," was all I said.

He cleared his throat. "I want you to come home. No, I need you to come home. I could never forgive myself if you didn't. Especially if something bad happened to you."

"I still don't understand how you could look at Melonie in a costume and think of me," I said. It sounded so ridiculous. Was that how he saw me? As Melonie in another hair color?

"I didn't," he said. His expression was full of sorrow and concern. "When I parked my bike, someone said my wife was dead inside. That was all it took. I was angry and afraid that it might be true with all the people you've put in jail. Seeing a female body on the floor was a punch to the gut. I swear my brain clung to the thought it was you on the floor."

"But you knew it was Melonie. You even said, 'Melonie?' and looked at her body with sadness," I reiterated.

"I don't remember that at all," he said. "I swear it was you. It was so surreal. After that, everything else, including you, was nothing but background noise. I became so focused on ensuring everyone did their job properly to find your killer that I didn't realize it wasn't you until you cuffed me. Then when you walked me out and up the stairs, all I saw was red. By the time I realized what I'd been saying and that *you* were still alive, you were gone."

"I don't believe you," I said. "I think you need more time to fix whatever this is going through your mind."

Mal got down and ran over to me, grabbed me by the pants leg, and pulled me toward Rex as if to say she was done with our tiff and wanted us to make up now. I let her and took a few steps closer. Rex met me and took my hands—something that always reminded me of our wedding and made my heart race. Darn it, he knew me too well.

"I don't blame you for thinking that way. I know it might take a while for you to forgive me. I'm so sorry. Come home with me."

I said nothing.

"Please?" He squeezed my hands lightly.

"I don't know," I said. "But if I were you, I'd never, ever do that again."

"I promise," he said. "Unless it's really you on the floor, and then, all bets are off. Besides, you wouldn't know, because—"

"I'd be dead."

"I don't want to ever have to think about that again. It's just . . ."

"What?"

"I couldn't live if anyone killed you."

Darn it, he knew he could always get to me. I grabbed him and hugged him.

He hugged me tight, tears welling up in his blue eyes,

and he wiped them off without letting me go. "Come home."

"I'll come home," I said. "Let me go tell Jenn."

"You might not want to go in there," he said.

"Why not?" I asked.

"They had a fight, too, and now they're making up."

"Why does that— Oh," I said and smiled. "And Mella?"

"Ran out as soon as I knocked and Shane opened the door with his eyeglasses half off, wearing nothing but his jeans." Rex grinned. "I asked if you were there. He said no and shut the door in my face. At this rate, they're going to have a second kid."

"About that," I said and took his hand in mine.

Chapter 9

The next morning, Rex brought me coffee while I slapped a small amount of makeup on my face. I had to wear it because of the demonstrations, and also because I was the "face" of the McMurphy. When I came out into the kitchen, he'd made bacon, eggs, toast, and slices of avocado.

"Is this an apology feast?" I asked.

"Yes," he said and pointed me to a stool on the counter between the kitchen and the living room. "I already took Mal out. Mella is on her cat tree, sleeping."

He put a plate of food in front of me. I couldn't believe how hungry I was, then I remembered I hadn't eaten much at last night's dinner. I'd spent more time listening to Rowan and Shane talk about old times, and glancing at Jenn's expressions of sadness, anger, jealousy, and worry. I reached over and squeezed her hand, noting that she wasn't eating either. Which was bad, since she was eating for two.

"Looks like I have the day free," Rex said. "Anything I can help you with?"

I swallowed a bite of toast with creamy egg and

avocado on top. Then I drank some coffee. "Is this to keep you busy and out of the investigation?" I asked.

"Maybe," he replied. It was the first time I saw the need to unofficially investigate mirrored in his expression.

"I don't have anything that needs getting done except maybe picking up some groceries," I said. "If you come up with anything on the murder, you have to promise to tell me."

"Only if you tell me if you discover anything," he replied.

"Fine," I said and gave the remaining food on my plate to the pets. "Do you know how she was killed?"

"Nail gun to the heart," we said at the same time.

"Shane?" I asked. He nodded.

"And you?" he asked.

"Rowan," I said. "It seems Shane told her, too."

"I heard she could get a priest to spill his guts."

We both laughed.

"Seriously," I said. "Do you know Rowan?"

"I didn't grow up here, remember? I had no idea who she was until Shane told me they went to school together. He even admitted to having a crush on her back in the day. But she wasn't interested, and they became close friends instead."

"There's still a spark there," I said. "Even if it's mostly on Shane's part. That and a couple of other reasons are why Jenn was so angry last night. I know I was angry, too, when you showed me yesterday how deep your feelings for Melonie still are. I mean, didn't she stay with you for a while?"

"Are you going to let it go?" he asked softly. "There's no spark, not even a flint strike between her and me. I would never lie to you about that."

I reached for his hand. "I know. That's why I was so shocked when you kept calling her your 'wife.'"

"I thought it was you," he said softly.

"As ridiculous as that sounds, I'm doing my best to understand," I said. "And I've accepted your apology. But that doesn't mean it's not going to take me a little while to shake it off."

"I understand," he said with a grim look. "I would be the same way if you went crazy for another man who had died. Let's say, Harry Winston."

I laughed and laughed hard. "He and Sophie are engaged. She's the one who would be devastated. Now, if you were talking about Trent . . ."

A possessiveness flashed in his eyes, and then anger. "Jessop." He spat out the name.

I laughed. Then kissed him firmly, grabbed a new chef's coat, and hurried downstairs. I had fudge to make, and Roxanne would be there already.

Jenn came in at nine to start work on a wedding she'd been hired to plan. She and I shared an office upstairs, mostly because one or both of us was usually out of the office working on other things. She had a happy glow about her and carried my overnight. I stepped out, leaving Roxanne to turn the fudge with the long fudge-turning implement.

"You never came back," Jenn said with little regret. "I thought I'd bring you your stuff."

"Thanks." I put the case behind the registration desk. "I understand you two made up?" I lifted my right eyebrow. "At least that's what Rex said when Shane came to the door."

"We made up in the best possible way," she replied, a blush rushing up her cheeks. "You?"

"Same," I said. "He apologized and claimed he thought it was me on the floor dead. Someone told him his 'wife' was dead before he even entered the building. That's why he was so crazy."

"Men." Jenn rolled her eyes, then smiled wide. "What would we do without them?"

"I don't know for sure," I said. "And I don't want to know." We both laughed. Then we hugged, and she went upstairs smelling of chocolate and her perfume, I went back to making fudge. But I couldn't seem to get over the fact that a murder had happened right next door. I needed to know who did it. Was it one of her customers? Was it someone Melonie knew but hated? Or was it a random stranger who'd been looking for a woman alone?

The random stranger theory didn't make sense, because Melonie wasn't alone—there were people in the shop. That meant the killer was likely someone she knew.

I finished the ten o'clock demonstration, then sold fudge for about fifteen minutes until the crowd was gone. "Roxanne," I said. "You knew Melonie better than I did. Who do you think might have killed her and why?"

"I don't really know who," she replied as she washed the big copper pot. "But as for why, you knew her. She was nasty to a lot of people. Always making them out to be the villain when she was the actual villain. Everything was all about how she was persecuted and then how she got back at people who persecuted her."

"Wait, so she thought she was persecuted? Isn't that a bit harsh of a word? I mean, when you treat people badly, you get bad back. Everyone knows that." I cleaned the marble fudge table for the next batch.

"Exactly," Roxanne said. "Several people tried to tell her the same thing, but then they found themselves on 'the list' of people who'd persecuted her."

"So, basically she'd had it in for everyone on the island," I said.

"Everyone but Rex," she continued. "Even after you got married, she told people she had something on you that would break you and Rex up permanently. She planned to use it to get to Rex. That way he'd divorce you, and she would console him until he fell back into her arms."

"What?" I couldn't believe my ears. I'd never heard any of this before.

"Oh, yes," Roxanne said. "All that and more when it came to you two."

I frowned. "Why didn't anyone tell me this before?"

"Because no one believed it," Roxanne said. "Melonie always schemed to tear people apart with her lies. The sad part is that it worked a great deal of the time."

"It wouldn't have worked this time. There's nothing she could have ever told Rex that would make him divorce me."

"Everyone agreed, but whatever it was, she thought it would be enough," Roxanne said.

"That's insane. If she believed she could do it, then why didn't she tell him before we got married? Why wait until after we were married a year?"

"She just wanted to make you look bad." Roxanne wiped down the copper pot.

"Great, now people might believe she got to me, and I was upset enough to kill her. That makes me look more and more like her killer."

"Yes," Roxanne replied and looked me in the eye. "Yes, it does."

Chapter 10

I didn't know what to do with the fact that Melonie thought she could somehow cause Rex to leave me. That she assumed Rex would come running back to her once I was out of the way. If most people knew about this, maybe whoever killed Melonie wasn't out to murder her as much as they were out to get rid of me by framing me for murder. I would lose everything. The McMurphy, my reputation, my pets, and possibly Rex.

That meant there were two sides to this murder. One to get Melonie, and the other to frame me. Maybe, for the killer, it was a win/win situation.

After the 2:00 p.m. demonstration, I left Roxanne to clean up the shop and went upstairs to shower. I couldn't stop my thoughts from going round and round. Who would want to get rid of me and Melonie? And more importantly, why?

Rex wasn't home, and neither was Mal. He must have taken her out for a walk. By the time I'd showered and changed, he still wasn't home. I called him.

"Hi, sweetheart," he said. I could hear the wind blowing around him. "What's up?"

"Simply checking to make sure you were still alive."

He laughed. "Yes, I'm still alive. Mal likes to walk far, and she thinks she's smelled something. I need to see what it is, so that's what we're doing."

"Basically, what I do, then," I replied.

"Yep."

"I wanted to tell you about a theory Roxanne had," I said and filled him in. "Do you think the killer murdered Melonie to try to frame me? If so, who would want to do that? Any idea?"

"We can talk about this when I get home, but offhand my answer is, maybe. You've made a lot of enemies catching criminals. Their families and friends can't be happy with you. If Melonie harmed them or further deteriorated their social standing, then it would stand to reason they would have no qualms about killing Melonie. Especially if they were angry with both her and you."

"I was afraid of that," I said. "I'm going to go for a walk. I need the exercise."

"Tell Carol I said hi," he said.

"How did you know I was going to Carol's?" I asked.

"Because that's where you go."

"Huh," I replied and decided then and there to go to the senior center instead. "I'll let her know if I see her."

"Have a safe walk."

"You, too," I said. "Don't let Mal get you into trouble."

"I won't."

I put my phone in the pocket of my blue jeans and headed downstairs. I was definitely going to the senior center. After that, I might go see Ida. She and Carol had yet to make up.

I walked out the back door to see Rowan coming down the alley.

"Allie," she said with a smile and a wave.

"Hi, Rowan. I see you've been walking Finn. How does he do with the crowds of fudgies?"

"He's great with a crowd," she replied. "Very laid-back."

I shook my head. "He's amazing."

"How's the investigation going?"

"Mostly I'm at the point of getting my head around what happened and considering possible scenarios."

"I had an idea," Rowan said. "What if they killed Melonie to frame you?"

"What made you think of that?" I asked.

"Well," she replied, "I have three reasons. One, Melonie wasn't known for her kindness. Basically she hated everyone but Rex, even if she was the one to run out on him. Two, there was the fact that it happened right next to the McMurphy, and three, you always seem to be the first one to find a dead body."

"Did Charlene fill you in on all of that?" I asked.

"Only the dead body part," she replied. "You're always the one to call her first."

"I suppose that makes sense," I commented.

"So, are you going to Carol's house again, or the senior center? Although my bet would be Carol's. Not only does she have more security but you're not carrying fudge, and you always take fudge to the center."

"Not always," I said and crossed my arms.

"That's not what Auntie Annie tells me. She said that if you're going to the senior center, you always bring fudge as a bribe."

Just then, Roxanne came hurrying through the back door. "Oh, good, I'm glad I caught you. You forgot your fudge." She handed me a plate of fudge, winked, and went back inside.

The whole thing took me aback. Was I so predictable? It appeared I was, and that wasn't good. Anyone who wanted me dead, or worse—framed—could have quickly guessed where I'd be and why. I swallowed the moment of embarrassment and the tingling anxiety that ran down my spine. "See?" I said and lifted the fudge. "Just forgotten."

"Finn and I are coming with you," she said. "It's not simply because I want to be a part of the investigation, but also because I want to ensure you're safe." She shrugged. "Besides, I might as well as go visit my aunt's friends."

"I certainly can't stop you," I said and headed toward the center. *From now on, I'm going to be less predictable*, I thought. The problem was that the island was so small and there were only so many ways to get anywhere. Perhaps I should change whom I talk to. Maybe I should talk to Liz first. She was the town's newspaper reporter and publisher. She had to know things about any investigation. I had no idea why I hadn't thought of it sooner.

Chapter 11

"Hey, Allie," Mr. Ryan called out from the table where the men played cards. "It's been a while since we've seen you. What kind of fudge did you bring today?"

"Larry, stop badgering her. The poor girl doesn't have to bring fudge every time she comes," said Bill Stanislav. He stood and rubbed his hands together. "Did you bring the Traverse City Dark Chocolate Cherry? You know that's my favorite."

"I sure did, Mr. Stanislav," I said.

"Rowan!" Mary O'Malley and Laura Morgan said at the same time. They got up and ran as best they could to hug Rowan. Instead of their usual tracksuits, they wore patterned shirts and one-color ankle pants. Finn stood beside Rowan, his tail wagging.

I put the fudge on the table and went into the kitchen to grab some small plates. When I got back, both men had several pieces of fudge resting on napkins on the table beside them. So much for the small plates. I shook my head and walked over to the corner, where Ida sat crocheting a lace tablecloth. “Hi, Ida,” I said. “How are you?”

“Terrible,” she replied, then looked up and grinned. “Have a seat.”

“Thanks.” I sat and watched the room. Rowan talked to a few other ladies while the rest helped themselves to fudge. I noticed Carol and Irma were missing.

“Need information on Melonie’s death?” Ida asked, keeping her eyes on her crochet. When she wasn’t out biking, Ida usually had a crochet hook in her hand, working on something while her sharp mind concentrated on other things. She liked to wear her long silver hair in a braid down her back.

“Yes, but that’s not why I’m here.”

“Why are you here, then?” Ida asked. Her busy hands calmed me. Today, Ida wore a pretty spring dress, cream in color with tiny purple flowers. The sleeves were three-quarter length, and the skirt came down to mid-calf. She wore comfortable purple tennis shoes.

“You look cute. Are you wanting someone in particular to notice you?” I teased.

“No,” she said, but I swear I saw a blush on her cheeks. I decided not to tease her further. “Now, tell me why you’re here if not to learn more.”

I frowned. “I’m really concerned that I’m horribly predictable. I never realized until today that everyone can guess where I’m going. Even worse, they still know even after I change my mind. For example, Rex told me I was headed for Carol’s—so did Rowan, and I just met her. When I changed my mind to come here instead, Roxanne came out with a plate of fudge before

I even asked. Before I said a word. It's like she read my mind. It's scary if I'm that predictable. I could easily be murdered—or framed."

"Framed?" Ida looked up, her hands making knots without her even looking.

I explained our theory. "It might be nothing. But I have to consider it like everything else."

"I see." She went back to counting her stitches. "Being framed is a strong possibility."

"But how would they know that I would choose that day to bring over fudge as a goodwill gesture to Melonie?"

"Did you discuss it with anyone else before you left?"

"Sure," I said. "Frances and Roxanne, but Melonie was killed long before I said anything about my intentions."

"Hmmm," she said. "Did Melonie say something untoward to you this week?"

"I don't think so," I said.

"You've been married for a year. Why would you pick this week to bring her fudge as a truce?"

That's when it dawned on me. "You're right. Why *did* I suddenly do it? If I remember right, she was tossing her trash in the big bin between us in the alley. I went out to do the same, and she threatened me. She said she'd have Rex back soon, even if it meant my demise. I thought that was odd at the time. We'd been married for a year. Why threaten me now? I replied that I really didn't think there should be this kind of animosity between us. After all, we were neighbors. Then she frowned at me and stomped off, slamming her door behind her."

"Was there anyone else in the alley at the time?"

"I don't think so," I said, shaking my head.

"Could anyone have overheard you?"

"Maybe someone with their window open at the hotel behind the McMurphy." I shrugged. "But it seems like a huge coincidence for that to happen. Think about it. The right person—the one who wanted Melonie dead—would have to happen to overhear our conversation and then kill Melonie and frame me to hide what they'd done."

"Unless it was someone who works nearby," Ida suggested.

"True," I said. "Or we could be off track altogether. It could be someone who wanted revenge not on me, but on Melonie. After all, there wasn't anyone Melonie didn't talk bad about. You know her hateful tone."

"True," Ida said. "But why now? What triggered it? Then again, the killer could be anyone on or off the island. Remember she was gone for a few years before she came back, even though she hates winter."

"It could even be someone from her past," I said thoughtfully. "How are we ever going to figure that out?"

"Let's rule you out first. Is there anyone from your time in Chicago who didn't like you?" Ida asked me.

"A few were jealous of my abilities in the kitchen." I shrugged. "But they knew I'd been helping Papa Liam my whole life. And as far as I know, after all this time no one dislikes me so much that they'd come all the way to the island and kill another woman to frame me."

"Are you sure about that?" Ida asked. "After all, you've become nationally known ever since that fudge-off. Jealousy can be very patient. Maybe they came up to see what you were doing and figured out how to frame you, to take you down a peg or two."

"That sounds ridiculous." I thought about it for a minute or two. "Okay, we'll rule framing me out. Which takes me back to the original question: Who could have done this to Melonie?"

"Oh, honey, I wish I knew. Melonie could be mean and rude. She hated everyone, and it showed. As you said, her killer could be anyone from anywhere. We both know she had to have been just as nasty when she left for all those years before she showed up again. I know she tried dog walking and pet sitting for a job, but even the pets didn't like her. There was something about her that was a bit off-putting. Maybe it was trauma. Or maybe she was just born that way."

"Trauma," I muttered. "I wonder by whom and why."

"You know, Rex was her second husband. I heard she had a way with men. She seemed to be a love-them-and-leave-them kind of gal. I'm surprised she didn't have a child or two."

"Maybe she couldn't have children and simply didn't care, or worse, she was using sex to cover up her grief." Ida stopped crocheting for a moment and put her hands in her lap. "Any idea if she was sleeping with anyone on the island recently?"

"I doubt very much she'd have told me if she was," I said. My gaze moved around the room. "Where are Irma and Carol?"

Ida shrugged. "I'm not their babysitter."

"You haven't made up yet?" Concern filled my heart.

"No." Ida shook her head. "Betty tried to get us all together for coffee and cake, but as soon as Carol and Irma heard I'd been invited, they backed out."

"What is wrong with them?" I said. "I thought Carol didn't mean not to invite you in the first place. That it was an accident."

"Yes, but an excuse is not an apology, and Carol knows that. I think that's why she's avoiding me," Ida said. "An apology is all I need. Even Irma knows that. Although why Irma won't visit me is beyond me."

"I hate to see my favorite people fighting," I said.

"Let's get back to your predictability problem," Ida said. "Have you tried mixing things up a bit?"

"It's a small island," I said. "Honestly, I don't know how to mix it up."

"What about going to see the girls your own age when you want to solve a case? I hear Sophie is on the island more often these days."

"I don't want to bother the girls. They have full lives."

"Maybe they feel the same about you," Ida suggested. "Are you still upset about the bachelorette party?"

"Oh, gosh, no," I said.

"What about Jenn? It seems to me that she knows about as much as Carol does when it comes to the island. Seriously. You should skip the book club and work with more young people like yourself. You might be surprised."

"You're right. I've been working with the seniors for

so long that it's become a habit." I stood. "It's time to mix things up a bit."

"Attagirl," she said. "Now, go on and get out of this dusty old place."

"I'll go if you promise me one thing," I said.

"It's not up to me to apologize," she said.

"It doesn't mean you can't be the bigger person and simply start showing up where those two go . . . like the book club. Or the card club. Bring cake. You know no one can resist your cake."

She made a face. "It won't be my fault if those two run out of the clubs as soon as I get there."

"Carol can't run out of the book club. It's at her house. Go with Judith. Then Carol has to open the door."

Ida shrugged. "We'll see."

"I won't quit nagging you until you do," I told her and bent over, giving her a kiss on the cheek. "Thank you for helping me understand how to be less predictable."

Chapter 12

I went to the police station to get Rex. I knew he couldn't stay out of things no matter how hard he tried. So, I figured it was my job to be sure he did.

"Allie," Charles said when I approached the desk. "Glad you're here."

I frowned. "I thought you were working the case. Why are you watching the reception desk?"

"It's Ashbury's lunchtime, and I needed to get away from Rex for a while to think."

"I'll get him." I shook my head.

"Perhaps now is a good time for a honeymoon," he suggested.

"We both know I'm a person of interest in this case," I said. "Leaving now would make me look guilty."

"With both of you gone, I might get some actual work done." He grinned.

"Get the district chief to tell Rex that he has two weeks of mandatory vacation," I said. "Then take his keys and don't let him back in. I'll keep him out of your hair."

"And what about you?" Charles asked.

"Well, it's not like you can make *me* take a vacation," I said with a wink. "But I promise I'll only follow a clue if I come across one. Otherwise, I'll concentrate on my wayward husband and the McMurphy. Deal?"

"Deal." Charles stood and shook my hand. "Now, go get him out of here."

I saluted him, and we both laughed.

Getting Rex to leave was as simple as threatening to perp-walk him out again. Many of the other officers grinned at me. But Rex was silently angry as I put my arm through his and walked out of the bullpen and into the foyer. Mal led the way.

"You're making me look like a fool in front of the other men," he groused.

"I think you're doing that all by yourself," I said. Mal barked as if in agreement. "Besides, who wouldn't want to walk around the island with their beautiful bride on their arm?"

Just as we made it to the door, another officer opened it. "Ah, Manning," he said. "It's been a while. I hear congratulations are in order. Is this your blushing bride?"

It sounded like a greeting on the outside, but Allie could hear the snideness in his tone. "Laird," Rex said. "This is Allie Manning." Rex sounded like the last thing he wanted to do was to introduce this man. "Allie, Officer Laird."

Officer Laird was short. At best he was five foot, five inches tall. Thin with very little muscle, it was easy to think that all he did was paperwork. Unlike Rex, it was hard to imagine him running down an offender. Like Rex, his uniform was perfectly tailored, and the seams were crisp. His dark hair was short on the sides and long and slightly greasy on top, as if he were trying to hide a bald spot with a comb-over. He had a sharp face, from the bones on his cheeks to his nose and chin. He reminded me of a horror-movie undertaker.

The man took my hand and kissed the back of it with his open mouth. It gave me the heebie-jeebies. I pulled my hand away and held on to Rex as I wiped it on my pants. Mal growled, and I agreed with her. "What a cute little dog," Officer Laird said. "I understand it bit a suspect once. If it bites someone again, the thing will have to be put down as a danger to those on the island."

"Officer Laird." I acknowledged the creepy man, then said, as calmly as possible, "You touch my dog, and someone will have to put me in jail because I will ki—" Rex squeezed my other hand. "—ensure whoever does it wished they had never come to the island," I finished.

"My, my, a threat already, and we've just met. I'll do you a favor and not put you in jail for threatening a police officer this time. See that you don't do it again."

"Why are you here?" Rex asked. His tone clearly simmered with something close to disgust.

"I can't believe no one told you," the man said with a grin. "I'm taking over the investigation."

"Officer Brown is fully capable—"

"Yes, yes." He cut Rex off. "The chief feels that—and I quote—'Brown is too close to the case' and had me step in instead. I'm sure this case will be easily cracked." He gave us a look that said he was better than everyone there, including Rex. I returned his expression with anger, and an up-and-down look as if I were surveying a cockroach. I couldn't help it. I was very close to telling the man he could take his attitude and go back from wherever he was from. But Rex patted my hand in an attempt to calm me. So, I kept quiet.

"I'm sure you can get back to your usual, bumbling ways once this case is closed. Unless, of course, the chief wants me to stay and oversee everything you've done here."

Knowing Rex as well as I did, I could tell he worked hard not to say anything he'd get into trouble for. It was clear the man was baiting him.

"When I say easily cracked, I mean it's an open-and-shut case." He looked me up and down before he turned and walked away from us. "Oh, and Allie," Officer Laird called over his shoulder. "Stay away from my case, or I will throw you in jail for obstruction of justice."

I narrowed my eyes and took three steps toward him. My hands fisted when Rex grabbed me around the waist and pulled me out the door. Mal growled again as the door closed behind us.

"What a loathsome man," I said. "How do you know him, and why is he really here?"

"We were at the academy at the same time," Rex said. "He's had it out for me ever since I came in first and picked Mackinac Island as my station." He paused. "Allie, he's right, you know. If you investigate, he can throw you in jail for obstruction."

"Don't worry," I said. "The last thing I want to do is to help that man find the killer. But that doesn't mean I can't throw hints Charles's way."

"Allie . . ." Rex said. "Please."

"My guess is that I'll be the first suspect," I said. "I bet he would love that. I was the one who found Melonie, and I do live next door. And everyone knows that Melonie hated me. It's not a difficult leap to think I hated her back. If I were to guess, he'll be knocking at our door first thing in the morning and dragging me down to the station for interrogation."

Rex's face grew dark with anger. "I'll put our lawyer on red alert. If he does that, don't say anything but the word 'lawyer.' I know he'll try to trick you into defending yourself. Don't do it. Whatever it takes to keep from saying anything but 'lawyer,' do it—except to leap over the table and try to kill the man."

I laughed, then grew solemn. If I was going to save myself and find the real killer, I was going to have to be careful and change everything I did. Including letting the seniors know where I was and if I was investigating. The last thing I wanted was for them to be hauled into the station and interrogated by that sleazy man.

Chapter 13

I was right.

It was eight in the morning. Frances had just come into work. Roxanne and I had finished the daily fudge and were discussing the kind we wanted to make for the ten o'clock and two o'clock demonstrations when Charles and Officer Laird arrived. They came through the lobby door and headed toward the fudge shop.

Stepping around the counter, I took off my fudge-coated baker's coat and hat. I'd worn a McMurphy polo shirt and black shoes to look more professional in case my prediction came true. As they approached, I opened the fudge shop door and stepped out. "Good morning, officers," I said and pasted a cheery smile on my face. "How can I help you? Are you looking for fudge? We've made some of my award-winning flavors this morning." I pointed to the cabinet.

"Allie McMurphy," Officer Laird started.

I smiled and cut him off. "It's Manning. Allie Manning. But do go on. Wait, let me guess. Your favorite fudge is . . . our nutty fudge. It's got black walnuts, pecans, cashews," I counted out on my fingers, "Brazil nuts, peanuts—although that's not really a nut—and coconut. Am I right?"

Charles had to work hard to keep a straight face.

"I'm not here for fudge," Officer Laird said with self-satisfaction in his tone.

"I see," I said. "Well," I continued to count, "I also have pralines, peanut brittle, chocolate-covered apples on a stick, and these wonderful lollipops I started making. They are a real hit with the kids. Do you have kids, Officer Laird?"

"No, but that's not the point." His voice went up an octave, and Charles had to cough.

"Are you laughing, Officer Brown?" Officer Laird asked, his face starting to turn pink. "There's nothing funny about a police investigation."

"Oh, right," I said with an innocent smile. "The investigation. How's that going? You must need some coffee by now. I have a coffee bar. It's free. I prefer that my guests use it, but you look like you need it." I walked right by them and went to the coffee bar.

"Allie, are you okay?" Frances asked, watching the two police officers stare.

"I'm fine. Could you let Rex know that I was right and to go ahead and talk to Jay Butcher?"

"Certainly," Frances said, her expression still one of confusion.

"Don't worry," I said, louder. "I'll be around when Jay comes to fix the thing. Sorry, officers, an owner's work is never done."

"I don't understand. Who is that man?" Frances asked.

"Don't worry, Frances. Rex will probably let you

know what we need from him when he gets here. But first . . ." I turned and smiled brightly. "Coffee for the gentlemen. Do you like cream or sugar?" I asked them, pouring them both a cup. "Let me guess. Black for you, and Charles, oh, right, you're working, excuse me, Officer Brown. I know you like two sugars with no cream." I handed them each a cup. Officer Laird took it out of habit.

"I'm not here for coffee or tea or anything to eat," Officer Laird practically growled as he set it back down on the counter.

"Too bad," I said. "I also have donuts from Michele's bakery. She makes the best—"

"Mrs. McMurphy—"

"Manning," I said. "Ms. Manning. It's easy to make that mistake. We've only been married for a year."

"Mrs. Manning," he practically yelled.

"Ms." I poured myself a cup of coffee. "And you don't need to raise your voice. I'm right here and listening."

Rex casually came down the stairs. "Officer Brown," he said and nodded. "Oh, yes, and Officer Laird. What can we do for you this fine morning?"

"I haven't a clue," I said. "They didn't want any fudge or homemade candy. Not even the chocolate-covered apples. So, I figured they were working very hard on the case. You are, aren't you?" I paused for a reply and then started again when Officer Laird opened his mouth. "I offered them coffee or tea and donuts. Still, it seems they don't want anything. Perhaps a guest room?" I turned to the two. "I mean, what does Officer Brown need a room for, since he has his own house?

Perhaps you, Officer Laird? We have some of the most accommodating rooms on the island."

Charles coughed again.

"Oh, Officer Brown, do you have allergies or a cold? I have a perfect medication for that. One my grammy showed me. It's a mixture of honey and hot—"

"Enough!" Officer Laird yelled.

"Please, Officer Laird, don't make me tell you again, lower your voice. We have guests still sleeping. It's their vacation, you know."

Rex had his arms crossed and leaned against the wall. Frances had grabbed Mal and held her while she growled.

"Besides, I was only trying to help," I said. "You don't have to yell."

"Mrs. Manning," he said.

"Ms." I corrected him as if he were a bit slow in the head.

"Ms. Manning." Officer Laird turned purple.

"Are you okay?" I asked. "You look like your blood pressure is too high. Perhaps you should sit." I pointed to one of the wing-backed chairs nearby. "Don't worry, we'll get this all sorted out. Frances, can you get a bag for Officer Laird to breathe in?"

Officer Laird took a deep breath. "Ms. Manning—" he began, getting it right this time. "We're here to take you down to the station to ask you a few questions."

"I don't understand," I said as innocently as possible. "Why can't you ask me your questions right here?

I have a perfectly good office. It's quiet, if that's what you need."

Officer Laird closed his eyes and appeared to be counting to ten. Charles coughed again, and Laird opened his eyes and gave him a dirty look. He started again. "Mrs. Manning, you are a person of interest in the murder of Melonie Manning. We need you to come with us."

"It's Ms." I was careful not to sound too much like he was an idiot. "Poor Melonie, I can't believe she's gone. Do you know I was the one who found her? I think I'll always remember her that way, and it's too bad. No one should be remembered looking like they look when they are found murdered. May she rest in peace."

"Come with us." I could tell he'd had enough. "Or we'll have to cuff you." Officer Laird finished.

"Oh, my," I said. "I've never been cuffed before." I glanced at Rex. "Have I?"

It was Rex's turn to cough, and Charles looked at him with one eyebrow lifted.

"I've had enough. Put the cuffs on her, Brown," Officer Laird said, very grumpily. So much for his snide self-satisfaction. "I'm done. Bring her to the station and put her in the interrogation room." He headed out the door, and I kept my mouth closed, but I did wink at Charles, who tried very hard to remain distant and professional. He cuffed me, then took hold of my forearm and gently walked me out. Rex, Frances, and Roxanne all frowned at Charles, but no one moved.

I took him seriously now. I didn't say a word, and neither did he. I knew he would most likely read me my rights the moment I said a word. So, I didn't.

What I did notice was everyone coming out of their shops and watching.

"Seriously, Charles?" Mary Emry said as she walked down the street with a Doud's delivery bag in her hand.

"Doing my job, Mary," Charles said.

"Oh, please, you know you don't have to cuff Allie. It's ridiculous," Louis Dupont said.

By the time we arrived at the station, there was a crowd behind us, demanding to know what was going on. They followed us into the lobby as Charles walked me to the interview room. He uncuffed me there.

"I'm sorry, Allie," he said when we were alone.

I still didn't talk, only smiled at him.

"Can I get you anything? Water? Coffee?"

"Water," I replied. "I've seen your coffee."

That made him smile. "When I come back, I have to read you your rights."

"I know."

He left the room, locking it behind him. I could hear my friends and the whole community arguing with whoever met them at the door and attempted to make them leave.

Charles returned with a small water bottle, put it down, and read me my rights. Then he quickly excused himself. It must be all hands on deck to get the community out of the station. The support made me smile.

Before they even came in to question me, there was a knock on the door, and Jay Butcher walked in.

"Why knock?" I teased. "It's not like I can open the door."

"Hi, Allie," he said, hugged me, then sat down, placing his briefcase beside him. "What's this all about?"

I let him in on everything, but not before looking to make sure there wasn't a camera on us.

"They can't record this," he said. "Not until they come in. Especially with your lawyer present."

"Thanks for coming," I said and touched his hand. "There's a new guy leading the investigation since Rex is too close to the victim. I knew as soon as I met him that he had some sort of vendetta against Rex. That's why I expected this ridiculous person-of-interest act, and we called you. I delayed them as long as I could."

"And the mob with pitchforks and baseball bats?" he asked.

I laughed, knowing no one out there had a weapon. "Charles had to walk me here cuffed. It was a direct order, and my friends and the rest of the community were not having it. Anyway, do I have to stay here? Can't you go out to them, tell them they have no reason to hold me, and take me home?"

"Did they read you your rights?"

"Yes," I said.

"I'll let them know we're done here," Jay said.

"Thank you."

Jay was in and out very quickly. There was a loud cheer when he walked me out. Everyone wanted to know what happened.

"It was all a mistake," I said. "Thank you! It's so wonderful to know that I can count on everyone here."

I applauded them, and they dispersed. Jay and I rounded the corner to the McMurphy.

He stopped me outside the door. “Are you sure you’ve told me everything?”

“Everything I know right now.”

“Good,” Jay said. “I think it’s best if you refrain from talking to anyone about what you know. You never know who might have a reason to frame you.”

“Like the killer?” I asked.

He said nothing.

“Okay,” I replied, more contrite.

“Keep me as your number-one contact for now,” he said. “What you did today isn’t always going to work.”

“Thank you,” I said.

“It’s what I get paid to do.”

Rocky Road Fudge

Ingredients

2 cups of semi-sweet chocolate chips
2 tablespoons of unsalted butter
1 14-ounce can of sweetened condensed milk
½ teaspoon of vanilla
1½ cups of coarsely chopped roasted nuts
2 cups of mini marshmallows

Directions

Line a 13x9-inch pan with parchment paper. Butter paper.

In a one-quart glass measuring cup, microwave chocolate chips, butter, and sweetened condensed milk on high for 3 minutes, stirring every 1.5 minutes until chocolate is melted. Carefully remove. It will be hot! Immediately stir in vanilla. Wait 5 minutes. Mix nuts and marshmallows in a large bowl. Gently stir in fudge mixture. Scoop into prepared pan. Cool completely and cut into 2-inch pieces.

Makes 24.

Chapter 14

"You okay?" Frances, her husband, Douglas, and Roxanne asked at the same time when I walked inside.

Mal greeted me at the door. I picked her up as my gaze landed on Rex leaning against the reception desk, watching me with his dark blue eyes. His expression was solemn, but there was a twinkle in his eyes.

"I'm fine."

"That looked pretty serious," Roxanne said. "Except for how you greeted them. You were hilarious, and I almost lost it. I had to work hard not to burst out laughing, but I figured it would make things worse. It seems that new guy is an"—she pulled back and searched for an appropriate word—"idiot," she finally settled on.

"What made him think you had anything to do with Melonie's murder in the first place?" Frances asked.

Rex came close and put his arm around my waist. I leaned my head into his shoulder.

"He has a bone to pick with me," Rex explained. "And Allie was the one to find Melonie, so he thought it would be easy to question her and get her to confess to the murder."

"But Rex got me a lawyer right away. Then, when Charles took me out cuffed, the entire community practically rioted inside and outside of the station. Plus, Officer Laird had no evidence," I said, then decided to change the subject. "How'd the ten o'clock demonstration go?"

"There weren't a lot of people," Roxanne said with a grin. "Many of the fudgies followed along to the station to see what was going on. But afterward, we were swamped until this lull. We're going to have to make some more fudge for the afternoon, if you feel up to it."

I glanced at Rex. He shrugged. "It's your call."

"Why don't we close up for thirty minutes," I said. "You go get some lunch, and I'll clean up to start again."

"Sounds good," Roxanne said.

I took Rex's hand. "Thanks for today."

"You don't need to thank me," he said as we walked up the steps to our apartment. "It was all you."

"You called Jay in the first place," I said. "All I did was keep Officer Laird busy until Jay arrived." I shook my head. "Poor Charles. He took a lot of heat for simply following orders. I guess he's going to have to do a lot to get back in good standing with the community."

"Oh, he'll be buying lots of drinks at the pubs," Rex said as we reached our apartment and went inside. I put Mal down and Mella slipped in between us and the door jam.

I thought about Rex's comment and stopped after the door was closed. "Wait, he didn't—"

"Assemble the mob?" Rex answered. "Now, why would he do that?"

"He did." I shoved Rex for not telling me the truth. "He had them follow us on purpose. Why? Ohhhh, to delay the questions until my lawyer got there."

"Maybe. . ." Rex said as I sat on a stool at the counter and he poured me a cool glass of lemonade.

I took a gulp of the sweet and sour, pulpy goodness, put down my glass, and narrowed my eyes as another thought hit me. "He didn't do it alone, did he? There were too many people. Which means you had a hand in it, too."

"I plead the Fifth," he said and put down two plates with grilled ham and cheese sandwiches and an apple.

"You two are cunning," I said, my admiration slipping out.

"You're not so bad yourself." He kissed me.

After lunch, Roxanne and I managed four new batches of fudge before the second demonstration. During the demonstrations, I always enjoyed telling Papa Liam's stories as Roxanne and I poured the hot fudge on a marble table with a cooling system underneath. We took the long-handled turner and turned the candy until the fudge cooled enough to use the small scrapers. I talked about choosing the type of fudge and how we made each fudge differently. To make the particular fudge we'd chosen, I poured chunks of crushed toffee and chopped mango down the middle. Then we folded and folded and folded it until the toffee and mango were well distributed and the fudge was cool enough to make a soft, sweet treat.

I cut it into one-pound slices while Roxanne passed out pieces to taste.

The toffee was sweet and crunchy, while the mango was richer, tropical, and creamy. It was a wonderful pairing I'd been trying out, and so far, it had gone over well. After the crowd left, I let Roxanne go for the day and texted my friends while I waited for any stragglers.

I included Liz, Sophie, and Jenn. *I need your help*, I texted.

Hello to you, too, Sophie teased me.

That was quite the show this morning, Liz texted. *What happened?*

Something happened? Sophie asked. *Now I need to know about this.*

Geez, I took one day off and something exciting happened, Jenn texted.

What happened? Sophie and Jenn texted at the same time.

I can't talk about it, I answered. *My lawyer said that if I did, I'd have to get another lawyer, and I may end up in jail accused of something I didn't do.*

They brought her to the police station in handcuffs, Liz texted. *It was quite the show. Charles walked her through town and down to the station, her hands in cuffs, while a mob of townies followed, shouting and angry with Charles and the police.*

Poor Charles, I texted. *He was only following orders.*

I was there, Liz texted back. *It was wild. I've never seen so many islanders upset.*

I can't believe that Charles would do such a thing, Sophie texted. *He's always so nice.*

He didn't, I explained. *There's a new officer in charge. Officer Laird.*

I met him, Liz said. *He's a creepy man with ulterior motives.*

What ulterior motives? Jenn asked.

I don't know, Liz texted. *But whatever it is, it's driving him to jump to conclusions. Which I'm sure he did with Allie.*

Allie, Jenn texted. *Tell us what he wants.*

He hates Rex, I answered. *He wants to pin the murder on me just to get to Rex. He told us it would be easily and quickly solved. But we all know that finding killers isn't that easy and it takes a lot of time. Especially if you don't know anyone on the island.*

I agree, Liz texted. *How would he know who to talk to and get the clues he'll need?*

That's where you come in, I messaged back. *Could you help me find this killer?*

And put you at risk for obstruction of justice? Liz asked.

Were you there when we met him? I texted.

No, Liz answered, *but one of my sources was.*

Why not go to your usual book club? Jenn asked.

Why go there when I have such beautiful friends who can help me? I'm so sorry I didn't ask you before, but my wedding taught me to reach out to my friends, I replied.

Jenn texted laughing emojis. *You just want to stop being so predictable.*

Maybe, I replied. *And maybe I need people I can*

trust to help me stay out of jail. So, are you in or are you out?

I'm in, Liz texted. *I've always wondered what it was like to search for a killer.*

I'm in, Jenn agreed. *Having Benji is a great cover.*

I'm in, too, Sophie responded. *I can keep an eye out on plane and ferry transportation. Nobody comes or goes on the island that I don't know about.*

Perfect, thanks, I texted.

When do we start? Liz asked.

Do you want to have a girls' night? I texted. *We should do one every month. We need to, really.*

They all agreed that a girls' night was a great idea, and it was set for Wednesday night. Now all I had to do was tell Rex about the girls' night and be as innocent as I could about it.

Chapter 15

Rowan Giles opened the door to the McMurphy, and Mal rushed over to play with Finn. It was an odd combination, a little white dog and a giant, silvery-gray-often-called-lilac Great Dane.

"How are you?" I asked. "You look exhausted. I mean that in the nicest way possible. Is there anything I can do to help?"

Rowan stopped at the front desk, where I was holding down the fort while Frances went to the doctor for her annual checkup. "I am exhausted," she replied. "After you were so excited about my photography, I called my Aunt Esther for advice about maybe opening my own store. She told me that opening a business was a lot of work. But I couldn't see how it could be. Rent the storefront, set up my equipment, add a few shots for example, and go. But no, there's the advertising and the signs and the logo and the big sign on the building and building permits for the remodeling to meet my needs and then handing out flyers and getting to know the neighbors so they don't complain about what I do even though I'm sure they won't complain. I've barely scratched the surface, and I can't imagine driving over an hour here and back, then adding a ferry trip every morning and every night." She took a deep breath. "It's just not possible right now. Oh, hey, I saw that police officer take you away in cuffs this morning. I thought you two were friends. Are you okay? Anyway, it looks like you made it out okay. Were they arresting you? Because I can tell them that when I got there, there wasn't a nail gun in sight, and you seemed as startled to find her as I was." She stopped to take another breath. "Long story long. I hope you're okay, and if you're investigating the murder, I'd love to join you."

Wow, I thought. *Okay. What do I say?* After all, it was still very likely she killed Melonie. She had more reasons than I did. She even showed up for the first time the day of Melonie's death.

Did I trust her?

"I'm not investigating this time, like I have in the past," I lied. "The new head of police has promised he'd charge me with obstruction of justice if I did. I'm sorry to disappoint you, but I wouldn't want to do anything to put myself or anyone else in the path of a police officer more determined to charge us with a crime than find the killer."

"I see." She sounded disappointed. "It's just that I've heard so much about you and your investigations that I had hoped to help you with one." She perked up. "Wait, I was also told that with your boyfriend–now–husband, Rex Manning, being the head police officer, you always had to hide your investigations."

I didn't say a word or even move a muscle, or my

expression would have given me away, and then she'd know and soon everyone would know, and I'd find myself in jail as promised.

"I understand you can't investigate." She winked. "It's too bad, because I have access to crime-scene photos and photos of people in the crowd, front and back. I may even have photos of the plumber and a few of the couples leaving out the back. Which is weird, by the way. People should always exit out the front door. It makes them look suspicious. Did they always exit out the back door of the shop?"

I thought about it for a moment. "No, actually, I would have seen people going out that way when I take Mal out for her walk."

"Like I said, I may have photos of the crowd. Of course, I know you're not interested since you aren't investigating. I'll probably delete them. I already asked the new officer if he wanted to see them, but he dismissed me. He said he only wanted official photos taken by Shane. Oh, and I'm not supposed to go anywhere for the next day or two."

"That's too bad about the photos," I said. "Staying is not a problem. I'll move some guests around."

"Thanks," she said then pulled her camera up to eye level and looked in the viewer. "It's a good thing the photos are digital. I can simply delete them."

I made a decision I hoped wouldn't come back to haunt me. "Listen, my friends and I are having a girls' night tomorrow. Would you like to come?"

"That would be wonderful," she said with a look of excitement on her face. "I could use a girls' night. It's been a while. I've been too busy the last eight years with school and stuff."

It was the shortest reply I'd ever heard her give. "I understand," I said. "When I first got here, I was too busy with work, too. But now I have a small group of friends our age. There's Jenn, my best friend who came to visit and never left. Then I met Liz. She owns the *Town Crier* with her grandfather Angus. And last but not least is Sophie. She owns a charter plane service for people who want to fly in. We're going to meet at Liz's house."

"They sound so special," Rowan said. "I don't think I've ever had that many girlfriends. I always did better with men. There's Shane, of course. Oh, I got the feeling that I somehow overstepped with Jenn. Do you think she'll be okay with my being there? I mean, I probably shouldn't have shown up without notice, told her her dinner was bad, then got yams and fixed them for everyone. I should have thought it through, but it's what my family does. Anyway, do you think she'll be upset? I have a tendency to upset women. I had a friend once—Heather—but she didn't seem to be interested in the same things as I was and dropped me to join the popular group. My sisters are so much older; they had lives of their own that didn't revolve around school. The younger brothers are closer to my age, so I hung around with them a lot. It's how I met Shane."

"What about Amy Hanson and Marijo Rooney? Didn't you tell me you were 'Charlene's Angels'?" I asked.

"Oh, you're right, I did tell you about them." She

leaned against the receptionist's desk. "Amy was hit and run over by a truck when we were eleven."

"I'm so sorry to hear that," I said.

"It's okay." She waved it away. "It's been a long time, and I'm mostly okay with it. Then Marijo's family moved to New Mexico. Her father couldn't take the winters here. We were fifteen. We texted at first. I talked every day on Messenger and Snapchat. But she was on there less and less until she wasn't anymore. Mom said it happens when you're that age and start dating and such. I also knew how outgoing Marijo was. She made new friends easily and didn't have time for me. Anyway, do you want me to bring my camera? We could look at the pictures, if you want."

"We might," I hedged.

"Cool, if it's okay with Liz, I can put them on the TV, and everyone can see them all at once."

A pair of guests arrived, and Rowan stepped back, as I checked them in.

Rex stepped down the stairs, and I looked at Rowan. "So, home videos? I can't wait to see Shane when he was in grade school."

At first, confusion showed on Rowan's face, but when she spotted Rex, she seemed to realize what was going on. "Yes, I'm excited for girls' night tomorrow and getting to know each other better. I'll meet you in the lobby, and you can take me to Liz's?"

"Perfect," I said as Rex came over and kissed me on the cheek.

"Come on, Finn," Rowan said, and the dog was

immediately at her side. "See you later, Allie, and thanks again."

We watched her climb the stairs before Rex gave me a knowing look. "Girls' night?"

"Liz wanted to spend some time with everyone," I said.

"I'm sure she did," Rex said.

"I would never put my friends in danger," I said as he put his arms around me.

"Just yourself," he replied near my ear, causing shivers down my spine. "I don't like it when you put yourself in danger. You put my heart in danger, and more than most of my joy and all of my love."

"Now you're getting all mushy on me."

"It's because I love you, Allie Manning."

"Aw," I turned and leaned against him. Then I placed my hand on his cheek. "I love you, too. Trust me, if I were to investigate this—and I'm not—the closest I'll get to danger is Officer Laird. The man is determined to see me go to jail for a very long time."

"I guess I'd better put Jay on retainer," he teased me.

"Why does Officer Laird hate you so much?" I asked. "You being the best in the class doesn't seem enough for this much retaliation."

"I might have been in a relationship with his girlfriend."

"What?" I said, aghast.

"*Shh, shh, shhh,*" he said and put his finger on my lips. "It wasn't my fault. She's the one who hounded me. She told me they'd broken up. I took her at her word, or I would never have done it. But it turns out she lied and didn't even have the guts to break it off with him. He's had it out for me ever since. Even when I apologized and explained what happened, he was certain I was lying and blaming his 'innocent girlfriend.' Guess what?"

"She blamed you, too," I said softly. "She sounds like a terrible person. Why did you even date her?"

"I was young, and I'd never had a girl throw herself at me. Plus, I didn't have a girlfriend. Hadn't had one in a long time because I was concentrating on school and training. And without any parents to offer me advice, I went with it. I assumed she was telling the truth. It took dating Laird's girl, the madness of my first wife, and Melonie abandoning me to realize I wasn't picking the best women. That's why when you were dating Trent Jessop, I stayed away. I wasn't going to do that again."

"Until you kissed me at that dance, and Trent saw us," I replied.

"If I remember correctly, you kissed me back."

"Trent and I had taken a break during that time," I defended myself. I didn't want to be like all the other women in his life.

"But then you got back together," he reminded me. "There was nothing left for me to do but stay away from you." He gave me a squeeze just as Frances came back.

"You two may own the McMurphy, but that doesn't mean you can act that way when you're at work," she teased.

"In our defense, the only people who arrived were the Dubbs. And Rex wasn't down here yet. Rowan needs to stay a bit longer. I told her she could and then moved the Wades into the Petoskey Room."

"Got it," Frances said. "Now, why don't you two take Mal for a walk or something." She waved us away.

I laughed and picked Mal up. I slipped her into her harness, and Rex opened the back door to let us out. You could tell Mal was happy to get some attention and be a part of our group. "Oh, Mal," I said as we walked along. "Have you been feeling neglected?"

"She shouldn't be," Rex replied. "I've taken her out twice already, and we've gone on long walks. Do you know that Mr. Beecher walks back here once a day?

I chuckled. "It's twice a day, actually. Where do you think I met him?" I glanced at my watch. "When are you and Charles going to buy drinks?"

"Are you trying to get rid of me?" he asked, his blue eyes twinkling.

"Oh, no," I said. "I want to know how much time we have together before I'm all alone again."

Rex lifted my hand and kissed the back of it. This time it was a warm, sexy kiss. I had goose bumps running up my arm. "Are you going to miss me?"

"I am," I said. "I really am. Do you want me to fix you some dinner?"

"No, that's not necessary," he said. "I imagine we'll be out until way past ten. Why don't you get some takeout and call one of your friends for a girls' night? I imagine you'll need to make plans. How's Jenn doing?" he asked. "Shane tells me she had a big wedding and anything that could go wrong did go wrong. She was running around like a crazy woman. It all turned out great anyway, and the couple and their family were very happy and have written her a glowing review for her social media."

"Thanks for letting me know. I knew she had a big event last weekend," I said. "I didn't know she was scrambling to make it right."

"Call her," he said.

"I will." We walked in comfortable silence holding hands and taking Mal as far as we could. Finally, I had to ask. "You probably knew Melonie the best out of anyone. Who do you think killed her, and why?"

"Really," he answered. "You're asking me that?"

"Curious is all," I said. "I mean, if you were running the police investigation, where would you start and why?"

"You don't give up, do you?"

"You won't tell me, even though you're a civilian right now?" I asked. "Did you at least tell Charles?"

"I can't," Rex said. "It would interfere with an investigation. Now, if they were to ask me, that would be a whole other thing."

I shook my head. "You are mean—just mean."

"I'd rather be mean than lose you, either to the killer or to Laird."

Chapter 16

I knocked lightly on Jenn's door with a bottle of the finest flavored bubble water in my hand. She let me in but put her finger over her lips. I nodded, entered behind her, and put the bottle on the counter. Benji was asleep on the couch. She picked him up without so much as a sound from him and took him back to his bedroom. Quietly closing the door, she returned to the kitchen.

"How are you?" I asked when she hugged me. "I heard you had quite the weekend. Also, I brought you Doud's finest bottle of flavored water." We both laughed. "Here, sit, and I'll pour us a glass."

"Pour yourself some wine," she said. "There's a bottle of white in the fridge."

I poured the appropriate beverages and sat with her as she rubbed her slightly rounded stomach. I put my glass down and held her hand. "Are you okay? Any morning sickness?"

She smiled. "I'm doing well, actually."

"Are you happy?" I asked. "Two kids can be a lot, or so I'm told."

"Yes, I'm very happy," she said. "I wanted a second baby so that Benji doesn't grow up an only child."

"Like me."

"Actually, like my cousin." She shook her head. "He was always precocious, and his childhood was more like being a third grown-up and less like being a child. I wanted Benji to have a better childhood, and I think a sibling helps with that."

"You might be right," I said. "I always wanted a brother or sister. If I haven't said this before, I'm so happy for you. Are you sure you're okay with . . . everything we're planning?"

"Speaking of girls' night—"

"Wait," I said. I held my hand up to stop her, then looked around. "Is Shane here?"

"No, he said something about Charles having to buy drinks for everyone and wanting to be there to support him."

"Then you know the crowd that followed Charles and me this morning and harassed the station about letting me out—" I started before she interrupted me.

"Was planned by Charles and Rex to give you time for your lawyer to get there," she finished.

"So now they have to buy rounds of drinks all night," I said.

We both laughed. Then she sobered. "You do know they would have done it even without the promise of a beverage."

"I do," I said. "That's why I love this place. People look out for one another."

"So, quick question," Jenn began as we both sipped

our drinks. "Does this new lead officer really think you killed Melonie?"

"He wants it to be me," I said and explained how he had unresolved anger toward Rex and why.

"I hate to say it, but I have a feeling he won't give up until you're in jail." Jenn looked at me with concern.

"I know," I said. "It's why I came to you, Liz, and Sophie for help. Here's the thing," I winced, "I invited Rowan Giles to girls' night, too."

Jenn sat back. "Why?"

"I know it's complicated—"

"We both know she's more likely to have killed Melonie than you," Jenn said. "And I'm pretty sure I don't like her after the other night. She's rude, and Shane . . ."

"Loves you," I replied. "But she also has the original photos of the crime scene and the crowd. Officer Laird dismissed them from his investigation, which makes it okay for us to view them."

"And you think we may see something the police missed. Besides, there is that old saying: Keep your friends close and your enemies closer." Jenn took a gulp of her drink. "Couldn't she have faked the pictures so that we don't suspect her? I mean, you saw how good she was at manipulating those pet pictures."

"Maybe," I said. "But I was there when she took the inside ones." I took a few sips of wine and tried to figure out how we could verify they were real. "Couldn't you somehow get Shane to verify the photos without letting him know you were comparing the two sets?"

"You are devious," Jenn said, then got herself more

flavored bubbly water and poured me another glass of wine. We both curled up on the couch.

"Time to change the subject. How far along are you?" I asked. "And why didn't you tell me sooner?"

"We've both been so busy," she said sheepishly. "And Shane and I wanted some time alone with the idea. Then I didn't want to bother you with something that can wait."

"Wait until when? When you're nine months along and about to give birth?" I teased her. "Now, how far along are you?"

"Five months," she admitted and pulled on her oversized shirt so that it was close to her body.

"I don't mean any offense, but are you sure it's five months—? Because you look six," I teased and took a swallow of my wine. The taste of berries and the tang of sugar and yeast filled my mouth.

"I know you're kidding, but I feel the same way. The doctor reassured me it was natural. I guess that for some women, after the first baby, your body gets bigger faster." She gently patted her tummy. "Remember how big I was with Benji? I can't even comprehend how big I'll be with this one."

"It'll be alright. I was teasing. Frankly, I didn't even notice that you looked any different except that you've been glowing lately. You always look so fashionable that I thought untucked shirts were in style." I tried to comfort her. "Are you planning on another island birth?"

"I haven't decided yet," she said honestly. "As much as I love the way Benji was born, I'd rather not have you off solving a murder when I'm about to give birth.

If we're off the island, there's less of a chance you'll be doing that."

I blushed. She wasn't wrong. I changed the subject. "Are you having Hannah Riversbend as your doula again?"

"Yes," Jenn said. "She was so much help. I love Shane, but he's not the best when it comes to labor. I think he's more scared than I am."

"And are you using Sarah as your midwife?" I asked and took another sip of wine.

"Let's have some cheese and crackers," Jenn said. "I'm starved." I got up, my head a little wobbly from the wine. But I helped her plate the crackers while she cut the cheese and arranged it.

Jenn brought it in and put it on her coffee table. I brought in little plates, and we helped ourselves.

"I believe I asked you about Sarah," I said.

"As much as I loved her, I want to go traditional with this birth. My gynecologist is affiliated with the hospital and will do their best to be on call around my due date."

"What about the ferry ride and then the car trip? Isn't there a possibility of having the baby on the way?"

"We're going to get a rental place for the last two weeks of my term. Hopefully this one won't be late."

"And Benji?"

"My mom is going to watch him."

"You already have a plan in place," I said with a smile.

"We started planning the moment we found out. Then we decided to wait to tell anyone until after the first trimester, in case I lost the baby."

"What a terrible thought," I said. "But necessary, I suppose. Are you still up for a girls' night?"

"To get out of the house? You bet I am," she said. "I haven't been to the office because I've been so crazy busy but I'll be in this week."

"I noticed you've been working from home a lot. I also heard last weekend was terrible. What happened?"

"Everything that could go wrong, did."

She filled me in, and I winced a time or two, but I was still proud of her. She never gave up. She responded to each disaster with the perfect solution, just like she did with mine.

"You're amazing. Doing all that while pregnant and probably still nauseous in the morning," I said, letting her know that I knew she was lying about her morning sickness. "Are you going to tell the girls? You know we're going to want to plan a baby shower."

"After we crack this case," Jenn said.

"After we crack this case," I agreed. I hoped that was soon, but I was afraid it wouldn't be as fast as I'd like. Especially when we needed to avoid Officer Laird.

Chapter 17

Mal and I were out for her evening walk when we ran into Mr. Beecher. He always dressed so dapperly in slacks, a dress shirt, vest, and a matching jacket. His head was bald, and he had twinkling hazel eyes. Mal loved him because he carried treats in his pocket.

"Hello, Allie," he said. "How are you doing after this morning's shenanigans?"

"I survived it," I said. "You're out late."

"Well, with all the business around Melonie's death, there have been a lot of people back here trying to solve the case. I decided to come out later when they weren't around."

It occurred to me that Mr. Beecher might have seen something on his walk. "Can I ask you, were you walking back here when Melonie was murdered?"

"Yes," he said as he gave Mal another treat. "Such a terrible thing, and I was practically there when it happened."

"Did you see anyone coming out of the back door?"

"Hmm, yes, I did, although you're the first to ask," he said.

"They don't know you like I do," I said. "Have you met Rex's replacement, Officer Laird?"

"I don't believe I have," he said.

"I hope you don't. Officer Laird is a blowhard who believes he knows better than the local officers. Not only did he call me a person of interest and try to pin the murder on me, but he said he'd put me in jail for obstruction of justice if I found the killer before he did."

"The man sounds like an idiot," Mr. Beecher said. "Come to think of it, I did see five people exit the photo shop. The first one to leave was Teddy Schmidt. I said hello, but he replied that he couldn't talk. He had to get something for Stan. I didn't realize he was in the shop working when it happened."

"He claims he was upstairs working and didn't hear anything. What about the other four people?" I asked.

"I may have an inkling of who one of them was, but it's hard to tell with their backs to you," he answered. "Especially when they were all wearing *Mackinac Island* sweatshirts."

"Then most likely they weren't local." I was disappointed. If they weren't local, they could be long gone by now.

"I think the group might have only been friends," he said. "But I think Ms. Maas may have been one of them. She could have taken the sweatshirt off. But I recognized her hair and slender body. I had no idea who she was with when she left the shop. It could have been anyone. What I do know is that he was shorter, with brown hair. The rest . . ." Mr. Beecher shrugged. "He had his back to me when he came out. The others both had dark hair and dark skin. I could recognize the sweatshirts from a distance, even if all I saw was the back of them. I doubt any of this is helpful."

I thought about it for a moment. "Wait—you were there when I came out the back door, right?"

"I was," he said.

"Were you the first one there?" I asked.

"Yes," he said. "Officer Davis wasn't far behind me. I introduced myself, again. I had no idea she was back after being reassigned last year."

"She's substituting for Megan Lasko while she's on vacation," I said. "Charles sent her around to watch the back door."

"That makes sense," he agreed.

"Who was second?" I asked

"David," Mr. Beecher said. "I found it interesting that he was so upset when he found out what was happening. I didn't realize he was friends with Melonie. Then there was Bill, he was also broken up by Melonie's death. Why they were both there is beyond me. Melonie wasn't nice to anyone, so why these two? Also, I found it strange they were there. How did word of her death get to them so quickly? Neither one even asked what was going on. They simply knew. Don't you find that odd?"

"I do," I said, making a mental note to check that out. Maybe one of them was the killer. But then I needed to know why. I needed motive, means, and opportunity. And above all, evidence.

"I also saw the book club," I said.

"Ah, the lovely ladies and Ms. Maas. They all came at once. I asked why, and they replied that they saw the police arrive, along with Shane and George Marron. When they saw that the front door was crowded, they tried around the back. I understand you called it in?"

"Yes, I did," I said and told him what happened. "And now Officer Laird is certain I killed her."

"Ridiculous," he said.

"I agree," I said. "Because I didn't do it. I mean, where would I get a nail gun so quickly? It's not like she had one lying around."

"A nail gun?" he asked.

"It's what killed her. Someone shot a nail through her heart at a very close range."

"I've never heard of such a thing."

"Did you happen to hear a nail gun being discharged?" I asked.

"Not that I'm aware of. Do you suspect one of us?" he asked. "Because I've never been a suspect before."

"Should I suspect you?" I asked, trying not to smile.

"Oh, definitely," he said, with a twinkle in his eye. Then he reached down and petted Mal behind her ears. "What do you think, Mal? Do I look guilty?"

She smiled her doggie smile at him.

"Too bad," I said. "Mal says no."

He laughed. "Well, she should know. Have a good night, and stay out of trouble."

"You, too," I said with a chuckle. At least I had a witness. If the killer was in that crowd behind the shop, I would have a head start.

Easy Orange-Chocolate Brownies

Ingredients

1 box of your favorite brownie mix (see box for ingredients required to make the brownies, for example 2 eggs, ⅔ cup of oil, etc.)
Orange juice, as needed
¼ cup of orange jelly/marmalade

Directions

Preheat oven to 350°F. Line pan.

Sieve marmalade to remove the larger pieces of zest. Make uncooked brownie dough using the instructions on the box, substituting fresh orange juice instead of water.

Pour into pan and smooth. Spoon out equal dollops of sieved orange marmalade.

Gently swirl using a butter knife.

Bake, cool and enjoy per instructions on the box.

Chapter 18

"There's no way any of those people could be the killer," Rex said the next night on our way to Jenn's to pick her up for girls' night. I'd already put Rowan and Finn in a horse and buggy taxi with directions to Liz's house. Everyone had a heads-up that she was coming.

"You can't know that," I said as we walked to Jenn's house. I carried a big bowl of my famous cream cheese and dried tomato dip along with a bag of chips. "You are as dismissive as Officer Laird."

"Don't compare me to him," Rex groused.

"You know who Melonie's first and second husbands were, don't you? Is there any way one of them could have done it?"

"I know they don't live on the island." He shook his head. "The only new person is Officer Laird, and he has no reason to kill Melonie. Of course, Officer Davis was here before, so she's not new, and I doubt she's a threat. And Officer Davis had been helping Melonie for the last two weeks."

"Helping? With what?" I asked.

"Melonie called regarding a possible stalker," Rex said. "I had Davis watch over her for two weeks, and no stalker showed up."

"What about the plumber?" I asked. "Stan Powell? The one who owns Powell's Plumbing Services? He's from the mainland."

"If he had anything to do with her first ex-husband, don't you think she would have recognized him?" Rex asked.

"Well, you certainly are a bucket of cold water tonight," I grumbled as we walked up to Jenn's house. I knocked on the door and turned to Rex. "I might have volunteered you for something."

"What?" he asked. "Escorting you two ladies to Liz's?"

"Not quite."

The door opened, and Jenn gave us both a hug. "Oh, thank goodness you're here," she said and waved us inside. Benji was up and bouncing on the couch, throwing building blocks around, his thumb in his mouth. "We finally broke him of the pacifier, and now he's sucking his thumb." Jenn was dismayed. "We're working on that. Anyway, thank you so much for doing this, Rex. Shane had to work late, and I have girls' night. I couldn't find a babysitter this late, and then Allie said you'd do it. Thank you, thank you. All the emergency numbers are on the fridge if you need them. You have Shane's and my phone numbers. Benji gets a cookie and milk in his sippy cup at seven o'clock, then a bath. I put his pajamas and a couple of disposable potty-training pants on his bed. You need to read him a book and he should fall right asleep. Let me get the storybook that's his favorite. Hang on."

She left, and Rex gave me the side-eye. "Babysitting?"

"He's not a baby—he's two," I said. "And he's your godson. Plus, you said you loved kids . . ."

"Not—"

"Here it is," Jenn said as she came out of the bedroom and handed Rex a book. "Do you know what potty-training pants are?" She paused, and Rex looked at me for help. 'I thought so," Jenn said. "They're for kids who are out of diapers but not yet potty trained enough to not need occasional diapers. We're getting him used to the idea of potty training, so there's a small potty in the bathroom. Encourage him to use it. Any questions?"

"Er . . ." Rex uttered, clearly trapped.

"Great," Jenn said. "Benji, Mommy's leaving. Come say goodbye." There was no reply. She looked at Rex. "He must be playing hide-and-seek again. His favorite place to hide is under my bed. Thanks again." Jenn picked up her dessert dish and stepped outside.

I kissed Rex on the cheek. "You're a doll."

"I'll get you for this," he muttered.

I chuckled as I left and closed the door behind me.

Our carriage was preordered and waited for us by the curb. "Are you sure he's okay with this?" Jenn asked. She looked worried.

"He can do it," I reassured her. "If he can handle all those bad guys, babysitting a two-year-old should be a breeze." But I knew he was already plotting his revenge.

Chapter 19

We arrived as Rowan introduced herself and Finn to Liz.

"He's really well behaved," Rowan said. "I promise he won't be any trouble."

She would have kept talking, but I cut her off. "He won't be," I backed Rowan. "Finn kept people away from the crime scene and does everything Rowan says. He makes Mal look like an untrained wild thing. She's here to help."

"As long as Allie vouches for you and your dog, you can come in," Liz said. "I like things the way they are, so be careful to leave them that way."

"Yes, ma'am," Rowan said.

"Are you sure this is a good idea?" Liz asked quietly as I passed her to go inside.

"She has crime-scene photos and may let you publish them," I said.

"Then she's welcome." Liz hugged me and Jenn. She showed us where to put our food. I set my dip and chips on a table full of veggies and veggie dip, plus two desserts. There were bottles of wine along with flavored sparkling water.

"You told them," I deduced.

"Yes," Jenn said. "I didn't want Rowan to tell them first or have them figure it out when I didn't have any wine." She sighed. "I learned my lesson with you."

Liz's home was a beautiful log cabin with a high, pointed roof and large windows that showcased the trees around it. The open design made you feel as if you were in the woods. It fit Liz and her curly dark brown hair, jeans, and flannel shirts. She was a beautiful woman with a good heart, and I wondered why she didn't date much.

I took my glass of wine into the living area, next to a large stone fireplace where everyone sat, and Finn lay down quietly next to Rowan.

As soon as I put my wine down, I gave Sophie a hug. Her long blond hair was smooth and flowed from her shoulders to the middle of her back. Her oval face and tilted blue eyes gave her a pixie look. I sat on the floor and faced everyone. "Thank you all for coming and helping me with this project that is *not* an investigation. It's a safer-community project. Okay? I won't have anyone arrested for obstruction of justice."

Everyone nodded that they understood.

"I brought some colored markers and a whiteboard," Sophie said. "It has a sticky back so that you can post it anywhere. We can use it to write down what we know. Maybe we can put together a plan."

"That's great," I said.

With Liz's permission, Sophie pasted the whiteboard

onto the interior sheetrock wall, then pulled the cap off a marker. "Let's start with who was there."

I let Rowan describe what happened inside the crime scene. I agreed, but then, once again, I had to cut her off to explain who was at the back door when I left.

Sophie wrote out a list of suspects, then made a crude drawing of the floor plan, showing where the body rested, along with a diagram of who stood where inside the building and outside.

"They do say murderers often like to involve themselves in the investigations," Sophie said, and she and Liz glanced at Rowan.

"I didn't do it," Rowan said. "I swear on a stack of Bibles. Plus, I have an alibi. I was talking to my Auntie Annie on the phone when I heard the camera clicking nonstop and I wanted to help the photographer understand how to take proper photos. Allie was there when I got there, and I went on and on about nonsense things because I was nervous about the whole thing. So, I took photos of everything. Would you like to see them?"

"Let's take a break." I cut her rambling off, stood, and went straight to Rowan. "You never told me about being on the phone with your aunt before you walked into the shop."

"I only remembered when she texted me the next day and told me she was glad she decided not to visit the island. The last thing she ever wanted to do was see a dead body."

"Did you tell the police this?" I asked.

"Yes, when I went in and asked if they wanted copies of my pictures." We followed the others to the food.

"Good," I said. "And I'm glad you have an alibi. Did they question your aunt?"

"Auntie Annie? I have no idea, she hasn't said," Rowan said. "These veggies and dips look good, but the desserts look better."

We filled our plates before we moved on to the photos. Rowan used her phone to cast them onto Liz's television. We went over them carefully, but the only real thing we discovered was a prescription jar on the bottom of three shelves that rested on the sideboard. It wasn't a prop like the ones in the window, because the bottle was too new. The ones on display were at least a hundred years old.

"Can you get a close-up of that?" I asked,

"Sure," Rowan said and stretched the photo.

It was a prescription used for anxiety and filled by David Peele. I explained to the ladies why that was suspicious. "David was there when I left the scene," I said, "and he could have given her something that would knock her out, making it easy to then kill her with a nail to her heart." I got up and wrote his name on the board with the word *pills* next to it.

"It doesn't explain the nail gun, though," Liz said. "He could have easily poisoned her."

"Don't they say that women are more likely to poison someone than a man?" Rowan asked.

"Not always," Liz replied.

"But we all know she didn't die of poisoning. What if the pills have nothing to do with it?" Liz asked.

"Rowan, can you show us Melonie's body? If you

don't want to see it, close your eyes," I warned the others, but no one did.

Melonie lay face-up. There was very little blood on her and the floor. It had to be pooled underneath her.

"Maybe it was a paralytic," Liz suggested. She stood and used her hand to emphasize her words. "She would go down and not be able to get up."

"How did they get her to take it?" Sophie asked. "And how would they know she had taken it, with enough time to drive the nail in and then get out between the last photo shoot and Allie arriving?"

"And why didn't the people in the back notice?" Jenn asked. "Someone had to be in the front with Melonie. But who?"

"Did Melonie always wear a costume when she took pictures?" Rowan asked.

"No," I answered thoughtfully. "Maybe she planned to take a photo with her killer. Think of it. They had to be in costume for the others not to care. I mean, I wouldn't care who was next after I had my pictures taken."

"Still, why weren't they in the back with the others after?" Liz asked. "They certainly couldn't walk down the street in Victorian garb and blend in."

"What about the plumber?" Rowan asked and flipped to a photo of the plumber as he came down the stairs. "He could have murdered her, then gone upstairs, changed, and come on down the minute he heard the police come in."

"That makes sense," I said. "Does anyone want to see if they can connect Melonie to Stan Powell? If he killed her, then they had to have known each other well enough to want to take a photo together. Plus, as a plumber, he'd have access to a lot of poisons."

"I'll look into Stan," Liz said.

"I don't understand how she could have been killed with a nail gun in the first place," Rowan said. "Don't people usually survive that?"

"Only if they're found early and taken to surgery right away. I looked it up," I replied. "If only I'd turned into her studio and not waited in the waiting area, she might still be alive."

"You can't think like that," Jenn said. "Even if you had called nine-one-one right away, she would have probably died on the way to the nearest hospital that could perform emergency surgery."

Rowan changed the picture to the people in the back of the shop.

"What about Ed?" Liz asked in an attempt to help me forget my pain. "What was the stable operator doing there?"

"That's a good question," Rowan said. "Since I'm new to the island, I can ask him to show me the horses and tell me about his business and what he does for hobbies."

"I can see if Shane knows anything about the drugs in her system. Maybe she was poisoned and then shot," Jenn said.

"What else do these pictures tell us?" Liz asked.

"Let's see," Rowan said and flipped through the next photo. We continued to look around the scene.

"Wait!" Sophie said. "Look at the flowers on the

small table under the outdoor screen. There's a card. Can you zoom in on that?"

Rowan moved in close and read the card. "*To Melonie, my forever love. Your favorite lover, Oscar.*"

"Who's Oscar?" I asked.

"I don't know," Sophie said, "but we have another name for our suspect board."

"I'd say," Rowan said. "Those flowers in the bouquet are lilies, daffodils, and wisteria. All poisonous. Oscar must not have loved her that much."

"So many questions and no answers." Liz frowned.

"I'm still thinking about the drug that made her not care that she was about to get shot with a nail. It had to be extremely fast-acting and timed just right. Otherwise, wouldn't the last people to be photographed have noticed her being woozy enough to pass out?" I asked.

"That would mean, again, that the murder happened after their picture was taken."

"Unless they were the killers," Rowan suggested.

"I ran into Mr. Beecher," I said. "He told me that he saw the five who left through the back. One of them was Teddy Schmidt. After he left the building, he told Teddy he had no time to talk. He had to get something for his boss."

"Is he the killer, or did he witness the crime?" Liz asked.

"I'll talk to him," I said. "But we would need to match him to a nail gun, and we would need a motive."

"All you had to do was spend two minutes with Melonie before you had the motive," Liz said.

"If she was that bad," Jenn said, "then why did Rex even marry her? It makes no sense."

They all looked at me. "Trust me, the last thing I want to talk about when I'm with Rex is his ex-wives."

They all laughed, breaking the somber mood.

"Speaking of which," I said with a blush, "we ought to get back. If nothing else but to see whether Rex is angry about my springing the babysitting job on him." I explained to everyone what I'd done.

Jenn laughed. "You'll know if he still wants to have kids after this."

"Before you go," Rowan said, "do you have any idea what the motive might be?"

"There really are very few motives that exist," I replied. "Revenge, money, jealousy, fear, and anger. They say the rule of thumb is that most women kill for jealousy and money. While most men kill for revenge or anger. Anyone can kill out of fear, but those rules aren't written in stone. Anyone can kill for any of these reasons, really."

"But Melonie wasn't stabbed multiple times," Liz said. "I doubt she was murdered out of fear or anger. And as far as I know, she didn't have a lot of money. That leaves revenge and jealousy."

"It could have been any of those reasons," Sophie said. "I mean, for all we know, Melonie might have had money or borrowed a lot of it and didn't repay it. She has moved on and off the island over the last few years. Maybe she comes here to hide when something bad happens."

"That might be why she stays close to Rex," Liz

suggested. "She figured no one would bother her if there's a cop nearby."

"She was wrong this time," I said.

"We'll never know. Will we?" Liz shook her head. "Anyway, you were heading out?"

"Yes," I said and gave Liz a hug. "Thanks for this."

"It was fun," Liz said. I opened my mouth, and she cut me off. "I know, I know, it's a community project, and it's all off the record until the killer is caught."

"You got it!"

"I'm leaving, too," Jenn said and gave Liz a hug. Then she patted her belly. "Baby wants to go to sleep."

"I should go, too," Rowan said. "Come, Finn."

The three of us grabbed a taxi. Finn didn't seem to mind at all that large horses pulled the carriage. It had taken Mal some time to get used to it. We dropped Rowan off at the McMurphy and took the taxi all the way to Jenn's house.

"Do you think he'll forgive me?" I asked Jenn.

"You did spring it on him." Jenn smirked.

"I didn't want to give him the opportunity to say no and ruin our girls' night."

"It wouldn't be his fault if he'd said no," Jenn said. "It would have been Shane's. Don't worry, it'll be alright."

"What if he's mad and won't forgive me for a week?" I asked.

"What if he had a good time with his godson?" Jenn countered. "It's always a possibility."

Jenn walked in the door, and I followed. Toys were scattered everywhere. There was a towel on the floor, clearly soaking up some kind of mess. A half-empty sippy cup rested in the sink. Cookies were mashed into the high-chair tray, and the wet mush had dropped on the floor around the chair. There were toys half on the couch, and half off. It looked like a hurricane had blown through the house. I glanced at Jenn. My eyes had to be as big as saucers as fear and regret shot through my veins.

"Where are they?" I whispered.

"Probably in the bedroom," Jenn whispered back.

We walked quietly toward the room. No noise came out of it. When we peered in, we could see why. Benji was in his crib—clean, in pajamas, and sound asleep. Rex was in the rocking chair beside it with a book in his lap, sound asleep, as well.

Jenn and I turned to each other and grinned.

"Aren't they cute?" Jenn asked.

"They are so cute," I replied and sighed. "But I'm going to have to wake mine up and take him home."

"I guess you'll find out tomorrow whether he's mad or not," Jenn whispered. "But it looks like it all turned out okay."

It did seem okay, at least while he slept, I thought. All I had to do now was figure out how to get him home.

Chapter 20

I made waffles with bacon and eggs, Rex's favorites for breakfast. He looked adorable when he came out of the bathroom showered, wearing a dark T-shirt and jeans. He didn't say anything about last night. In fact, he didn't say anything at all. I drank orange juice, kissed him, and then took Mal out for her early morning walk. My heart raced. Had I gone a bit too far by springing Benji on him? I wouldn't know until he said something or sprang something on me as payback.

Mal pulled on the leash and took my attention away from Rex. As we went by the photo shop, Mal sniffed the door and then the alley, as if she knew what to look for. Finally, she pulled me along until we were on the street, then she turned to the right.

"Where are you going?" I asked her. She ignored me and followed her nose. It was odd because she also ignored all of her favorite places to sniff in the morning. I called it her reading the "morning news." Instead, she practically ran with her nose to the ground like Scooby-Doo. We turned left on Market Street until we got to the pharmacy, where she sat and looked up at me, her tongue out and happiness in her eyes.

"Good girl," I said.

The pharmacy wasn't open yet, but I saw David was at the store, standing at the back of the shop. It was clear he was a suspect. Mal was never wrong. Now all I had to do was find his motive, along with the means he used and any evidence. Evidence other than the bottle of pills on the shelf in the photo shop.

"Let's go home," I finally said. Mal shook her head as if to get something out of her ear, then led me again. But instead of going home, she went to the stables and panted her smile. What was up with her? First David, now Ed? Were they working together? Is that why they'd been in the alley? If so, why?

"Okay, Mal," I said. "Good girl. Let's go home now." But again, she ignored me and instead pulled on the leash until we were in front of the police station. She sat again and looked at me expectantly. "I'm sorry, baby," I said. "We can't go in and visit Charles. They might even arrest us for interfering in an investigation."

Mal sat and wouldn't move. Sometimes she could be so stubborn. I finally picked her up and walked away while she whimpered and looked back at the station. As I walked, I ran into Charles on the way down the street.

"Hi, Allie," he said. "You're a bit off-route from your usual early morning walk."

"It's Mal," I said. "She's being stubborn today."

Mal reached for Charles until he pulled her from my arms.

"Good morning, good girl," he said and scratched her

behind her ears. "Why are you being a naughty, stubborn girl today? Do you want your mama to get thrown in jail?"

She whimpered again and turned to face the station.

"Does she want to go to work with me?" he asked with a chuckle in his voice. "I'm pretty sure Officer Laird won't throw *her* in jail for interference."

"That's the weird part," I said. "She sniffed the back door of the photo shop and practically ran to the pharmacy. Then she pulled me to the riding stables, and finally straight here, as if she wanted me to tell you about her clues."

"Do you have a clue for us, little dog?" he asked her.

She barked, and he laughed. "Okay, I promise to go check out the pharmacy and the stables." Mal turned and licked his face.

I wished I could tell him about what we'd seen on the shelf in the pictures. But I had to leave that part out. Otherwise, Charles would know I was investigating and get me handcuffed for good.

"Come on, Mal," I said. "Mama's got fudge to make." I took her from Charles. "I'm sorry if she's bothering you. I know you have work to do on the case."

"It's quite alright," he said and scratched under Mal's chin. "I already talked to David. He has an alibi. He was helping Betty Olway at the time of the murder, and she confirmed it. Everything's going to be alright, little dog. Okay?"

Mal licked his hand.

"Have a good day," I said.

He winked at me. "Tell Carol and the book club that I said hi."

"I haven't been to the book club," I replied, and that was absolutely true.

He looked me in the eye and seemed satisfied with what I said. "Good, Officer Laird would not hesitate to put you in jail."

"I know. It's why I stayed away." I put Mal down. "Come on, baby, it's time to go home."

"Tell Rex I said hi."

"I will," I replied. As we walked away, my mind went to Betty and her alibiing David Peele. Was it true? Or did she get the timing wrong? Betty didn't always get things right, and it was a bit too convenient that she was his alibi. If he was helping Betty, then how did he know about the murder? And how did he get to the back door so quickly?

Then there were the clients in the photo shop. They should have at least heard something—even if it was Melonie hitting the floor when she passed out. And yet no one called nine-one-one.

Which means they either didn't know or didn't care. Until one guy saw me and ushered everyone out the back. Why? To keep them from getting involved? Or so they could get lost in the crowd? None of this made any sense. And what about Ed? He was the most suspicious of all. As far as I could tell, there was nothing to tie him to Melonie. And yet he was there—with tears in his eyes.

The store was open onto the street. Why didn't passersby see or hear anything? Then I remembered the front window had been completely covered with the old-timey pharma scene. Whoever did this had to have known the display would obscure the murder.

My thoughts went round and round as we walked toward the McMurphy. The drugs. The bouquet. This scene was carefully planned and staged. Right down to Melonie in a Victorian costume. What they couldn't have known was that I would show up. Or was I that predictable? Did the killer have a partner who saw me leave the McMurphy with a plate of fudge and head toward the shop?

I must have messed with their plans. Maybe they wanted to pose her? But I surprised them.

Which meant they'd killed her shortly after my first fudge demonstration. In fact, the killer had to have been in there long enough for me to pack up some of her favorite fudge, plate it, and take it over to the shop.

Since there were customers in the back and I came in through the front, the time frame had to have been short. Very short. Maybe less than five minutes before I came in. That caused a shiver of fear to spike down my back. One minute earlier, and I might have shared the same fate.

Five minutes. Five minutes kept going through my head. The killer must have stood right outside the door, lost in the crowd, listening to the *pop* of the lights. When the last group moved into the costume area, the killer must have walked in, made sure she'd passed out or was close to it, then shot her with the nail gun. Whoever the killer was, they had to know how to cause her to pass out quickly so they could be in and out before anyone else noticed.

Their presence in and around the shop also had to be natural enough that no one paid attention to them. Even me, I thought with a moment of shock. I could have witnessed the killer walk out and not thought twice about it.

Chapter 21

It was well after five when I finished scrubbing the fudge shop. I had hoped the work would help me remember who I'd seen when I walked toward the photo shop. So far, nothing. Roxanne was long gone, and so was Frances. Carol walked in, grabbed a cup of coffee, and asked me to join her at the wingback chairs and end table near the coffee bar in the back. I grabbed a bottle of water out of the small fridge under the coffee counter.

"What's up?" I said as I nearly fell into the chair out of exhaustion.

"You haven't been over to discuss the case," she accused me. "Why not? The ladies want to know. Did we do something wrong?"

"Oh, no," I said and rubbed my temples. "It's simple. I was told if I investigated this one, I'd end up in jail, along with anyone who helped me. I'm not about to see you ladies get thrown in jail because of me."

"That never kept you from letting us help you investigate before." Carol pouted.

"That was Rex. This guy, Officer Laird, is different. He can't wait to make Rex squirm or feel pain. It has to do with something between them in their past. Officer Laird wouldn't hesitate to grab me, cuff me, and put me in jail for good whether I did anything or not."

"Oh, yes, I heard that Charles handcuffed you and pulled you through town to take you in. Was that because of this Officer Laird? And whatever did they handcuff you for?" Carol asked.

"Yes, it was on Officer Laird's command. He wanted to make an example of me. And to question me. He was certain that since I found Melonie first and had a plate of my fudge on the ledge to 'cover my true intentions,' I must have killed her. He even told Rex and me that it was an easy open-and-shut case."

"That's ridiculous," Carol said.

"True," I said. "But that doesn't mean he wouldn't badger me for hours to get me to confess."

"What did you do?" she asked, horrified.

"Rex called in a lawyer while I stalled." I leaned in toward her. "Here's the thing—it's not only me he wants. He told me if I go anywhere near 'that book club of yours,' he would take us all in. That's why—"

"You haven't been over to see us," Carol finished.

"Exactly."

Carol shook her head. "This is the first time you've shut us out, but now I understand why."

"I do have a few questions," I said. "Do you want to get a cup of coffee?. We need a public place where the music and crowd noise aren't very loud."

"Are you sure?" she asked. "Shouldn't we stay here? Why risk being seen together?"

"That's part of the point," I said. "If he sees us together, I'm going to give him what-for for not letting me visit with my friends. Everyone will notice, and he'll look like a fool in public."

"I see," she said.

"Oh, let's walk Mal." I stood. It was nearly 6 p.m., and my seasonal night receptionist, Kaylee Morgan, was at her post, scrolling through her phone, waiting for late guests to arrive. "Rex hasn't been home all day, and I don't know whether he's taken her for a walk or not."

"Why hasn't he been home?" Carol asked.

"I sort of sprung babysitting Benji on him last night." I felt worse every minute he was gone.

Carol laughed. "I would love to have seen the look on his face."

We went up to my apartment, and my pets greeted us as if they hadn't seen another person in years. Rex still wasn't home, and from the way my pets acted, he hadn't been home at all. I fed them both their dinner while Carol and I chatted. When Mal was ready and at the door with her leash in her mouth, I haltered her up and opened the door. Mella slipped out before we went down the stairs.

"Do you have any questions?" Carol asked as we started down the alley, getting straight down to business. Thankfully, the way to the coffee place kept Mal away from the pharmacy and the stables. I didn't want to give Carol any ideas. Not until I knew more.

"I do," I said. "But let's wait until we get to a more public place."

"Oh, right," she said.

Once we got our coffee and sat down, I asked my questions. "The entire book club was at the back door of the shop the day of the murder. How did you know to be there?"

"Laura ran into Valentine a few blocks away. Valentine told her that something strange had happened while she was at the photo shop changing out of her costume."

That caught my attention. "Valentine was changing out of her costume during the murder? Then, she told Laura something strange had happened?" Here was the clue I'd been waiting for. "Did she say what it was? A thump on the floor? Someone walking in and then back out?"

"She didn't say," Carol replied, her eyebrows drawn together in concern.

"Sorry," I said. "Please continue."

"Well, Laura said she heard the ruckus coming from the photo shop, so she called us. When we got there we tried to look into the front of the building, but by that time, the police had roped it off. We hoped it wasn't you or Melonie who was hurt, but then we heard your voice through the open door."

"Wait," I said. "You were all at home, and yet you got there at the same time?"

"Oh, no," Carol said. "We were all at my house to discuss the upcoming horse festival. Laura was on her way to my house when she called."

"Can I ask another question?"

"Sure," Carol answered. "Ask all the questions you want."

"Was Betty with you that morning?"

"Oh, yes," Carol said. "She's having her house remodeled and stayed with me the last couple of nights."

"Did she ever leave your place?" I was pretty sure of the answer.

"No, why?" she asked, looking confused.

"Did she go to the pharmacy around the time of the murder?"

"I would think not," Carol said. "She was at our festival committee until we got the call, and before that we had breakfast with tea."

"Can you swear to that?" I asked.

"To Betty not leaving? Sure, I'd swear it on a stack of Bibles. You can ask the other ladies, too. Betty was at my house when Melonie was murdered—or 'allegedly murdered'," Carol said. "Why all the questions about Betty?"

"David told the police that Betty was at the pharmacy at the time of the killing, and she agreed. Carol, she gave David Peele an alibi."

"Well, that's nuts. She must have gotten her days mixed up," Carol said. "Like I said, we can all vouch for her being with us."

"That means David could still have done it," I said softly. My thoughts whirled.

"Why would you think David might have done it?" Carol asked.

"Yes, Allie, why would you think David might have done it?" Officer Laird stood beside us and pinned me with his smug gaze.

"Hello, Officer Laird. Let me introduce my friend Carol Tunisian," I said.

"Goodness, aren't you a hunk of man?" Carol said. "It's so nice to meet you. Why don't you get a beverage and come sit with us? It's not every day we get to have a drink with a man as handsome as you."

He scowled. "Don't try to distract me again. Mrs. Manning—"

"It's 'Ms.'," I told him yet again.

"Mrs. Manning," he replied. "I told you if I caught you investigating the murder, I would put you in jail for obstruction of justice."

"Oh, goodness," Carol said with a laugh. "You don't think we were talking about your case, do you? Of course you do. We're simply playing a game of who-dunit. Have you never played? A name is pulled out of a hat and whoever wants to play that day is separated into groups of two. You get a full day to figure out who did it. Allie and I were talking about David's alibi. He claims he was home with his mother. But we're sure he was really at Alice's house. Alice is a character in the game, you see. Her brother Jason is dead. We're trying to figure out whodunit."

Officer Laird gave us the stink eye, but we both looked at him innocently.

"That's part of the surprise," I answered. "You never know how far ahead of the others you are until you solve the puzzle."

"Who starts the puzzle?" he growled.

"Frances Devaney, my manager at the McMurphy," I replied.

"I'll just go down there and see what she thinks of the game." He stared at us with narrowed eyes to see if we would flinch.

"Go ahead, she'd be happy to explain, but she's home for the night," I said. "It's past her shift time."

"Fine." He turned and left. I waited until he was out of sight before I called Frances. She tried to give me a strong talking-to, but then she suddenly hung up. I stared at my phone, then grinned.

"Did she go for it?" Carol asked.

"I think so," I replied. "She hung up as if she didn't get a call from me."

"We should go," Carol said. "I need to talk to Betty and ask her what the heck she was talking about when it came to David and why she thinks she was at the pharmacy that day."

"Thanks," I said. "It might be best if you take Betty to see Charles and tell him what you told me. That way they'll be no obstruction of justice charge. Okay?"

"Are you sure we can't help?" Carol asked.

"I'm certain," I said. "You met Officer Laird. If he finds you and the book club with a murder board, he'll throw all of you and me in jail.. We don't want the ladies in jail now, do we? Some of them wouldn't last very long."

"No, I suppose not," Carol said, disappointed. "We can still look for clues and share them with you, though, can't we?" She perked up. "We're very good at passing notes without getting caught."

"I'm not investigating," I replied. " Please be very careful. That man has someone watching you."

"Investigation or not, we'll keep you up to date. I'll put notes in envelopes and put them in your mailbox down at the front desk," Carol said. "He can't check your mail. It would be illegal."

"Fine," I said.

"Great!" She answered, her eyes twinkling.

I paid the bill and said goodbye to Carol. Mal and I headed home with two things on my mind: *Where was Rex, and did David have a motive to kill Melonie? If so, would he kill again?*

Black Forest Fudge

Ingredients

2 cups of dark chocolate chips (semisweet can be used if preferred)
2 tablespoons of butter
¼ teaspoon of salt
⅓ cup of cherry preserves
1 14-ounce can of sweetened condensed milk
dried tart cherries
powdered sugar, as necessary
½ cup of marshmallow fluff

Directions

Line 13x9-inch pan with parchment paper. Butter parchment paper.

In a microwave-safe bowl, mix chocolate chips, butter, salt, cherry preserves, and sweetened condensed milk. Microwave on high for 90 seconds. Stir and add dried tart cherries. Microwave for another 90 seconds. Ensure chocolate chips are melted. Remove and stir until thick. If it is too runny, add sifted powdered sugar a tablespoon at a time until it is the proper consistency. Pour into pan. Dollop marshmallow fluff on top. Gently heat a butter knife in hot water, then swirl marshmallow fluff throughout fudge before it sets.

Refrigerate until set. Remove from pan. Flip upside down on a cutting board and remove parchment paper. Cut into desired size pieces, then serve. Store remainder in an airtight container in the refrigerator or freeze for later.

Makes 24.

Chapter 22

I walked into the pharmacy, and the doorbells announced I was there. I looked around and grabbed something off the shelf, then went to the back to see David behind the counter filling prescriptions.

"Allie, good to see you," he said, welcoming me in.

"It's nice to see you, too." I handed him the bottle. "Can you tell me if this is good for allergies?"

"It's okay," he said. "Let me show you what's better." He came out from behind the counter and walked me over to aisle twelve. "Now, this is the best thing except for prescription meds. It'll help with sneezing, runny and itchy nose, and itchy eyes. You take one tablet twice a day until allergy season is over, and it should help."

"Are there any side effects, like dizziness or drowsiness?"

"Not usually," he said. "I say that because some people report one or the other symptom. If you get either, bring it back. We'll try something new. Or you may want to see Dr. Young in Cheboygan—he can get you something that's stronger than over-the-counter stuff."

"Thanks," I said. "I'll take it."

We walked back to the counter, where he rang it up.

"Melonie's death is such a shame," I said.

"Yes," he said without looking up. "That'll be six dollars and seventy-five cents."

I pulled out my credit card. "If you don't mind my asking, what brought you to the scene?"

He shrugged. "I had just picked up my lunch when the commotion broke out. I had some time and was curious. Poor Melonie. She had such a difficult life."

"I didn't know that," I said with honesty. "I would have been more forgiving. What made her life so difficult?"

He looked around, but the shop was empty. "I heard her father was abusive, and so was her first husband. She ran away to the island and married Rex. But I think it was to find some sense of safety in her life. Even then, she found the winters here too long, too cold, and too boring for her."

"Huh," I said. "I think the winters here are lovely."

"Not Melonie. She left Rex before he even realized she was gone. Look, I can't speak for her, but my guess is that she felt stifled in safety. I mean, someone who's used to drama rarely escapes it. She divorced Rex and wasn't seen on the island again until a couple of years ago."

"Rex and I were dating before she came back," I said. "She hated me on sight."

"See? Drama. That's probably why she begged Rex to let her stay at his house," David said.

"And he let her," I said. "Sometimes his heart gets in the way of his head." I sighed. "That's when the harassment started. She told me he was hers, and she wouldn't stop until we broke up and he came back to her."

"But that didn't happen." David paused. "She must have been really angry about that, especially when you two got married. Yes, she had a difficult life, but that doesn't give her the right to make others' lives difficult, too." He sounded like he'd known her harassment firsthand.

"How did she hurt you?" I kept my tone soft and understanding.

"The way she treated my dying mother—let's just say, I'm not sorry to see Melonie dead. My guess is that you feel the same."

"No, not really," I answered. "Even though she was horrid and a constant thorn in my side, I always tried to see the best in her. In fact, I'd brought her some fudge that morning to mend fences, since we're neighbors."

He patted my hand. "I'm sorry you'll never get to do that now."

"Thank you," I said. "Can I ask you one last quick question?"

"Sure. What can I do for you?"

"There was a prescription bottle on Melonie's shelf. Can you tell me who filled it or what was in it?"

"What shelf are you talking about?"

"The one in her studio. She had a bottle of pills there."

"Huh," he said. "Why there, I wonder. Most people keep them in their bathrooms—although with the moisture, I wouldn't advise it. Do you have any idea what was in it?"

"No," I replied. "The bottle was too far away. Whatever it was, would it be easy to replace the drug with something else? Something that would make her pass out?"

"Usually, I wouldn't be able to tell you what she was taking. HIPAA rules, you know."

"But she's dead," I countered.

He leaned over. "Are you investigating?" he asked with a wink.

"I can't do that," I replied. "It's considered obstruction of justice. I'm curious is all."

"I see," he said. The he turned around and put a large bottle of pills on the counter. "These are for anxiety. A common side effect can be lowering the blood pressure too much. That could have made her pass out if she stood up too fast."

I snapped a picture of the bottle with my cell phone. "Thanks."

As I walked off, he added, "Don't forget—if that allergy medicine doesn't work for you, go see Dr. Young. She can write you a prescription for something stronger."

That stopped me cold. I turned around. "Who was Melonie's doctor?" I asked. "Is he any good?"

"Like I said, Dr. Young," he replied. "She's great for pretty much anything, including allergies. But she's only on the island once a week. If I were you, I'd make an appointment as soon as possible."

"Thanks." If David was the killer, then he was very

good at covering it up. Truthfully, I couldn't say one way or another at this point, but at least I knew the name of the pills on her shelf. When I got back to my office, I planned on looking them up on my computer to see if they could have been what made Melonie pass out so quickly.

Chapter 23

Jenn waited for me in the office under the guise that we were both working late. Which we were, really. I had inventory to go over, and she had another wedding to plan.

"How did you get away from Benji and Shane tonight?" I asked.

"I usually work after Benji goes to bed," she explained. "After he went to sleep tonight, I told Shane I had to come to the office to get stuff done and kissed him on the cheek while he played video games."

"That's one thing Rex doesn't do," I said as I looked up the pills on my computer. "He doesn't play video games."

"Huh. . . . Any information on the pills?" Jenn asked. "Are they what David said they were?"

"Yes, they're for anxiety. But we need Shane to verify that those were the pills on the shelf and that the pills in the bottle weren't switched." We both looked at each other, and a bit of sorrow for Melonie moved between us. "Simply knowing she took medication for anxiety gives me a new understanding of why Melonie acted the way she did."

"She was scared," Jenn replied. "Huh. Why didn't she tell anyone?"

"Would you if you didn't have any friends here? Or worse, if you were afraid people would make fun of you?"

"No," she said. "I guess I really wouldn't."

I read on. "Wait, it's like David said, if you take too many of these, it can cause you to pass out."

"Yikes," Jenn said.

"If I remember right, she did have a refillable water bottle nearby. Anyone could have spiked it with her prescription pills."

"A few gulps, and she'd pass out?" Jenn asked.

"We do have a working theory that she was sedated before the nail gun killed her. Wait—" I read on. "It says it could take over an hour to work."

"Well, shoot, if they overdosed her, how would they know when she would actually pass out?" Jenn said.

"It would most likely put her to sleep." I read on. "You're right, though. I doubt that's what made her pass out."

"We're back to nothing." Jenn sounded disappointed.

I drummed my fingers on the table as I thought. Then it hit me. "Why do women dance with their drinks in their hand? Or keep an eye on each other's drinks?"

Jenn stared at me for a moment. "It's been a while since I've danced." Her expression was thoughtful. "Is it to keep from being slipped the date rape drug and carried off?"

I nodded. "GHB's fast acting. But where would you get it? What is it commonly used for?"

"Isn't it sometimes used as a horse tranquilizer?" Jenn said, her expression growing more intrigued.

"Who would have it?" I asked.

"The vet," we both said at the same time.

"Aren't there five veterinarians here on the island?" Jenn asked, the hope on her face suddenly collapsing.

"Who would be nearby when they treated a horse?" I asked.

"Ed," we said it at the same time again.

"Could he have stolen a pill when the vet wasn't looking?" Jenn wondered. "I mean, it only takes one."

"I don't know," I said. "It does seem like a stretch, but it's the best lead we have right now," I said. "Plus, he was at the scene."

"But Mr. Beecher said he saw Teddy run out, not Ed," Jenn said.

"True," I agreed. "And if Ed did it and Mr. Beecher only saw him come to the back later, it would mean he had to go out the front in that short of a time frame. If he went out the front, I would wonder why."

"What do you mean?" Jenn asked.

"I think I'm a witness." I explained to her why.

"Wow," she said. "But you don't remember anyone coming out at all?"

"I was nervous about how Melonie would react, and I wasn't really concentrating. Still, if someone like Ed had walked out the door, I think I would remember."

"Could you have seen the fudgies walk in? That's something you expect and don't think about."

"The timing's off," I said. "I'm still thinking about those people in the back room and why they went out the back door instead of at least trying to go through the front. Oh, did I tell you what Carol told me when I asked her how she and the book club ladies got to the murder scene so fast?"

"No," Jenn said.

I shared what Carol had said.

"Odd, very odd," Jenn said. "At least we know one of the people who went out the back."

"True," I said. "What about the plumber? Did you find out anything there?"

"I mostly talked to Teddy. He said, 'Stan won the bid on a big job at the Grand,'" Jenn said.

"Is that good, or is that bad?" I asked.

"It's hard to tell. Teddy's very nice. He was happy to answer any questions I had. Oh, and I might have told him you were looking for a plumber for the McMurphy."

"That's fine," I said. "Mr. Devaney can cover the usual stuff, but if the mainline breaks or the boiler quits, it wouldn't hurt to have another professional on call."

"Good, whew," Jenn said, then winced.

"Are you okay?" I asked.

"Yes, I'm fine," she said. "The doctor said these little cramps are simply my body remembering how to stretch to give the little one room."

"Do you know the gender yet?" I had to ask. "I know you wanted it to be a surprise when Benji was born. Are you doing that again?"

"We haven't decided yet."

"Wouldn't a gender reveal party be cool?" I asked.

"It does sound like fun, but we have to decide whether we want to know the gender or not first."

"Of course," I said, trying to contain my excitement. I bet she was going to do it, and I couldn't wait. I began to imagine how much fun it would be. We could even combine it with her baby shower.

Jenn snapped her fingers in my face. "Earth to Allie. Come in, Allie."

"Right." I cleared my throat. "What else did Teddy say?"

"That Stan had a crush on Melonie. Teddy had strict instructions to let him be the one to work the job if Melonie ever had a need for a plumber."

"Maybe he found her with someone—like whoever 'bouquet Oscar' was—and his anger made him kill her. He could have bought the drug from Ed, slipped it into her drink," I said. "Once she was out, it would be easy to kill her. We may have our first motive."

"He was at the murder site and supposedly came down the stairs without knowing what was going on, but he had to have heard photo lights popping over and over again," Jenn surmised.

"Wait! No one heard the nail gun because the murderer covered it with the pop of the lights." I loved it when things started to come together.

"Yes!" Jenn said. "That's brilliant. And how easy it would be for Stan to be the murderer. He was supposed to be working upstairs. He could have easily spiked her water bottle, then brought it down for her as a nice gesture. Teddy said Stan had put in a whole house filter, so he would have an excuse to get her to taste it."

"Then when she passed out, he could have exchanged the bottle and put it on the shelf, making it look like she had left it there herself," I said.

"Clever! He'd call Teddy for an alibi. If you think about it, plumbers don't usually need nail guns. But if he finished with the plumbing and needed to reattach baseboards or drywall sections, he might need one. That means he could have been the one to have a nail gun nearby," Jenn said.

"It's kind of a stretch," I said. "But it makes more sense for him to have one than anyone else at the scene. Unless Melonie had one in a box of tools. Either way, we have opportunity, means, and motive for Stan," I said. "But we also have means and opportunity for David. Just no motive . . . yet."

"Don't forget Ed." Jenn sighed. "This is hard. I wonder what the other girls dug up. I mean, what if all of them have means, motive, and opportunity?"

"We'll just have to dig deeper," I said. "It still bothers me that we don't know who the other fudgies were. Did you get a chance to ask Teddy about that?"

"He said he was upstairs helping Stan when he asked him to go get more caulk. His bottle had run out. Teddy hurried down and raced off to get it. He was so focused on the task that he didn't see or hear anything else," Jenn said. "Then, when he came back with the caulk, Stan told him to go get some washers, and stat. Stan met him at the top of the stairs and gave him the address of the next job, and for the third time Teddy ran out the back door."

"With all that running, we can rule out Teddy," I said.

"Darn, I hate to be stuck. But that leaves us with at least three suspects and no real evidence. The good news is that Officer Laird must have run up against the same roadblocks."

"I had a thought. Melonie had to have written down the names and addresses of her clients," Jenn said. "She'd need to know who they were and where to send the proofs."

"That was my first thought," I said. "There's only one issue with that. The police must have her appointment book because I never saw one. I highly doubt they'd let us see it."

Chapter 24

"Where've you been today?" Rex asked. "Mal and Mella have missed you."

I could have said the same thing to him when he'd crawled into bed with me at 2 a.m. last night. But I hadn't because I didn't want to know how mad he was about the babysitting gig. I gave him a kiss, then sat on the couch and gave my pets the attention they needed. "Dinner smells wonderful," I said.

"Don't change the subject. I heard you were talking to Carol and Laird interrupted you." Rex stood with his legs splayed and his arms crossed, giving me his cop stare. "Have you been investigating?"

"Have you?" I asked much more politely, but enough to prove my point. "You were gone much later yesterday."

He frowned. "That's beside the point."

"Is it? If you must know, I picked up some allergy pills at the pharmacy," I said and pulled the bag out of my pocket. "David said if these don't work, we should go see Dr. Young for a prescription."

"You know Laird is watching you like a hawk."

"Oh, yes, Carol and I got a coffee. When he showed up acting so smug thinking he'd caught me in the act of investigating, I looked at him and said, 'What? Now I can't have coffee with a friend?' He's a total idiot."

"And you weren't investigating," Rex said sarcastically.

"No," I said. "Carol wanted to know why I hadn't come to the book club, and I told her that I wasn't investigating this one. Then I explained the obstruction of justice threat and how the last thing I wanted was to send anyone else to jail."

"Right." He harumphed. "And you and Jenn in the office?"

"Believe it or not, I do have office work to do. You don't normally see it because you're at work."

"So, you weren't talking with Jenn about who killed Melonie?" he asked.

"We talked about Stan. You know, the plumber? And how I should keep him in mind should the McMurphy have a bigger problem than what Mr. Devaney can do by himself."

"I see," he said. "It took a long time to talk about that."

I narrowed my eyes. "If you must know, we also discussed a gender-reveal party for her baby. But you'd better check that out. It might be code for an 'investigation'." I stood. "I can't believe I'm being interrogated in my own home!" My temper rose. "How dare you demand to know everything I've done in my day? What if I stood looming over you and commanded you to tell me what *you've* been doing all day? Especially when you don't come home until two a.m." I picked up Mal. "Come on, girl, let's go for a walk." Ignoring him, I snapped on her halter and took her outside, slamming the door behind me. It took three blocks before I calmed down. I know Rex was used to being the cop in situations like this, but this time he wasn't. I wouldn't let him continue to treat me like a suspect when he was no more a cop on this case than I was. I let Mal walk where she wanted to, her little nose to the ground. "What is going on with him, anyway? He's been pushing my buttons ever since Melonie died," I muttered.

Mal drew me back to the pharmacy, the stables, and then the police station—the same route as before. "Come on, girl," I said and pulled her away from the station. "We can't tell them anything or Mama will get in trouble. Besides, we have no evidence. Let's go down to the lake."

But Mal didn't want to go to the lake. And since I hadn't done anything she wanted me to do, I let her go where her nose wanted to go. She turned away from the lake and moved down Market Street. Then she stopped at the house at the end of the street across from the Beaumont Museum. It was a lovely Victorian with a covered porch in the corner.

"Mal," I said. "What are you doing?"

She simply looked at me with her big brown eyes. "Fine," I said and sighed. It was a bed-and-breakfast, and maybe one of the couples were guests. I took her inside and smiled at the receptionist. "Hi, Ellen," I said.

"Allie, what are you doing here? Checking out the competition?"

"No," I said. "Mal thought we should come in."

"Hi, Mal." Ellen came around the desk and leaned down to pet Mal. "Do you want to know if our bed-and-breakfast is better than your hotel?"

Mal licked her face. Ellen laughed and straightened. "She's so cute."

"Listen," I said. "Between you and me, did any of your guests get their pictures taken at the Old Tyme Photo Shoppe about the time Melonie died?"

"You know, the police were here this morning asking the same thing. Mr. and Mrs. Elwood are on their honeymoon, and they have a heck of a story to take home. They told me all about it. But they weren't here when the police came by. How did you know they were here?" she asked.

I pointed at Mal. "She likes to help solve murders." We both laughed. "As if newlyweds are suspects," we said together.

"But maybe they saw someone there who shouldn't have been," I continued. "Could you have them stop by the McMurphy tomorrow? I'll give them some free fudge."

"Sounds yummy," she said. "I'll let them know, but I'm not responsible if they don't show."

"That's fine," I said. "I'm glad to have found them. Maybe they can tell me about the rest of the people in the back of the photo shop. Only, could you keep this to yourself? I'm 'not investigating,' I'm only curious.

Mostly because Officer Laird is looking for any reason to put me in jail."

"Gotcha," she said. "I don't trust anyone from off the island, anyway. Especially if they're after Rex and his wife."

"Thanks," I said. "Come on, Mal. Let's go home." I had a cop of my own to handle.

Chapter 25

Mal refused to go home and sat on the sidewalk until I practically had to drag her. I finally sighed and let her lead. Again. This time she turned left and took me up the hill for about a block. She seemed to be onto more than me in this investigation. At least, if Officer Laird said anything, I could say I was simply out walking my dog. Halfway down the block, she stopped and rushed up to the door of a 1930s two-story home. I hated to keep knocking on strangers' doors, but I knew if I didn't, Mal would simply make me come back. Resigned, I stepped up on the wrap-around porch and rang the doorbell. When it wasn't answered, I knocked on the door.

"Mal," I said, "no one's home. We'll have to come back." Mal started whining. I knocked one more time. "See?" I said.

It was then that the door opened. A man stood there in his shirtsleeves, a vest, slacks and dress socks with slippers on his feet.

"Mr. Beecher!" I said at the same time Mr. Beecher said, "Allie, what a surprise."

Mal put her front paws on his leg and stretched, hoping for a treat.

"Come in, come in," he said and held the door open. The hallway was paneled in old walnut. The parlor had old walnut trim and bookcases on both sides of the fireplace. Wherever there was a wall, it was painted dark green. The carpet was a thick, long-looped gold and walnut.

"I've been to your home before," I said. "But I didn't remember it being here."

He smiled. "My old house was too large to keep clean, even with a service. That's why I sold it and bought this two-bedroom place."

"Well, Mal found you," I said. "I think she was hoping for a treat."

"Let me get that for her. What can I get you? I have hot tea, lemonade, or coffee."

"Coffee would be great," I said.

"You look hungry," he said. "I'll bring some of Sheila's homemade cookies."

"You don't have to—"

He was gone, and Mal followed him. I sighed, stepped into the living room, and sat on the thick brown leather couch. The end tables and coffee table matched the woodwork. Everything put together looked like a very masculine library.

He walked into the parlor with a tray, cups and plates of cookies, and a carafe of coffee. Mal grinned and followed him, then jumped on the couch and into my lap.

"Traitor," I said to her.

Mr. Beecher laughed. "I only gave her two."

I sighed. "She's the one who brought me here. It seems she's looking for Melonie's killer."

"A good sniffer, then," he said. "How's your 'non-investigation' going?"

"I'm not sure. There are at least three suspects, but no real evidence. It's all circumstantial. Nothing like guesswork to ruin a good investigation. Jenn talked to Teddy, and he was kind but had little to add. I spoke to David, and again he was willing to answer my questions and even shared his reason for being there, but he had no motive—and no nail gun."

"Have a cookie, or the coffee will hit you hard."

I took a cookie. "Oh, these are so good! Please tell Sheila I said thank you."

"I will," he said. "Can I ask you something?"

"Sure," I said.

"How are things at home? You've seemed very emotional lately."

"Rex is driving me crazy," I said. I didn't know what it was about Mr. Beecher, but I always seemed to spill my guts around him. Maybe he reminded me of Papa Liam. "First it was his wife this and his wife that, when he talked about Melonie. Then tonight, he interrogated me like a suspect in my own home. I don't know what to do about it. I even had him babysit Benji to try to get his mind off of this whole murder thing, but it didn't work."

I see," he said. "I heard that the new Officer Laird had it in for Rex and was trying to get you for obstruction. Perhaps he's scared of losing you."

"If that's the case, he's going about fixing it the wrong way."

"He's going about fixing it the only way he knows how," Mr. Beecher said gently. "Have another cookie. After all, Mal had two. Let me tell you something." He leaned in closer. "Sheila and I have had our fair share of arguments, but they all stem from either misunderstanding or fear. Perhaps you should try to listen to him a bit more with the thought that he really is trying to keep you safe."

I sighed. "I hate it when you're right."

He chuckled. "Sheila says the same thing."

"Before I go," I said and brushed the cookie crumbs off my lap, carefully putting them in my napkin, "do you know who might have had a motive to kill Melonie?"

"She wasn't the nicest person to anyone," he said. "I do know that she took the location next to the McMurphy for safety. She figured with Rex so close, that nothing would happen to her."

"How do you know this?" I asked, leaning forward.

"People tell me all kinds of things." He grinned. "I seem harmless, and I listen. You see, her ex before Rex was not a good man. He was very abusive, hitting her and even throwing her down the stairs. The divorce was quite contentious because he thought of her as his property."

"Oh, my goodness. Poor thing, just another reason for her to push people away. Do you have any idea who her first ex-husband might have been?"

"No, she never did say," he said. "But she wasn't the

best at hiding. It would have been easy to find her here. Her name and face were even on the flyer for the shop. Which meant it would be easy to run an internet search and find her picture. No one on the island knows what he looks like or what his name is. It could be anyone."

"Oh, no, it also means he could have left already or be here watching and we wouldn't know. He could even have changed his last name so we wouldn't suspect a thing. Do you have any idea what he does for a living?"

"She didn't say," he said. "I'm sorry."

"Oh, it's not your fault. You've given me so much information already, plus good coffee and delicious cookies." Mal barked. "And treats apparently." We laughed, and I put my cup down and stood. "Thank you, Mr. Beecher," I said. "I'm going to see if Mal will let me go home now."

"She's a smart pup," he said, petting Mal behind the ears. "I suggest you go wherever she takes you. Do be careful, though. It's dark out now."

"We will be," I said. "Come on, Mal. Let's go home this time."

We left Mr. Beecher's warm and welcoming home and walked out into the cool street. I was glad to have a jacket on and a sweatshirt under it.

I let Mal go wherever she wanted, but as we left the street, I heard footsteps nearby. I stopped to let the person through, but no one passed. I glanced back. No one was there. Mal cocked her head when I stopped, but then she pulled behind me and growled. Since she only growled when necessary, I felt a chill go down my spine.

"Come on, Mal," I said. "Let's go home before your daddy comes looking for us." I hoped the threat of Rex coming to look for us would stop whoever was following us. We hurried down Fort Street. The footsteps followed, but every time I turned around, no one was there. Mal continued to growl. It occurred to me to let her go and chase whoever it was away, but I worried for her safety. What if they had a knife and hurt her?

Suddenly, Mal slipped out of her halter and ran back behind me. "Mal!" I called and raced after her. She turned down the alley behind Market Street, and the footsteps hurried off. I raced after Mal to see her disappear into the darkness of the alley. "Mal!" I called, my fear for her rising. Then I heard her barking. Whoever it was, Mal had them cornered. I turned on my phone's flashlight and continued to run until I caught up with Mal. She *did* have someone cornered.

It was Officer Trainee Barry Ashbury.

"What are you doing, Barry?" I asked. Mal looked up at me with pride.

The poor kid gulped, his Adam's apple going up and down. "I'm sorry, Mrs. Manning. But Officer Manning asked a few of us to keep an eye on you and make sure you stay safe. We're supposed to not let you know we're doing that, but I'm not very good at following a suspect."

"A 'suspect'?" I raised my brows and narrowed my

eyes. So, Rex was having me followed like a suspect, too.

"Um, not an *actual* suspect." Barry tried to walk it back. "But like, a person of interest."

"A 'person of interest'," I repeated, my tone communicating my anger.

"I'm sorry, I'm sorry. I'm not good at this." He gulped again, and I could tell he was thinking hard. "Witness protection?"

I bit my lip. "Who's a 'few of you'?" I asked, circling back to let the poor kid off the hook.

"I don't know, actually," he said. "I know that it's me and Officer Davis and a couple others."

"And does Officer Laird know about this?" I asked. If he did, then my investigation was over. I'd have to give it to someone else.

"Not as far as I know," Barry said, his voice shaking a bit. "We're doing it off shift. Officer Manning is paying us out of pocket. Someone could have told Officer Laird, though. I mean, not everyone likes your husband."

"I see," I said. "Well, you might as well walk me home."

"But I'm not supposed to let you see me, and Officer Manning might not be happy with me."

I sighed. "Okay, then just walk us to the alley and stop behind Doud's. You can still see me, but it will look like I can't see you. Does that work?"

"Yes, ma'am," he said, his eyes lighting up. "Thank you, ma'am."

"Call me Allie," I said.

"Yes, ma'am—um, Allie."

I turned my flashlight off and slipped Mal back into her harness. Then I turned toward Fort Street. Mal seemed pretty happy with herself and proudly led us home. When we arrived at Doud's, I thanked Barry, and he watched us get home and go up the stairs. I took a deep breath before entering the apartment. I was madder now than I was when Rex had given me the third degree, treating me like a suspect rather than his wife.

I unlocked the door, took off Mal's halter, and without a word to Rex, went to the bathroom, cleaned up, then went into the bedroom and locked the door. I hated to leave my babies out, but I didn't want to give Rex a chance to come in and try to continue his *interrogation*.

I was so mad I paced the floor. He tried the door a couple of times.

"Come on, Allie," he said through the door. "Let's talk about this."

If he could treat me like a suspect, then I could treat him like a suspect who called for their lawyer. In fact, I could call my own lawyer in the morning.

"Allie," he said. "I'm sorry. I'm used to pushing people for answers."

"But I'm your wife," I grumbled without letting him hear me. "I want a lawyer," I said loudly, and then continued to keep walking.

"Allie, that's ridiculous. We can settle this ourselves."

Ridiculous! Oh, he was in worse trouble now! I called Jenn and explained everything, from the interrogation to being followed to him saying I was being ridiculous when I'd said I wanted a lawyer.

"Oh, he didn't," she said.

"He did," I replied.

"I'd lock him out of the room as well. And I'd call the lawyer. Let Rex pay for it. Maybe Jay can put some sense into that man's brain. Interrogating you, having you followed, then telling you that you're being ridiculous. Huh. Call that lawyer right now."

"Oh, he did not," I could hear Shane say in the background.

"He did," Jenn said.

"What is wrong with him?" Shane asked. "This is going to take a houseful of flowers and jewelry and an expensive date before he's out of the doghouse."

Chapter 26

I got up early to avoid Rex. The poor guy had slept on the couch. When I went to go to work he had one arm over his head and his blankets were on the floor. I picked up the blankets and draped them over him. He rolled over to face the back of the couch. I didn't want to wake him. If I did and saw his sleepy face, I knew I'd give in. So, instead, I took Mal out for a long walk. This time, she didn't drag me anywhere, and I was relieved. We took our usual walk down Market Street to the beach, then to the library and back. Halfway back, we ran into Rowan,

"Oh, Allie, I'm so glad I caught you." Rowan walked up with Finn by her side. "I know for sure what made Melonie pass out."

"Come on, Mal and Finn. Time to go home. I'm late for work. Rowan, what brings you out so early in the morning?" I asked, not so subtly letting her know we don't talk about the community safety project on the street.

Rowan became quiet and walked without looking at me. "I get up early to see if I can photograph any wildlife. I have some great pictures of the red crossbill and a yellow warbler. They were so beautiful in the sunrise."

Once inside the McMurphy, I poured her some coffee, and she waited while I poured mine. "Okay, very quietly—and look for Rex," I said. "He could be down any minute. Tell me what you know."

She turned so that we were side by side, both looking for anyone to go by. "The water bottle was laced with GHB. The date rape drug."

"Just as I thought," I said. "That makes Stan our top suspect. I can't believe Shane would tell you this. Are you sure?"

"Shane doesn't do all the testing," Rowan said. "My cousin Caleigh does the fluids work. It's good to have a chemist in the family. Anyway, she told me."

"Oh, that makes sense," I said. "Who else knows about this?"

"People have a tendency to overlook me," she said. "Especially when I'm out photographing wildlife. Shane and Officer Laird were talking about it yesterday while I was shooting a turtle near the police station."

"Are you sure they weren't messing with you?" I asked. "After all, who could overlook all your red hair? Are you sure they aren't out to get us for interference?"

"No, my cousin told me first. They just confirmed it," she said and sipped her coffee while Finn and Mal played.

I needed to take Mal's halter off, and a glance at the clock told me Roxanne would be in at any moment.

"Thanks," I said. "This is great. But for now, I need

to get to work before Rex comes down and asks too many questions."

"Got it," she said. "Do you want me to tell the rest of the girls?"

"If you want," I said, "but do be careful. The cops are watching everyone I talk to, including you."

"I'll be careful," she said. "I'll simply manage to 'run into' the other girls."

"Good," I said.

"Here's the thing, though," Rowan said. "The GHB isn't much of a clue. Really, anyone could have walked in off the street and slipped it into her bottle. Had their picture taken. Left and then come back to supposedly pick up their picture and finish her off."

"It had to be someone she knew," I said, disappointed that this new clue still didn't help us find the killer. "They would have had to walk in, spike her water bottle, go around the waiting room wall until the last group was in the dressing area, then go out, shoot her with the nail gun, and leave. All without anyone seeing them or the nail gun."

"What if the nail gun was there all along—you know, stashed somewhere, and the killer put it back to come get it later?"

"You could be right. Shane and the others didn't find a nail gun when they searched the crime scene. But it could still be in the building," I said. "We need to get in there and look."

"I agree," Rowan said. "All we need to do now is figure out how to do that."

Rex came down the stairs, and I turned to Rowan.

"I have to get to work," I said. "I'm glad you're staying a few extra days. Text me if there's anything else you need."

"Will do," she said and walked me over to the fudge shop. I went inside, locked the door, then put the ingredients into a big copper pot.

Rex walked by without so much as a glance. I didn't know what made me angrier, his interrogation or his ignoring me altogether. Either way, I was unsettled, and I wasn't sure if I'd ever get over it.

Cinnamon Peanut Butter Fudge

Ingredients

1 cup of cinnamon chips
1 cup of peanut butter chips
2 tablespoons of butter
1 14-ounce can of sweetened condensed milk.

Directions

Line 13x9-inch baking pan with parchment paper.

Place all the ingredients in a microwave-safe bowl. Microwave on high for 3 minutes—stirring at 90 seconds. Ensure all the chips are melted. Remove from microwave. Stir and pour into pan. Refrigerate until set. Cut into 2-inch pieces and enjoy. Store remainder in an airtight container in the refrigerator.

Makes 24.

Chapter 27

The day went by quickly. My fudge demonstrations were very successful, and I left after helping to clean up. Roxanne stayed to serve any customers. I went upstairs, showered, and then took my babies for a walk. Of course, my kitty, Mella, went out on her own, but Mal liked her halter. We set off to see Liz at the *Town Crier*. Maybe she had some info on Ed that she could share. As the manager of the stables, it would be reasonable for him to have a tool belt with a nail gun on it. What we needed was a motive. Maybe Melonie and Ed were having an affair, and she'd broken it off. Men had killed for less.

I frowned. Did Melonie have money? Most of the time, they say to follow the money. The problem was, I had no idea how to access Melonie's bank accounts to know how much she had. We needed someone who could.

Mal and I walked into the office, the doorbells jingling as we entered. Liz's grandfather Angus was usually at the front reception counter, but not today. The newspaper building was small. The walls were white, adorned with framed newspapers from throughout the years. I stopped to look at the stories while waiting for Angus. When he didn't come, I frowned and hit the desk bell. Mal put her front paws on the smooth blond wood of the counter, looking for Angus, but he wasn't there.

At the sound of the second bell, Liz came out from the printing area behind the reception desk. The two areas had a wall between them for sound dampening. "Allie!" She came around, and we gave each other a big hug. Mal joined us by putting her front paws on Liz's legs.

"How are you?" I asked. "How's Angus? I expected to see him."

"He's got pneumonia," she said with a worried look on her face. "They're keeping him in the clinic until he starts to look better."

"Oh, no," I said. "Pneumonia can hit older people especially hard. I hope he gets better soon."

"Thanks," Liz said. "In the meantime, I've been ordered to stay busy."

"Don't you worry about helping with the investigation. We'll figure it out."

"Oh, no," she said. "I love helping, and I have done quite a bit of investigation. After all, investigating is what journalists do, and nobody can put me in jail for that."

"If you're sure," I said.

"I found out that Ed and Melonie were dating," Liz said. "Ed was quite in love. He bought her diamond jewelry and flowers. Expensive dinners. They went on cruises and so on. Then, out of the blue, she broke up with him, and he discovered she had been dating Lochlan Forester and had only stayed with Ed for the gifts he gave her."

"Wait, I heard Rowan tell Charlene that she moved back here because of her boyfriend, Lochlan Forester," I said. "That dirty guy. I'm going to have to tell her."

"Don't be so fast to do that," Liz said. "This puts her back on the suspect list. Jealousy is a strong motive."

"She told me this morning that her cousin said there was GHB in Melonie's water bottle. She said her cousin works at the lab as a chemist identifying liquids at the crime scene."

"She could be telling you how she did it," Liz said. "Too bad, I really liked her."

"And she thinks the killer stashed the nail gun before they came in, took it out, killed Melonie, and put it back. She was going to see if we could get in and look for it."

"That makes her seem even more like the killer, hoping to find the murder weapon and wipe it clean for prints, if she hasn't already."

I frowned. "I don't buy it. I can't see a murderer having a pet like Finn. Finn is so well trained that it shows Rowan's patience. And she has an alibi, along with a million relatives and half the island who know who she is. It would be hard to get away with anything like this. Especially since I'm convinced the killer was someone no one would notice going into the shop. They had to be someone that went in and out a lot. Someone even I would miss, which puts Rowan far down on the list. My money's on the fact that she has no clue about Forrester's multiple girlfriends. I think I should tell her and watch her reaction."

"Remember that no woman wants to hear that kind of news. They usually don't believe their friend, and that's the end of the friendship," Liz warned.

"Well, darn it. I really like her, too," I said with a frown. "Let's circle back to Ed. He had a reason to be angry with Melonie. But was that enough motive to murder her?" I asked.

"Ed does have access to a nail gun. He's been remodeling the stables to update them for the horses to make them more comfortable." Being used, then jilted could make anyone angry enough to kill.

"Means, motive, and opportunity," I said. "But so does Stan. We need to remove all the other suspects, to be sure."

"This is hard," Liz said with admiration in her voice. "I can't believe you do this all the time. Sounds like we need to meet on Friday and go over our murder board to see where we are in terms of removing people from our list."

"Maybe," I hedged. "Except I found out yesterday that not only does Laird have people watching me, but so does Rex."

"What?" Liz sounded as insulted as I felt.

"Yeah, turns out that officer trainee Berry not only stinks at surveillance, but also interrogation. He told me that Rex has been paying people to follow me for my 'protection.' There is most likely someone watching this building, right now."

"I'm going to go out there and give them a piece of my mind!"

I touched her arm and shook my head. "It's no use. Why don't you set up a video meet for all of us instead?"

Liz glared at the door. "Fine."

"Are you going to be okay, with Angus in the clinic?"

"I visit him every day for a few hours until he kicks me out," she said, then looked back at me. "You know him and what a stubborn old coot he is. Now, tell me, how's your investigation into David going?"

"Well, he had the means to make her fall asleep." I shook my head. "He even admitted it, but what he had access to is slow acting. So far I haven't found a motive for him, and if he had a nail gun, wouldn't people have wondered why he was walking around with it?"

"So, do we cross him off the list?" Liz asked.

"I'm not sure," I said. "I mean, she could have been having an affair with David, too."

Liz shook her head. "What is it with these guys? I'm lucky to get a date. Meanwhile, she has them all lining up at her door. In my opinion, she wasn't even that good-looking."

I sighed. "There has to be something we're missing. We still don't know who Oscar is. You know, the guy who sent the flowers."

"Maybe, since you've finished with David, you have some time to look into Oscar?" Liz asked.

I took a deep breath. "Sophie's looking into him. I'll check in with her later. Meanwhile, I have to figure out how to keep Officer Laird away from our community safety committee."

"I believe in you," Liz said.

"Thanks."

As Mal and I stepped out, I noted that it was past dinnertime. If I wanted to stay away from Rex's interrogations, I'd have to go pick up dinner from one of the pubs. Then lock myself in the bedroom, unless Rex got there first.

Chapter 28

Mal and I went up the back stairs to the apartment. Half of me felt sad. Rex and I had never fought like this before. The other half of me was still upset that he would treat me like one of his suspects instead of his wife. It was like he kept forgetting I was his wife. One time, okay. But twice? If there was a third time, then he might just find his things out on the stoop. And that would break my heart forever.

I removed Mal's halter and leash and unlocked the door. When I stepped inside, I saw immediately that the apartment was full of lilacs and peonies—the same flowers from my wedding bouquet. The smell of steaks and baked potatoes filled the air. It made the hamburger in my takeout box seem like dog food. Mal would love that.

My pup went running, and I put my to-go meal in the fridge as Rex came around the corner from the bedroom.

"Hi," he said.

"Hi," I replied. "The flowers are pretty."

"They're your favorites," he said. "But you already

know that. Look, I'm sorry I've been treating you so badly. I have no excuse. I wouldn't blame you if you weren't ready to forgive me yet. I also know the flowers and steak dinner are far from enough to make up for it."

"Okay," I said and crossed my arms to keep myself from diving right into his arms. Rex had a killer *I'm sorry* face. "Should I expect you to do this often?"

"The flowers or the interrogation?" He tried to get me with his heart-pounding smile.

I crossed my arms and glared at him.

He sobered. He must have realized his teasing fell short. "I hope not," he said. "If I do, please stop me right away. I'm afraid it's a built-in habit from my years as an officer. It's not an excuse." He put his hand up like a stop sign. "I'm asking you to let me know right away so that I can stop and apologize."

"That didn't work last night."

"It will now. I'm going to be working hard on my listening skills." He stepped closer. "I miss you. Can I hold you?"

My heart melted. I was such a sucker when it came to Rex. He held me tight, and we kissed. Then he took my hand, sat me down, and served some of the best steak I'd had in a while. It made me feel a little guilty that I was investigating when I wasn't supposed to be. But not guilty enough to stop.

Chapter 29

I decided the fudge of the day would be good, old-fashioned Million-Dollar Fudge. I made milk chocolate fudge, but then, for the center, I poured in dark chocolate chips, German chocolate chips, pecans, walnuts, black walnuts, peanuts, almonds, cashews, hazelnuts, and macadamia nuts, followed by marshmallow fluff. We folded that all in, then cut it and put it on a tray while everyone watched and listened to my stories.

I wondered if Melonie had a million dollars. A lot of people would kill for that much money. But if she did, where did it come from? And who inherited it once she was dead?

We finished the second demonstration at 3 p.m., and the Million-Dollar Fudge sold out very quickly. I left, took a shower, got dressed, and went into the office, where Jenn worked.

"Did Rex apologize?" she asked.

"Yes," I said. "With a lot of my favorite flowers and an amazing steak dinner."

"Well, good, I'm glad he listened."

"'He listened'?" I asked.

"He was complaining to Shane, and bless my husband, Shane gave him the talk."

"'The talk'?"

"That when you're wrong, you're wrong, and pretending you're not doesn't work with women. The best you can do is apologize with flowers—a lot of flowers—along with a good meal and maybe even jewelry."

"Ah, that explains things," I said. "At least he understood that he was wrong. I still worry. That's twice in one week. A third time, and he's going to have to do a lot more than say he's sorry. How's the event planning going?"

"Hard, but it appears to be on track."

"That's good," I said, and, following a thread, I opened the browser and looked up lottery winners for the last two years. If a group of people had won the lottery and Melonie had stolen it all, then that could have been the motive. But no matter where I looked, Melonie Manning was not on any list. The ones who were anonymous either won the lottery when she was here or when she was married. I frowned. Melonie had married again after she'd married Rex. So why did she keep his name? Or did she return to his name after her last divorce?

Jenn stood and pushed her chair back. "I've got to go home and make dinner. Are you okay?"

"I'm fine, thanks. I'll stop here in a minute." I glanced up at her. "Be careful, okay? There's a killer on the loose."

"I will," Jenn said and touched her tiny baby bump. "There are two of us to worry about."

I didn't know why I worried for Jenn. She'd helped me a couple of times before. But this time, something was different. Something dangerous. Maybe I shouldn't have involved her at all.

At dinner, I asked Rex, "What have you been doing since your sabbatical began?"

"I've been working in the community garden," he said. "We've placed raised beds and mounds. So far, we've added flowers, like an old English garden. There's the rose garden, the hollyhocks, foxglove, columbine, lady's mantle, peony, sweet pea, English daisy, yarrow, geranium—"

"That's a lot," I said, cutting him off. "Are you planting any vegetables?"

"Sure, the usual, plus corn, squash, and beans to represent the First Nation's three sisters."

"It sounds amazing," I said. "You make me feel bad. I've been working, walking Mal, and stopping in to see my friends. Remember, you told me to keep in touch with them."

"I did," he said, then took my hand and kissed the back of it. "Shall we leave the dishes for later?"

With everything going on, I wasn't about to miss out on an invitation like that.

Chapter 30

It was 8 a.m. the next morning when Frances and Douglas walked in. Officer Davis followed. I asked Roxanne to continue making fudge and went out to see what was going on.

"Officer Davis," I said.

She turned around. "Mrs. Manning."

I rolled my eyes. "It's Ms. . . . never mind. Do I need to call my lawyer?"

"No," she replied.

I felt relieved. "Then how can I help you?"

"I'm here to question and arrest Rowan Giles."

"Rowan?" I asked, confused. "Why?"

"You don't really need to know this, but if it will keep you from asking questions, and I'm certain it will," she said, "not only were Giles and Melonie Manning enemies in school, but Manning was having an affair with Giles's boyfriend, Lochlan Forester. Officer Laird thinks that's enough to bring her in and arrest her."

"Ridiculous," I said. "Where's the evidence?"

"She was at the murder site. That gives her opportunity and motive."

"Technically *I* had opportunity and motive," I said. "This is outrageous. You can't go around arresting people just for being there. What actual evidence does he have?"

"Like I said," Officer Davis said, and I could tell she wanted to roll her eyes, "we have motive and opportunity, and that's enough."

"Enough what?" Rowan asked as she and Finn came down the stairs. Finn looked at Officer Davis and growled. "Finn, enough," Rowan said with a stern voice. "Come." Finn went straight to her side. So did Mal.

"Rowan Giles," Officer Davis said, "you're under arrest for the murder of Melonie Manning."

This time, Rowan rolled her eyes. I would have laughed if it hadn't been so serious. "Sure, pick on the new girl. That's what locals do, isn't it?"

"I'm not from here," Davis replied. "I'm substituting. You can't call foul on this. Now, turn around."

"But you've been here before—and for a long time," I pointed out to Rowan. "It doesn't really make you a new girl, now, does it?"

Rowan turned and put her hands together so Davis could easily cuff her. Finn growled again and stood between Davis and Rowan. "Finn, go to Allie and stay." Finn did as he was told, but it was clear he was upset so I petted his back. His hackles were up, and Mal whined, wanting me to pick her up so she could see eye to eye with the person who would hurt her friend. Both dogs made low, rumbling sounds in their chests. I didn't blame them.

"Don't say anything," I told her. "I'll call my lawyer."

"Thank you, but no need," she said. "My brother is a lawyer. Please call Shane. He'll know what to do."

"I will."

"I'd call that a conflict of interest," Davis warned me.

"I'll call Jenn. There's no conflict in calling my friend."

Davis walked her out.

I called Jenn immediately. She said she'd talk to Shane right away.

I heard through the grapevine that Rowan's brother Patrick was there within half an hour, and Rowan was out within an hour.

Finn was so happy when she arrived. Oddly, so was I, even with the circumstantial evidence. I never believed Rowan killed Melonie. I walked out of the fudge shop and gave her a big hug. "I know there's no way you could have done it," I said.

"Thanks, Allie." She smiled. "Allie, this is my troublesome brother Patrick."

I looked at the tall, thin yet muscular, heartbreakingly handsome man with orange-red hair. He had wide shoulders, blue eyes, and freckles everywhere. "Nice to meet you," I said. "I'm glad you could get Rowan out."

"She's not one hundred percent out," Patrick said. "We had to post bail, and she can't leave the island."

"She can stay here as long as she wants." I looked at Frances, and she gave me a short nod. I knew Frances would be able to move guests around to continue to accommodate Rowan.

"Rowan isn't the first one Officer Laird accused of Melonie's murder," I told Patrick. "He went after me first."

"Sounds like he's desperate to find the killer—fast."

"And he's making a lot of mistakes," I said. "He and my husband, Officer Rex Manning, have some kind of ongoing rivalry. It seems that he has something to prove."

"That would explain why he arrested my sister on circumstantial evidence alone," Patrick said. "Rowan tells me you're good at sleuthing out killers. I hope you find this one soon. I don't think my sister can afford my fees."

Rowan punched his arm, and he grinned at her. For a moment, Allie wished she had a brother.

"I've got to go." He looked at me. "Keep her out of trouble, okay?"

"I will." I watched as he walked out.

"Sorry about this," Rowan said. "I was going to break up with Lochlan anyway. Auntie Charlene, my Aunt Kathryn, and well, everyone in the family disapproved. We dated in New York because I was lonely, and he was someone I knew. I also knew I wasn't his only girlfriend. He was like that at school, and a leopard doesn't change its spots, you know? Anyway, I wasn't surprised to hear about Melonie. I certainly wasn't attached enough to Lochlan to kill her over it. I broke up with him a few days ago, and the cops would have known that if they'd only asked."

Roxanne knocked on the glass, and I looked at my watch. "Oops, I have to go. It's almost ten o'clock."

Rowan looked around and then leaned into me. "I've decided to do some digging. We need to know who Melonie's first husband was in order to rule him out. I know an app that will let me search open records.

I should be done by the time you're done with your demonstration."

"You know how to do that?" I whispered back.

"Yup," she said and grinned.

"Crazy," I shook my head. "Good luck." The demonstration is exactly what I needed. It felt nice and normal to pour and stir the fudge while telling one of Papa Liam's stories. It also gave me a break from worrying about Rowan being wrongly accused. Or that the real questions remained the same: Who did it and why? And what was with all the spurned lovers?

Chapter 31

When we were done, I left Roxanne to deal with the stragglers.

"She's up in her room," Frances told me.

"Thanks," I replied. Then I took off my chef's coat and hat, hung them up, went up to Rowan's room, and knocked on her door.

Rowan and Finn both answered. Her dog was clearly more than well trained. He was protective. "Hello, Finn," I said and petted him behind the ears.

"The app is still running," Rowan said as she waved me in. "I had no idea how many Melonie Mannings there were in the United States."

"How will you know it's her?" I asked.

"I'm using the parameters of Mackinac Island and St. Ignace for Melonie Manning." Rowan sat and let me look at the computer over her shoulder. The app cycled name after name after name and compared each to the parameters of Melonie Manning, Mackinac Island, and St. Ignace until one popped up.

"I think we have it," she said with a little awe. "Look—her ex-husband is some guy named Cal St. John."

"Great," I said. "I haven't heard anything about a guy named Cal St. John on the island. Not that I would if he was simply part of the day crowd. I can ask around at the various hotels, but he could have taken the ferry home or stayed in Mackinac City or St. Ignace."

"It does seem impossible to track him down. It would be too easy for him to come and go. But I was thinking about it—he most likely didn't have an electric nail gun. That would have been too hard to hide." Rowan tapped her desk. "And there's no way he could have gotten close enough to put GHB in her drink."

"You're right, it doesn't make sense. Still, I suppose he could have had a tool belt on," I said. "And a tool bag. Everyone would have assumed he was a contractor and not even thought twice about it. Is there a picture of this person?" I asked with my fingers crossed.

"Well, I have their marriage certificate, but no picture. Let me check some of the job profile sites," she answered. "They can give us a lot of information." The site came up with close to a hundred Cal St. Johns. The pictures went on and on. We took out anyone who looked younger than twenty-five and older than sixty-five.

"Melonie was thirty-two when she died, which means she was around twenty-two when she first got married," I said. "Rex is four years older. I bet she only dates guys four to five years younger or four years older than her."

We searched for anyone who looked like they were between the ages of thirty-eight and forty-five and came up with five possibilities. Neither of us had seen anyone who matched the pictures, but we were both relatively new to the island. At least we had some photos to take around the island and see if anyone else had.

"Wait," Rowan said.

"What?" I asked.

"It looks like three of our men are married already." She pointed at the screen. There were pictures of three Cals with wives who were clearly not Melonie. We both sighed at the same time. "The other two have girlfriends. I found them on their social media."

"Then there was no reason for any of them to track Melonie down." I said, surprised at the disappointment running through me. I'd thought it was a wild goose chase to begin with. My fingers gripped the cold metal chair. "That takes us back to the beginning." I was frustrated. "Could you find anything that might suggest money as a motive?" I asked.

"There must be an app for that," Rowan said. "I'll check after I take Finn for a walk."

"Okay," I said, somewhat amazed. Geez, at my age I was supposed to be up on all the new apps. I mean, I had TikTok, Reels, Insta, Snapchat, Threads—all the popular ones. So why didn't I have the apps Rowan used? Come to think of it, I did have one baking app and two fudge apps, plus all my banking and travel apps. Even smart people couldn't have it all. "While you do that, I'm going to go talk to Sophie and see if she found out anything about our mysterious Oscar."

Chapter 32

I needed to see Sophie to find out what she'd discovered about the mysterious Oscar. She spent a lot of time with Harry Winston these days, but I hoped she had time to find out something. I found her at the airport in her small office. Her desk and her files barely fit inside it. She must have had a moment between flights.

I knocked and walked in. "Sophie. Are you busy?"

"Allie," she said with a smile, then she up and gave me a hug. "Sit, sit. It's not every day you come visit me at my office."

Okay, honestly, I'd only been there once before. "How are you?" I asked. "How's business?"

"I'm good," she said with a smile. "Business is booming, and well, Harry and I are getting closer."

"I'm so glad for you both," I said sincerely. "I was wondering if you'd had a chance to look into Oscar yet. It turns out there was GHB in Melonie's water bottle, and that's why she passed out. I figured this Oscar could have done it and no one would know. It's the perfect crime, if you kill someone and no one knows who you are or where you live."

"I checked with the florist," Sophie said. "The flowers were an online order, which meant they could have come from anyone, anywhere. I don't know what they mean, but it doesn't make sense to leave flowers with your name on them at a crime scene."

"Huh, I agree, it doesn't make sense. I suppose it could be a nickname or a middle name or—"

"Put there to throw everyone off the scent of the real killer," Sophie interrupted me.

"Exactly," I said. "Perhaps Oscar was someone from her past that the killer wanted her to worry about."

"Possibly, but it would be very difficult to prove. By the way, we ran into the book club the other day," Sophie said.

"Yes, Carol's been poking around. I tried to tell her to leave it, but the ladies are insistent about investigating," I said. "I asked her how she knew about the murder so fast, and she told them Valentine called them and told them there was something weird going on at the shop. It turns out she was one of the five who went out the back."

"That means we know two of the five," Sophie said. "Teddy and Valentine."

"Yes," I replied.

"I feel like the ladies are doing better than we are. When Harry and I walked by they were questioning Ed's workers. Carol waved us over and told us they'd discovered that Ed is doing some repairs on the stables and that a nail gun would be easy for him to get his hands on."

"Better than us or not, I warned Carol that Officer Laird had someone watching them. She told me they could ask around without looking suspicious, and yet here they all are obviously investigating. Don't talk to them again," I cautioned. "I don't need them leading Officer Laird to us."

"Got it," Sophie said. "If he asks, I'll simply ask him why he's so interested in why I'm talking to my friends. Then I'll ask him if he doesn't have something more important to worry about—like solving a murder." She grinned.

"And if he brings you in for questioning, look at him as if he's gone mad and say only one word . . ."

"*Lawyer*," we both said at once.

"Okay, we may be whittling down our list." I said with relief. "We already have means, motive, and opportunity for Ed. He has a nail gun. It would be easy for him to swipe a GHB pill from the vet. And Melonie had used him until he discovered she was having an affair with another guy."

"It sounds pretty damning," Sophie agreed.

"But I have a couple of suspects like that. Both Stan and Ed could have done it. Except, something seems off to me. Think about it, flowers, a shot through the heart, a romantic Victorian dress, and two spurned lovers in the crowd. It's too—"

"Contrived," Sophie said.

"Yes!" I said. "It feels like a setup. Same thing with David. He had access to the drug, was there with the crowd, and is rumored to have had a fling with Melonie.

But I don't think it actually has anything to do with heartbreak or jealousy."

"I have to agree," Sophie said, then paused. "I heard they arrested Rowan today. Do you think she did it?"

"No," I said honestly. "She didn't have a nail gun, and her motive is weak. They're saying it's jealousy over Melonie sleeping with her boyfriend. Rowan said she already knew about it and was breaking up with Lochlan anyway. Seems her entire family hated him."

"Good, we can scratch her off the list. I'm surprised they arrested her." Sophie had her hands under her desk, and I wondered why.

"Me, too, but Officer Laird can't wait to find a killer and beat Rex on a case."

"Sloppy," Sophie said. "Just sloppy."

"It's okay. Her brother Patrick is a lawyer. He was able to post bail for her and get her out within two hours."

"Good, good," Sophie said, then paused. "Can I share some news with you?" she asked shyly.

"Of course," I said, trying not to grin as I guessed what she was going to tell me.

She pulled her left hand out from under the desk. There, on her ring finger, was a huge diamond surrounded by sapphires, all on what was probably platinum.

"Oh, my gosh!" I squealed and grabbed her hand to look closely at the gorgeous piece of jewelry. "It's beautiful! Congratulations." I ran around her desk to give her a hug. "Harry is a great guy. There's no one better I would wish for you!"

"Thanks," she said and blushed. "It happened last night. We had a table next to a window to watch the sunset. As soon as it was over, Harry got down on one knee and opened the ring case and proposed. I said yes immediately. He put the ring on my finger, and we kissed. Then we heard the clapping and catcalls of the other people in the restaurant. Harry grinned, and I blushed. The restaurant brought us a special dessert of a flourless cake shaped like a heart that said, 'Congrats!' The thing is, Harry didn't order it or even tell them what he was going to do. It was like they knew. It was amazing."

"It sounds terribly romantic! And the ring is completely you. If I were to see a ring like this, I would know it was for you. Did you see it before he proposed?"

"No, actually," she said. "Harry had it handmade for me. I'm stunned that he loves me so much because I love him and that has never happened before in my life."

"Then it's meant to be," I said. "I remember the feeling when Rex and I finally got engaged. I made it difficult at first. But it all worked out in the end. Do you have any idea of when and possibly where you'll get married?

"No, silly." She pulled back her hand and shook her head at me. "It just happened last night, and it was a surprise. Why would I know the where and when already? You should know I'm not one of those women who've had a dream wedding in mind their entire lives. I don't think weddings are as important as the marriage, but my family may have other ideas."

I laughed. "Trust me, they will. Just be firm about what you like and what you don't like. Promise me."

She laughed. "I promise."

Chapter 33

I was so happy for Sophie. Mal enjoyed the long walk and the time spent visiting. She didn't seem to care about the diamond ring, but she did like the excitement, and she joined in, wagging her little stump tail.

That happiness aside, I couldn't keep the worried expression off my face. None of the events of this murder made any sense. There was Rowan, who didn't have means. And the five people that went out the back. One was Teddy, who left out of the back in a hurry, but again, he had opportunity, but no motive or means. There were Mr. and Mrs. Elwood, the honeymooners, in the back of the shop. I still needed to talk to them to see if they knew anything, including asking why they went out of the back of the shop rather than the front. Then there was Valentine and one last mystery man. Valentine had to know him. After all, Mr. Beecher said it looked like a single man and two couples. So why didn't Valentine mention who she was with? I made a mental note to see her, too.

Who else was gathered around the back door? The book club, who all had alibis. Stan, Ed, and David, who all seemed to have motive, means, and opportunity along with questionable alibis, were there. I disqualified Mr. Beecher and Officer Davis.

Who was left, and why did they have to be there? Then I realized there was a whole other set of people in front of the store. The killer could have been there, too.

Most likely, they'd left the island already if they were someone off the island in the first place.

I needed to talk to the Elwoods.

Once again, Mal and I walked into the bed-and-breakfast from the side porch.

"Mal simply can't stay away, can she?" Ellen said with a chuckle. "Still looking for the Elwoods?"

"Are they here?" I asked.

"Sure, but you'd better hurry if you're going to catch them. They leave this morning," Ellen said.

"Where can I find them?"

"Room sixteen, but do be careful. Officer Laird just left, which means—"

"He might come back with more questions," I finished her sentence.

"I'll try to stall him, but . . ."

"We'll hurry, won't we, Mal?" The last thing I needed was to explain to Officer Laird why I was in a rival hotel, although with people following me, he most likely already knew.

I knocked on the door of room sixteen, and a lovely woman answered. She had brown hair, with wide brown eyes and the glow of the newly married. "Mrs. Elwood?"

"Oh, I love the sound of that," she said with a wide smile. She was shorter than me and curvy.

"Mrs. Elwood, I'm Allie McMurphy. I own and work at the—"

"McMurphy Hotel and Fudge Shop," she said. "Come in. I heard you found that poor woman's body. And to think we were there when she was killed." The woman shivered.

A tall man with coco skin and warm brown eyes stepped out of the bathroom with a shaving bag in his hand. "Honey, I think that's every—Oh, hello," he said. He seemed suspicious I was there.

"This is Allie McMurphy. She's the one who found the body. Oh, and her sweet little puppy."

Mal jumped up on the lady until she petted her.

"Hello," I said. "Mal and I are sorry to bother you. I came to see if you were alright after your photo shoot."

"Oh, we're fine," the woman said. "What a crazy story we'll have to tell about our honeymoon. And we finally got our picture. The police had it for the longest time, but then they realized it was digital, and so they sent us a copy. Do you want to see it?"

The man walked up and put his hand on his bride's shoulder, telling me through his body language that he would protect her. It made me smile. "Yes, I'd love to see one of Melonie's last shots."

She pulled the photo out of an envelope and passed it my way. "What do you think? Isn't it the cutest? I love the costumes so much. It was fun to pick the backdrop, too. See, we picked the one that looked like a very wealthy library. Books are kind of our thing. Aren't they, babe?"

"Yes, they are," he said in a soothing baritone voice.

The photo was well framed, with the backdrop pulled down so that no one could tell what it was. The new 3D backgrounds seemed so real. All in all, they really did make a lovely couple. I scanned the photo quickly yet carefully, and something popped up in the back of my mind, but I couldn't put my finger on it. "So nice," I said. "You two look like you belong there." I handed it back. "When I was here before, I told Ellen that I would give you a free pound of fudge from my fudge shop for the trouble you've been through. I'm practically a newlywed myself."

"Really? When did you get married?" she asked.

"Our first anniversary is in two weeks," I replied.

She put down the picture and hugged me. "Were you married here?"

"We were," I answered.

"That must have been amazing. We were married in our hometown of Grandville. This is our honeymoon."

"Congratulations," I said and picked Mal up to stop her from begging for further attention. "I heard the police were here. I hope they were kind to you."

"I wouldn't say 'kind'," Mr. Elwood said, his hand back on his wife. "More like badgering."

"Oh, honey, it wasn't that bad."

"It was bad enough." He frowned.

"Well, I hope this terrible murder doesn't keep you from coming back," I said. "Please don't forget your fudge. It's on me, and I'm so sorry you had such a bad time. Don't tell Ellen, but if you ever want to come back, the McMurphy will give you a special rate. See you soon. Thanks for showing me your beautiful picture."

Mal and I left. It was nearly 2 p.m., and I had to be back in time for the demonstration or Officer Laird might arrest me this time, and that wouldn't be good.

Red, White, and Blue Fudge

Ingredients

3 cups of white chocolate chips
2 tablespoons of butter
1 14-ounce can sweetened condensed milk
¼ cup of blueberry preserves
¼ cup of raspberry preserves

Directions

Line 13x9-inch baking pan with parchment paper.

Place the white chocolate chips, butter, and sweetened condensed milk in a microwave-safe bowl. Microwave on high for 3 minutes—stirring at 90 minutes. Ensure all the chips are melted. Remove from microwave. Stir and pour into pan. Alternatively dollop blueberry and raspberry preserves. Use a gently warmed butter knife to swirl the preserves into the fudge. Refrigerate until set. Cut into 2-inch pieces and enjoy. Store remainder in an airtight container in the refrigerator.

Makes 24.

Chapter 34

I figured whatever it was that tickled my brain would pop out eventually, but right now I would be cutting it short for the demonstration. I decided I'd go see Teddy Schmidt after my demonstration. He was in and out the back door. He had to have seen something.

Then I'd go see Valentine. It had to be the man with her who said, "Let's go out the back." More than anything else, I needed to understand why he said that. I had a feeling it was the one missing piece of this puzzle.

"Allie, Allie, hold up." It was Carol, and Irma was with her. Unlike Carol, Irma preferred to have her hair cut into a shoulder-length bob and colored champagne blond, just enough to blend in her grays. They wore their tracksuits and were clearly power-walking again. I was going to have to ask them if they had taken up pickleball. I'd heard it was a lot of fun.

Mal and I stopped while they caught up. Thankfully we were in the mouth of my alley, far from the prying eyes of the police.

"Hi," I said. "I'm kind of in a hurry to get to my

demonstration before a certain officer comes looking to see if I'm where I belong."

"We have something to tell you," Carol whispered.

"We think we know who at least one of the couples was," Irma said with pride.

"Who?" I asked.

"The Elwoods," she said. "They're from out of town on their honeymoon."

"I've met them," I said.

The two women looked defeated, as if I'd popped their happy bubble. "Why don't you come in, and we can talk after my demonstration?" I said. "There's coffee."

"Yes." Carol perked up. There was nothing she liked more than free coffee. They followed me in as I took Mal's halter off and went to work. It was a good thing I did. I saw Officer Davis looking in the window. Clearly, the cops were watching me. Well, if they thought they were good, I had to be better.

After the demonstration and the cleanup, I went out and smiled at the ladies. "Why don't you give me about fifteen minutes to shower and change. Then come up to my office. I have to do some paperwork."

They nodded and went back to their conversation. When I got upstairs, Rex wasn't there, and it had me wondering how much gardening he could do on his days off. I never knew he was so into it. Maybe he'd start one for us. I loved fresh vegetables. I certainly hoped he wasn't part of the crowd watching me.

Showered and changed, I opened the office door to find the two ladies talking to Jenn.

"She's going to have another baby," Irma announced.

"How did you know?" Jenn asked, her eyebrows drawn together in confusion.

"It's the glow, dear," Carol said and patted Jenn's hand. "Pregnant women always have that glow."

"How do you know that glow isn't from finally getting your toddler to sleep through the night?" Jenn replied.

"At our age," Carol said, "we can tell the difference. Now, ladies, let's talk about the investigation."

"Carol, I told you there is no investigation," I said and watched Irma's expression fall. "It's too dangerous. Officer Laird said he will toss anyone investigating the murder into jail for obstruction of justice. So, no, this one we have to leave to the police."

They both went silent, and I hoped I had finally gotten through to them. Nope.

"But we have a copy of the last picture Melonie took right before her death."

"How'd you get that?" I asked.

"We ran into that couple—"

"The Elwoods?" I asked.

"Yes," Irma replied. "They were on their way to the police station to demand their pictures since they'd paid for them."

"We were sympathetic, of course," Carol said. "And we agreed that they should demand their pictures. If the police were going to hold them as evidence the least they could do was print off a copy."

"They were up in arms about it after we met," Irma said. "And the best part . . ."

"The best part is they promised to make a copy for us!" Carol said with glee.

"A copy?" I repeated. "Why?"

"We told them we were—"

"Friends of Melonie and would like a copy of the last picture she took." Irma's eyes sparkled, and Carol had an expression of self-satisfaction.

"Get this," Carol began. "They told us their photo wasn't the last. The last was of a lovely couple from Iowa."

"They talked about how fun Mackinac Island was and how nice the people were. I guess neither couple knew the other, but they bonded over coming into the photo shop on a whim."

"Huh," I said. I hadn't thought about the fact that the police have the SD card with all the photos on them. One of those final shots could have been a picture of the killer. So why were they using all this time to arrest me or Rowan? It doesn't make any sense. It means they know and have known from the beginning who those two couples in the back were. "Has Officer Laird interrogated Valentine yet?" I asked.

"Not that I know of," Carol replied and drew her eyebrows together in confusion. "Why?"

"Didn't you say that it was Valentine who called you all to come to the back of the shop? And that she felt something wasn't right at the photo shop?"

"Yes," Carol said.

"Then Valentine had to be part of the last couple getting their picture taken," I said. "Do you even know who was with her when she got her photo taken?"

"No," Carol said suddenly quiet.

"You haven't asked?" I questioned.

"No," Carol repeated.

"Hmmm," I said. "Listen why don't you two go home. Seriously. Stop investigating. No one needs to get hurt. Okay?"

After a long moment, Carol looked at Irma and Irma looked back. Both had disappointed expressions as they got up.

"Well," Carol said. "You're right, I suppose."

"Thank you." I walked them both downstairs and out the door. Hopefully I had finally gotten to them, and they would give up and find something else to entertain themselves with. Meanwhile, I had to find and talk to Valentine. Surely, she knew something important about the case.

After they left, I was working on inventory when it dawned on me what was amiss with the Elwoods' photo. I looked at Jenn. "Where's Shane?"

"At work," Jenn said. "Why?"

"Remember I had the chance to see the Elwoods' picture?"

"Yes," she said.

"Well, I knew something wasn't right about it, but I couldn't put my finger on it."

"Okay." She leaned her elbows on her desk. "I'll bite. What was off in the Elwoods' picture?"

"Their photo backdrop was the Victorian library. The same backdrop that was down in Rowan's pictures."

The idea made me smile. This might all come together after all. "But unlike Rowan's picture, the braided rug was not in the Elwoods' photo."

"And . . ."

"We talked about the killer having stashed the murder weapon in the shop somewhere. Remember?"

"That sounds familiar," Jenn replied. "Are you thinking that—"

"The murder weapon was stashed under the floorboards."

"And you think Shane missed it?" Jenn sounded one part disappointed in me for thinking so little of her husband and one part amazed that we might have figured out the answer.

"I think Shane was so busy with the scene that he had them take the carpet, but without seeing the Elwoods' photo . . ."

"He wouldn't have looked under the floorboards," Jenn replied.

"And we need someone official to find the nail gun if it's there," I said.

"I'll call Shane right now and have him meet me next door," Jenn said. "Allie, you might be on to something."

Chapter 35

When I got back to the apartment, Rex was packing.

"Wait, I thought we got over our arguments," I said, worried. He was carefully packing his uniforms. Mella sat in his suitcase on top of his T-shirts, and curious, Mal jumped on the bed to watch him.

He came over and kissed me hard, then hugged me closely. "With Laird here, I've been reassigned."

"No, no, no, no, no!" I said as tears sprang into my eyes. "Why? Where? For how long? We have a life here. Everyone hates slimy Officer Laird. No one even knows his first name, and he isn't even living here. He's staying in Mackinac City." I hugged Rex harder, as if I could keep him home with a hug.

He slowly untangled me. "I'm due to show up tonight." He stepped away and finished packing.

"But it's late." I struggled to hide my emotions as I worked to wrap my mind around the whole thing.

"I have to go where the chief wants me," he said.

"But this is your home. I'm going to call and have a

word with the man." I pulled out my phone, but Rex gently pushed my hand down.

"We already had a talk. He said it was temporary." Rex pulled Mella out of his suitcase and closed it, zipping it up.

"Temporary can become permanent," I argued. "Especially when they find out how good you are. Where is your assignment?"

"A few hours south of here." He pulled the suitcase off the bed, and I followed him into the kitchen.

"What do you mean, 'a few hours south of here'? Can he do that? It can't be his jurisdiction," I argued.

"I can't talk about it," he said, then kissed me hard, holding me tight.

"Is that what you've been doing during the day? Setting all this up? How long have you known?"

"Sweetheart, I have to go, or I'll be late."

"I'm walking you down to the ferry." I grabbed Mal's leash.

"Stay here," he said softly. "There's a killer out there, and I know you're stirring up trouble. You can't help yourself."

"But—"

He looked stern and sad at the same time. "I need to know you're here and safe."

"It's only a few blocks away," I argued.

He brushed my wavy hair off my face and behind my ear. "If you go, everyone will notice that I'm leaving, including the killer. Stay home—for me—and lock the door behind me. Keep the doors and windows locked at all times. I'll call every night."

"I hate this," I said, holding on to him one last time.

"I know. Me, too. I love you."

"I love you, too." Mal, Mella, and I stood near the door, confused and sad. He kissed me one last time and was gone. I ran to the window to watch him go down the alley until I couldn't see him anymore. With tears in my eyes, I locked the door and slumped to the floor. Maybe If I solved the murder before that nasty Officer Laird, they'd fire him and bring Rex back.

Chapter 36

I was exhausted the next morning. I hadn't slept all night without Rex by my side. It was unusually chilly out for our morning walk. Mal didn't seem to notice. I had hoped the cold air would help wake me up, but I was sure I'd also need a lot of coffee. My thoughts tumbled as I tried to figure out how to explain Rex's reassignment to Frances, Douglas, Roxanne, and Jenn. I didn't know how I was going to sleep until he got home. Even Mal and Mella were confused and sad.

I decided the best thing I could do was to throw myself into my work and the investigation. Keep myself as busy as possible. That way I didn't have time to think about it and would come home too exhausted not to sleep.

The walk was simple. It seemed that Mal had stopped with her obsession with the pharmacy, stables, and police station. Maybe because Rex was gone.

Brown sugar fudge with tart cherries and English walnuts was the fudge of the day. While I worked hard making fudge, my thoughts kept flitting from Rex to the murder investigation, going over it again and again in my head. I thought about Teddy, Valentine and the mysterious man who told them all to go out the back of the shop.

I knew I had to do two things after my demonstrations. One, I had to go see Teddy. He really wasn't a suspect. Teddy was always so happy-go-lucky that it made no sense for him to be the killer What would be his motive? All I could do was hope he saw something. Then I needed to see Valentine and ask her who she was with and why he thought it was better if they called.

Maybe Melonie had kids, and her custody suit was contentious. That could explain her time off the island. But if she had children, wouldn't we have seen them at some point? Or maybe she wasn't allowed to see them and was trying to get visitation rights back.

Ugh! None of these theories made any sense. I suppose sometimes there was no sense for murder.

"Allie? Allie!" Roxanne's voice cut into my musing.

"Hum, yes?"

"It's nearly ten o'clock, and the crowd is starting to gather to hear your stories as we make the fudge. Brown sugar with tart fillings, right?"

"Yep, tart cherries, English walnuts, and let's try some dark chocolate chunks," I instructed. "The brown sugar is a favorite, but super sweet. If you add tart ingredients, you balance it out."

I shook off my thoughts and worries to tell my stories. We were done and handing out samples by a quarter to eleven, and I let Roxanne go to lunch. I was so distracted and tired I realized I had to be more mindful. Some days I'd be so far inside my head I'd forget about her. Which meant she'd have to have a hurried lunch between 1 and 2 p.m. I had to tell her to let me know when it was her lunch break. I asked her to let Frances know, as well, in case I forgot, and the fudge shop wasn't covered.

Which reminded me, I hadn't told anyone about Rex leaving yet.

Finally, there was a slow moment, and I asked Frances to watch the shop until Roxanne got back. I went up to my office. Jenn hadn't come in that morning, so I called her. I needed to talk to her first to bolster me so that I could tell everyone else without crying. I'd thought about calling her last night, but between Benji and her pregnancy, I thought she needed more rest.

"Hey," she said when she picked up the phone. "Are you okay? Whatever it is, it's not good if you're calling and not texting."

I sat down in my chair and then got up to pace. "I don't know where to . . ."

"Start?" she finished. "Talk. Ease into it. Tell me anything. Ask me how my day's going. Ask me about Benji. Then tell me what's going on."

I swallowed back the tears, but my voice cracked, and I took a deep breath. "Is now a bad time to call?" I asked.

"For you, it's never a bad time to call. Unless it's in the middle of a wedding, and there usually isn't one in the middle of the week."

I took another deep breath. "Did Shane agree to look at the scene again to see if the murder weapon was stashed there?"

"He did," she said. "I went with him with Benji on my hip. It was strange to take my two-year-old to a crime scene. Shane said it was okay because the place had already been processed. You were right, by the way. There was a loose floorboard. When he pried it up, it was just the size needed for the nail gun. But the space was empty. The only thing that remained were a couple of nails. He took pictures and collected them. Oh, and he says thanks, by the way. It's too bad the killer got back to the gun before we did."

"As much as I hope the murder gets solved, the last thing I want is for Officer Laird to solve it," I said with a bit too much anger.

"And there it is," Jenn said. "Good, you're angry. Now tell me what's going on."

I told her what happened with Rex leaving because of Laird.

"Oh, I knew I hated that slimy guy, but this. This is so wrong," Jenn said. "Everyone should know what happened so that they'll stop helping him."

I sighed. "It's probably best that only a few of us know," I said. "If Laird solves this murder, I'm afraid he's going to stay. And then it wouldn't be right for the whole island to hate him."

"I don't like it," Jenn said. "Wait, do you think Shane knew this and didn't tell me? I'm going to kill that man!"

"Don't say that—he's the father of your children, and you love him," I said. "So far, you're the only one I've told. Thanks for listening."

"Anytime," she said. "And if you get lonely, stop by.

Benji will keep you too busy to think about anything else."

I laughed. "Thanks, Jenn."

I hung up, went downstairs, and told Frances and Douglas what was going on. They were also supportive and reminded me that Rex had told me it was only temporary. Which meant, solving the case or not, it didn't mean Officer Laird would stay. That made me feel better.

The rest of the day went fairly smoothly, considering I was exhausted and unable to turn my brain off about the investigation. Finally, Roxanne pushed me out and told me to go. She would handle the stragglers.

Frances had to go up and check on a couple of guests, so she asked me to watch the desk. While I did, I opened my phone and started taking notes. Mr. Beecher had told me that Teddy Schimdt had run out of the back of the shop and left in a hurry. Teddy had excuses, but that didn't mean he didn't see anything. He could have either hidden the nail gun or seen who killed Melonie. Jenn talked to him, but she didn't get much except that he seemed okay. If I put him back on the list and he was the killer, why would he have wanted Melonie dead? He was new to the island and a brawny man with the opportunity, and possibly the means, to do it. Especially after we found that the murder weapon had been stashed and then removed. But there was no proof of a motive. At least right now.

Not being able to go back to the crime scene without going to jail bothered me more than anything. It meant Rex, my work family, my best friend, and my guests were all in danger. Jenn was pregnant, and I had put her in danger. I hoped Shane had asked her not to come back here until the killer was caught. I'd call her later and tell her myself. I couldn't live with myself if anything happened to her or her baby because of me.

I had to figure this out in order to keep everyone safe, and I had to figure it out now. Ugh, I needed to go back and talk to Teddy myself.

Then I needed to get serious about listening to Mal and figure out what my pup had wanted when she went from the pharmacy to the stables to the police station. Did David have something to do with it? Did Ed? Had they worked together? Was that what Mal had been trying to tell me? I added that question to my list.

I should also talk to Charlene. I needed to ask her if Lochland was the jealous sort and perhaps had heard Melonie was flirting with someone else. If so, who? David?

Teddy. It all came back to Teddy. The thing was, from the few times I'd met him, he didn't seem like a mastermind who could orchestrate a murder this complicated. Teddy was a big guy, but despite his lumberjack size, he was the kind of guy who was more of a follower than a leader. I'd guess he was maybe thirty-five years old. He had a congenial smile, broad shoulders, and big hands, and he was nearly bald, with only the hair around the sides of his head left. It was still dark brown. The gray of age hadn't hit him yet.

Why couldn't I figure this out? Then it dawned on me. Rex wasn't doing his thing, and I couldn't trust anyone except Charles, and I hadn't even seen him in a few days. Now with Rex off the island, my deductions felt off more than ever. I glanced at my watch. It was before five. Maybe I could catch Teddy before he left for the night.

Roxanne came by to get a water bottle from the mini fridge before she left for the night. She dug one out and came over to me. "You'll never guess what I heard at lunch," she said, her dark eyes twinkling with secret knowledge.

"What?" I said, looking up. "Don't make me wait."

"David is having a secret affair." She wiggled her eyebrows. "He should know that nothing on this island stays a secret for very long."

"I'm pretty sure I knew about that. It's Valentine Maas, isn't it? Laura Morgan's friend?"

"It's not her," Roxanne said. "That's why it's a secret affair."

"Who's he having an affair with, then?" I asked, digging through possibilities in my head.

"That's the odd part," she went on. "No onc knows. Those two are very good about hiding it. It's almost like a game."

"If no one knows who she is, how do they know he's having an affair? Don't you need to be with someone to have an affair? Who's this rumor coming from anyway?"

"Carol and Irma," she replied. "They noticed there were a lot of takeout bags with dinners for two in the pharmacy trash."

"They went through the trash?" I knew I sounded as appalled as I felt.

"They wanted to know if David had a motive for the murder."

"I told them not to investigate," I said.

"You know there's no telling any of the seniors anything," Roxanne said. "Carol told me that they started to stake out the place, taking note of who visited the pharmacy the most. Where David spent his lunches, his evenings. They figured it had to be someone we know or at least someone the ferry captains know."

"I don't understand, why keep an affair secret?" I asked.

"Maybe she's married or has a boyfriend or maybe she's famous. We do get famous visitors you know." Roxanne's eyes sparked with excitement.

"The ladies think this secret affair gives him a motive for murder? How? Why? And why are you getting mixed up in this?"

"Oh, honey, I love a good mystery," she said. "And a good rumor. Yes, everyone knows they may be at risk for obstruction of justice. But truthfully, he can't arrest the entire island."

"I suppose not," I said. "It's probably just me he wants to arrest."

"Don't worry, we've all got your back," she said. "Especially since Rex has been transferred."

I leaned back and closed my eyes. Small town, indeed. "How did you know?"

"We all know you two have been having a bit of a rough time with Officer Laird here and all. Then Mary Emry saw Rex leaving with a suitcase, and everyone was worried. So, Charles calmed us all down by letting it slip about Rex. We weren't supposed to let you know we knew." She shrugged. "Do you think no one would notice that you didn't sleep last night?" Roxanne gave me a sympathetic look. "Don't worry, we're all looking out for you. No one's telling anyone that you're investigating. We don't want to give that nasty man a reason to arrest you."

I wanted to pull my hair out. "How many times do I have to tell everyone I'm not investigating?"

She simply looked at me.

"Right, I'm being followed," I said and blew out a long breath. "I don't understand. If everyone knows so much, then why can't I find the killer?"

"Well, we don't know *that* much," she explained. "And the killer must know that you're looking for them. I'd say one hundred percent of us don't want to go to jail, but that doesn't mean we won't do our best to figure out who David's secret lover is." She rubbed her hands together. "Finding out is going to be a lot of fun. I'll be a sleuth like you, only without a dead body."

I laughed. "Knock yourself out, but if you do find out that David has a secret lover and you figure out who she is, please tell me. I'm curious."

"No, you're not just curious," she said. "You think it might help you solve the murder. At least I won't be arrested for obstruction of justice." She grinned, and we both laughed outright.

"What's up?" Rowan and Finn came down the stairs and walked by when they heard us laughing.

"David, the pharmacist, is having a secret affair,"

Roxanne said. "I'm going to help the book club figure out who it is."

"Sounds fun," Rowan said.

"Rowan, you might want to rethink getting involved," I said. "You've already been arrested for murder. Unlike Roxanne's sneaky fun, you could be seen as planting evidence or getting in the way of the murder investigation, which is obstruction of justice. Either could be added on to your charges."

"Planting evidence or obstruction of justice?" Rowan asked while Roxanne kept quiet.

"Even if this was part of the case," I explained, "don't you think Mr. Beecher would recognize them? And how secret would they be if they were seen in public? And if, and I mean if, you find out who else was part of the group that was there when Melonie was killed, all you'll have is circumstantial evidence."

"Wait," Rowan said. She hit her forehead. "I can't believe I didn't think of this before. She was taking pictures when she died, right?"

"Right," I answered, wondering where this was going. "But we all know that already. The camera and SD card are in evidence."

"But that doesn't mean we can't get the photos online," Rowan said with a glint in her eye. "Most studio photographers upload their photos automatically to the cloud in case anything happens to the SD card or if they want to make some quick touchups. If we can hack her account, then we'll know who those customers were."

"Ooo," Roxanne said. "I would love to be a part of that."

"It could be considered tampering with evidence." I sighed. "Please don't do it, Roxanne. I need you to help me with fudge making, not sitting for twenty-four hours or more in jail. And Rowan, I'm serious. Doing anything like this will be bad for your bail hearing."

"What's another thing when you've already been arrested on circumstantial evidence?" Rowan asked.

"They will put you in jail and keep you there this time," I said. "Trust me, I know."

"She has a point," Roxanne said.

"I'm not worried. I have Patrick to get me out of things," Rowan said.

"I'm worried," I said. "There are some things a lawyer can't help with."

"Okay, I've been warned. But that doesn't mean I can't help. Right, Rowan?" Roxanne said. "After work, of course, boss."

"Of course," I replied and told myself that I'd tried. "I do have another clue."

"What is it?" they both asked at the same time.

"Mal," I said. "She keeps going from the pharmacy to the stables, then to the police station. I thought maybe David and Ed were the murderers. You know, working together? And maybe Mal wanted me to go tell the cops."

"Why didn't you?" Rowan asked.

"Because I had no evidence, and unlike Rex, Officer Laird wouldn't take Mal seriously."

"That little dog has sniffed out more murderers than Allie," Roxanne said.

"She has," I agreed.

"Finn's good at sniffing things out, as well," Rowan said. "Should we put them both to work?"

"You could," I said. "But I can't figure out why a secret lover would want Melonie dead, and worse, I have no proof. A lot of people on the island own nail guns, and there isn't any way to get evidence from one without taking them all into the lab. Checking that could take months."

"What about any bloodstains on the nail gun?" Rowan asked. "They had to shoot it pretty close to get it to embed in the heart far enough to kill her."

"That means she was most likely already on the ground when they nailed her," I said.

"Ugh." The two groaned.

"What?" I asked, confused.

"Terrible pun," Roxanne pointed out.

"Ohhhh," I said.

Roxanne turned to Rowan. "Sometimes she's a little slow to catch on."

"I heard that," I said. My thoughts started to come together. Melonie might have been killed by two people. Someone who slipped the GHB in her drink, knowing exactly how soon she'd be incapacitated. And another who hit her with the nail gun. It would be easy to stash the murder weapon where Shane couldn't find it, then come back and get it later, when no one was looking. Once the crime scene was released, anyone could have snuck in and taken the nail gun home.

While it sounded plausible, it all came back to the why. Why do it? My brain kept telling me to follow the money. But if her murder was about money, why?

Did Melonie have something on the murderers? Was she blackmailing them? I wouldn't put it past her, but what was she blackmailing them for? Or was it only one person? Mal might have been going to the pharmacy because David was selling prescriptions on the side. The killer could have paid someone to get the prescription for them. That way David wouldn't be able to identify him if he wanted to. Together, no one would suspect a thing.

"There she goes," Roxanne said. "Lost in thought again. You're going to go see Carol and then talk to David, aren't you?"

"Carol, yes, but I'm not going to see David. We already know he had means, opportunity, and motive. It would be a waste of time. Besides, I think there's someone else who might be able to provide proof of who killed Melonie," I said. "Someone who knows about nail guns."

Chapter 37

"Hi, babe," Rex said on the other side of the line. I was cuddled up with Mal and Mella on the couch. Teddy had already left the island by the time I'd finished with Carol. I would have to wait until tomorrow to talk to him. I'd invited Rowan over for a movie night, and she and Finn sat beside me. Finn acted like a lap dog, but he could take up the entire couch if Rowan let him. So, he sat on the floor with Mal, his eyes going from the popcorn bowl to Rowan and back, as if he could will her to give him some. When Rowan brought in the popcorn, I'd asked her not to feed my begging fur babies. I knew someone whose pup had died after choking on popcorn, and I wasn't taking any chances.

"Hi," I said in a low voice, then got out of my seat on the couch, motioning to Rowan that I was taking the call in another room. I went into the bedroom and partially closed the door. Meanwhile the traitorous animals stayed with Rowan, watching the popcorn bowl with keen eyes.

"How are you?" I asked. "Do you like the job? Are you going to be there long? Are they stricter or more lenient there? Do you have a good place to stay? Did you eat? Please tell me you ate."

He laughed a husky laugh. "It sounds like a bit of Rowan has rubbed off on you. So many questions. The good news is that I do have a nice short-term rental. The bad news is that I may be down here for six weeks or more."

"No!" I exclaimed loud enough that Rowan stuck her head into the room and asked me if everything was all right. I mouthed that I'd tell her after. She nodded and went back to the couch. This time Mal came in and jumped on the bed, then turned in a circle three times and sat down next to me. Mella stalked in, jumped up onto Rex's pillow, and began to lick her feet. "Six weeks is too long," I said. "I'm not sure I can make a week without you."

"Sometimes you have to do what you have to do," he said. His warm voice poured through me, giving me goose bumps.

"Please tell me there's a chance you'll come home sooner," I said. "Lie to me if you have to."

"There is a small chance I'd get to come home early," he said. "They've had a double homicide, and since I've had a lot of experience, they brought me in. It's not going to be an easy case, and it looks like six weeks is the minimum."

"But we need you here," I said. "There's a killer on the island, and Officer Laird is barely trying to find them. He's too busy flaunting his new position around town."

"He may be self-centered and thinking he's already

got the killer after arresting Rowan, but be careful, he's out to get you. I can't stress enough how much you need to be careful. Leave this one alone. Please, I'm asking you."

I couldn't promise since I was deep into my investigation, so I changed the subject. "You know, Jenn is pregnant again. What if we were to try to start a family?" I asked.

There was a long pause. "Are you trying to tell me something?" he asked.

I laughed. "No, sweetheart, I'm not. I was just wondering, and I think it might be time to start talking about it."

"Now? While I'm gone for six weeks?" He sounded suspicious. He probably should be, but now that I'd mentioned it, I'd started to warm up to the idea.

"Why not talk about it now?" I asked. "You're away with no distractions, and I'm here. We won't be influenced by desire. We can make independent decisions."

"You understand that if and when you get pregnant, you absolutely have to give up sleuthing for the safety of the baby."

I frowned. I hadn't thought about that, but he was completely right. If I were pregnant, I would have to give it up, at least for a while. Maybe no one would get murdered for those nine months. "I know," I said softly.

"And I know you're sleuthing now," he said, with more of a resolute tone than an accusatory one. "Please be careful, there are only so many times Jay will be able to help."

"*If* I was sleuthing," I qualified the statement, "I'd

simply get others to help me. He can't watch everyone all at once, no matter how many people he wants to put in jail."

"Be careful," he repeated. "Not everyone wants to keep you safe."

"I know," I said. "Now, don't sidetrack me. Do you want kids? If so, when?"

"I do," he said. "You know I do. I was waiting for you to bring it up. After all, it's your body. Plus, I wasn't sure if you could give up sleuthing for over a year, maybe for the next eighteen years. And it's a big commitment for the fudge shop, too, let alone all the other things you do, like the committees and the book club."

"It's not like life would stop completely. Jenn seems to do okay with everything."

"She's not handling hot sugar every day," he said with worry in his voice. He wasn't wrong.

I diverted the conversation again. "I miss you."

"I miss you, too."

"I could find a pet sitter and come down to see you," I suggested.

"I want that more than anything," he replied. "But you have to know, I'm working all day and most nights. So, I can't guarantee you'd even see me."

"It's enough for me to just be close to you," I said in almost a whisper. "To be there whenever you came home and hold you while you went to sleep."

"I miss you with all my heart," he said. "But you can't. It wouldn't be safe."

"Be careful out there," I said, disappointment rushing through me.

"*You*, too," he replied. "I'm worried that this murder will be more complicated than ever before and that Laird will be there waiting for you to mess up."

"I'll be careful," I said. "I won't let him find out." At least I hoped.

Chapter 38

I went to see Teddy after my first demonstration was done. He seemed to be the missing piece in all of this. I found him working on the public toilet near the docks. "Oh," I said as I walked into the ladies' room to find him, as if I didn't know he was there.

He had the wall under the sinks torn out, and what looked like rotted wood was underneath. Mal went over to sniff it. Teddy greeted her. "Hello, little doggie, what brings you here?"

"Hi, Teddy, it's me and Mal," I said.

"Ah, Mal, I should have recognized her. I see her everywhere." He looked up at me. "What brings you here? There's a sign on the door that says out of service."

"I was looking for you, actually," I said and sat down with him under the sinks. I made a note to get home early and change my clothes before I did anything with fudge. "Wow, this looks like it's been leaking a long time."

"It has." He sighed. "I wish I'd known before all this

damage. It seems they told Stan, but he kept forgetting and finally threw me in here today."

"I see you have the leak fixed," I said. "At least, I don't see any water dripping. It looks like it should remain fixed for a long time. Now, who fixes the wall?" I asked. "Surely not you."

"Oh, yes, it's me," he said. "I've been in construction for years, but while the pay is decent, it all depends on the weather and the market. So, I thought I'd do something that pays even better and is not dependent on the weather or the economy. Sooner or later, everyone needs a plumber, rain or shine. I'm apprenticing with Stan. Now, see these cut studs? I'm going to reinforce the rotting ones with new ones and then add this drywall. Nail it in, tape it, and putty it. Then the painters will come in and repaint so that it all matches."

"Wow," I said, then grabbed Mal and put her in my lap.

"I'm also going to create an access panel for next time."

"That's smart," I said. "How do you attach the new studs and the drywall? Do you use a hammer and nails? Isn't that hard under the sinks like this?"

"I use a nail gun," he said. "See?"

I covered Mal's ears, and he put three nails in the stud, attaching it securely. "That's fast," I said. "But don't you need to plug in your nail gun?"

"No, nearly all of them are battery-operated now. It's easier and lighter."

"Can I feel it?" I asked. "Listen, I was looking for you because I may have some work I want done on the

McMurphy, and Mr. Devaney is busy with a different project."

"Sure, here." He handed me the gun. It felt heavy. I would need two hands to hold it, but Teddy needed only one. I looked at it, secretly looking for blood, but I saw nothing. I handed him back the gun.

"Is it safe to have more than one person around when you nail things?"

"Oh, yes, it's perfectly safe as long as you wear a good safety hat and goggles."

"Oh, no, I don't have either," I said. "Should I move back so you don't accidentally hurt us?"

"I suppose, but I'd practically have to hold it against your skin like a piece of wood."

"Ouch," I said. "Well, I'm glad it's not like TV." I glanced at my watch. It was fifteen minutes before my two o'clock demonstration. "I've got to go. Thank you so much for answering my silly questions. I'll be sure and call you. Like I said, Mr. Devaney needs help every now and then when things get backed up, and I pay well."

"I'll consider it," he said with a grin. "Thanks, Allie."

Mal and I hurried back to the outside steps to the apartment to change my clothes and get downstairs in time for the demonstration. When I arrived, Charles was sitting on the top of my stoop. "Hi, Charles," I said as I opened the door, and we went inside. "How are you? Sorry if I'm a little short. I was sitting on a restroom floor getting a lesson in plumbing, and I have to shower and change before my two o'clock demonstration.

Please tell Officer Laird I'll come in as soon as I'm cleaned up."

"It's not Officer Laird, Allie. And I already told Roxanne she'd have to do the demonstration by herself."

I stopped. He looked very serious. "What's happened?" I asked. "Since they sent you, it must be serious." I looked at his face and must have turned white. I felt dizzy and could barely talk. "It's Rex, isn't it?" He gave a small nod, and my mouth went dry. "Is he alright? I'm sure he's alright. I spoke to him last night. Please tell me they got the murderer and he's coming home early," I whispered.

"Allie, sit down."

"I'm fine because he's fine."

"Sit." Charles pointed to the kitchen bar stool. "Rex got into a tangle with the wrong people, Allie. He's been shot."

"What?" I sat down hard on the bar stool. "No, you have that wrong. It can't be Rex. He's a good shot."

"He's in surgery right now to take the bullet out."

"A bullet? I don't understand." Mal jumped up in my lap, and I held her so tight she squeaked. "Did you say he was in surgery? Right now? Take me to him. Let me grab a bag. I'll have Frances watch my fur babies. Where is he? Is it far? Sophie will fly me there."

"I can't tell you where he is," Charles said. "He's undercover."

"I don't care what he is, I'm going to be by his side, and I'm going to be there *now*! Where is he? If you don't tell me, I will find out on my own," I warned him.

"That's what he thought," Charles said. "I have his

direct orders to keep an eye on you day and night and ensure you don't go anywhere."

"What?" I exclaimed. "No, no, no! I will find a way to get around you."

"That's why there'll be an officer stationed at every door of the McMurphy—and a few windows, too."

"Are you crazy? That's the entire police force making sure I stay in my home. I'm not about to stay in my home, and you know it. Not when Rex is out there somewhere shot and in surgery. I can do undercover," I insisted. "What does he need? An ex-wife? A girlfriend? A fiancée? I could even be the fudge maker he used for his mom's gifts."

"You can't go, Allie. It's for the best. He's on a very important assignment."

"What about Mal?" I asked. "She'll need her walks. People will wonder with all the police here and me not walking Mal. They'll think I murdered Melonie. There will be talk about why I wasn't taken in. What does Officer Laird think of all this? You know I'm going to find out where Rex is, and you won't even see me leave. But make no mistake, I will leave. I won't even pack a bag."

Charles sighed. "Give it a couple of days, okay? Then you'll get to see him."

"I can't, and you know it. Could you?"

"I don't know," he said quietly.

That slowed my brain down a moment. "Oh. Charles, I didn't mean anything. Still no favorite woman? No love of your life?"

"Not for lack of trying," he said softly.

"Don't you worry; Jenn and I will set you up with someone perfect."

He cleared his throat. "No, thanks. If I'm going to find her, I'll find her on my own."

"Wait a minute." I narrowed my eyes and put Mal down. "You did that on purpose."

He raised his right eyebrow. "Did what?"

"Stopped me from thinking about the love of my life in surgery and not being able to get to him. Don't think I'll forget." I turned and left.

"Where are you going?" Charles followed me.

I stopped him with a hand to his chest. "Can't a woman get some privacy?" I pointed to the bathroom, and Charles's face turned red. I went in and closed the door behind me. It was ridiculous for Charles to think he could stop me. I didn't need a change of clothes. I could buy that and a toothbrush anywhere. I sat down on the toilet lid and thought things through. Frances would take care of my babies. Everyone else would just have to take care of things without me. I'd swim across the darn lake if I had to. But I was pretty sure Sophie would smuggle me out.

I quietly opened the bathroom window. It was the right size for me to wriggle through. Yes, it would be tight to reach the staircase, but if Charles was right, they'd be watching it. I'd have to take the rain pipe up onto the roof, and then go from my roof to the next roof and the next, until I was sure they weren't still searching. Then I'd shimmy down and run until I found Sophie. I bet she was at Harry's and they'd check her plane, but I wouldn't be there until after they checked.

My plan seemed flawless—until I was halfway out the window and saw Charles standing there on my stoop. "Need a hand?" he asked.

"Oh," I said. "You startled me."

He gave me a serious stare. "You know I'm going to have to nail that shut now. And if that doesn't keep you inside, I'll have to assign a woman to go into the bathroom with you. Bedroom, too, of course. Which means you'll be seeing a lot of Officer Davis."

Officer Davis was not the person I cared to see. She kept to herself, and I didn't really know her, so it was odd to think of her following me into my most private places.

I tried another way. I snuck out to the staircase that went up to the roof, but when I got to the top, a cop was patrolling it. I waited for him to move away from the door and slipped out into the shadows. When he moved again, I hurried to the next rooftop, only to be grabbed by Charles. I sighed.

"You need to stay away from the crime scene," he said.

"You mean you aren't done with that crime scene yet? What's going on?"

"Allie." He looked at me, disappointed, then picked me up and tossed me over his shoulder, wet, stinky clothes and all.

"You can't keep me here. I won't let you. It's Rex. I'm getting to my husband, no matter what. You can't stop me. I'll jump if I have to." Tears rolled down my cheeks. "He is the love of my life, and I won't let him be in surgery without me. I have to be there. He went into surgery alone. *Alone!* What if he wakes up and I'm not there?"

"There are plenty of men in blue there for him. He's not alone. Trust me, he'd be *more* upset if you were there. You'd be putting yourself in unnecessary danger. Plus, he'd have my hide, and you don't want to kill me, do you?"

"I will if it means getting to Rex. I'd go through anyone to get to him."

"How would you even know where to find him?"

"I'll figure out where he went, then I'll start with the closest hospital and move out in a circle from there until I find him."

"I'll let you know. Seriously, I'll keep you in the loop."

"I can't stay here." He carried me back inside the apartment, and I sat down and let the tears fall. "I can't take it. Not being there. Not knowing if he's going to be okay or not. What if it were me? Who would stop him? Not you. Not anyone."

Charles sat down beside me and awkwardly patted me on the back. "It'll be okay."

Tears flowed. "What if I'm pregnant and he dies in surgery? People die in surgery all the time."

"Allie, are you telling me that you're . . ."

"I don't know. And you don't know," I said slowly. "Would it make a difference if I was?"

He thought about it for a moment. "Yes," he said, shaking his head. "It would put you in even more danger."

"You would never say that to him. He'd clock you

and then come find me. I'd do the same if you weren't so big. Don't you think I couldn't take Officer Davis down. Because I can."

"Allie, don't make me put you in jail to keep you safe," he said softly.

"What is it with everyone trying to put me in jail? You can't hold me without violating my rights. Jay would get me out in an hour. We both know that. I'm going."

"I won't let you." I could tell I was wearing him down. It was simply a matter of time and creativity, and I'd be gone. "Can I at least go see Jenn?"

"Only after Shane gets home," Charles said.

"But you can walk me there, and even come in if you think I'll run."

"Why? So you can go out a bathroom window again?"

"Wouldn't you move mountains to get to the one you loved? Especially one who has been shot and is in surgery?"

He looked me in the eye. "Yes."

"Then how can you do this to me?" I asked. "How can you keep me from him when he may be dying under some strange doctor's scalpel? Just tell me where he is and let me go there," I whispered.

"I can't," he said.

"Why!" I screamed my frustration.

"Because I don't know."

Chapter 39

There was a knock at the door. I looked at Charles, and he opened it. I crossed my arms, my emotions all tangled up. He didn't even trust me to open the door. Why didn't anyone know where Rex was? Where was I supposed to go? To every hospital in the Lower Peninsula until I found him? It might be a little extreme, but that wouldn't keep me from doing it.

Maybe Charles knew that. Maybe that was why he opened the door, because he knew I would run. But still.

"Allie, are you okay?" I glanced around Charles to see Rowan and Finn standing on the stoop.

"Come in, come in," I said and grabbed another tissue to wipe my nose and then add it to the pile beside me. Mal stayed at my side and Mella on the chair above me. I was done with Charles anyway. After they'd come in the apartment, he closed the door behind them and stood at it, with his arms crossed like some kind of bouncer.

Rowan glanced at him and then at me, her eyes wide. "I thought *I* was the one in trouble with the cops," she whispered.

"It's Rex," I said, tears falling down my cheeks. I grabbed a full box of tissues. Right now, I was scared for Rex and mad as a hornet at Charles. Big guy or not, at some point I'd take him down. I mean, he had to sleep some time, and then, *bam!* I glared at him. All I had to do was figure out how to get off the island without him hunting me down. What if he lied to me about not knowing where Rex was to keep me from going there? If he'd lied, I was going to kill him, and then I'd be a murderer, but it would be worth it. The feeling made me a bit happier. I had to be smart about this. "He's been shot and is in surgery. They won't let me be with him."

Rowan patted my hand and sent Charles a dirty look. Finn growled. Then Mal growled. Maybe Finn could take Charles down. "Thank you, baby," I said to Mal and then buried my face into her little warm body. "It's going to be okay," I said to Mal, then grabbed another tissue for the tears still running down my face. Mal licked them as if that would make them stop. "Daddy's going to be okay," I whispered, but I could still feel the angry rumble move through her as she stared at Charles.

"Shh, Finn," Rowan said. "Down." The big dog lay down but kept his eyes on Charles. "What can I do?" Rowan asked. "Make you some soup? Some coffee? I'm actually very good with beef stew or any kind of dessert. What do you have in your cupboards? I'll make you something."

"I can't eat anything," I said. Nonstop tears ran down until my nose started running as well. Rowan reached out and moved the tissue box closer to me. "Thanks," I said and blew my nose.

"Why won't they let you go?"

"I don't know, ask him." I pointed to Charles. "They seem to think it would be dangerous for me to go."

"Well, they won't know danger until we get them." She narrowed her eyes at Charles, who simply looked back at her. "I have brothers," she said. "I know how to hurt someone." Charles didn't even blink. She gave him the stink eye. "Come on, I'll make you some pastry. It's always relaxing to watch."

She looked through the cabinets until she found my pots and pans and whipped up a potato soup. She poured me a bowl, and it was delicious, but I couldn't eat anything but a spoonful or two. Then she found Grammy Alice's baking bowl, a mixing spoon, and a cupcake pan. If nothing else, my cupboard was well stocked. Then she got down flour, cold butter, baking powder, and sugar, then found strawberries in my fridge. I'd had no idea what I was going to do with the berries when I saw them in the store, but they were fresh and on sale, so I had to get some. I watched, mesmerized by how Rowan whipped up flaky strawberry tarts in forty minutes.

"How did you do that?" I asked as the dessert baked.

"It's an old recipe of my grandmother's," she said. "The perfect comfort food, as far as I'm concerned. And he can stand there all he likes, but he's not getting any of it." Charles raised his right eyebrow as if he wasn't bothered by her, but we could hear his stomach growling across the room. Rowan leaned in and spoke low. "You need something else to think about."

"No, I don't," I cried. "What if he's dying and in pain? What if he's already dead?" I touched her arm. "What if he's crying out for me and I'm not there?"

"Don't think like that. You can't think like that," Rowan said. "Thinking like that will drive you crazy. Let's take your mind off all that and put it on something else."

"Like what? What else could be more important?"

"Right here and right now, your babies need dinner. Feed them. Then we'll go for a walk." She turned and glared at Charles. "We're going to take our dogs for a walk. You can walk behind us if you must, but keep far enough back to stay out of our conversation. I'm sure a guy your size can outrun a fudge maker."

Charles looked at her as if she were crazy. But I didn't care. She was right. I sniffed and used a tissue to wipe my eyes. One thing at a time, and right now there was no way to find Rex. I couldn't stop the tears, but there were two fur babies that still needed love, attention, and dinner. Besides, the more people who knew, the more help I'd have getting away.

I leaned in. "Do you really think you could take him?" I whispered. "I don't know where he is. He said he'd be in the UP or somewhere south of Mackinaw City, but once I'm off the island, I can start making phone calls."

Rowan glanced at Charles. "I could take him, but not for long. We'd have to be somewhere you could make a quick escape."

"I can hear you, you know," Charles said.

I jumped at the sound of his voice. I have no idea how he could sneak up on us that way but apparently he could.

We both scowled at him.

After seeing to the animals' dinner and treat needs, I put a halter on Mal, and we walked outside. The sun started to go down as we walked. Rowan was right. Fresh air and leaving the apartment helped. I was an emotional mess of tears and anger. Still, Mal followed her nose. I was tired of her going from the pharmacy to the stables to the police station, so we walked in the opposite direction.

As we walked, several people stopped me and asked what was wrong. I told them, and they all glared at Charles, who seemed impassive to the whole situation.

Then each of them would whisper, "If you need off the island, just come to me, I'll help smuggle you out." All I could do was wish I'd never closed off the smugglers' tunnel in the McMurphy basement.

"So," Rowan started a conversation as people were farther and farther apart. "Rex is your number-one preoccupation right now, and he should be, but there's no way to know where he is. Are you sure that Officer Brown doesn't know? Rex and Officer Brown are good friends, right? He has to know where Rex is. Maybe we can get him to tell Shane. Jenn said Shane talks in his sleep. It's just a matter of waiting it out."

"I can't wait. I *won't* wait." I blew my nose.

"Okay," Rowan said with sincerity. "We can have

Carol start the phone tree and everyone can divvy up areas—"

"A few hours away," I finished.

"A few. Around two hours away and ask about incoming gunshot victims. Once we get a hit, we'll get you out under the cover of night. But for now, take heart. Officer Brown and Rex are good friends, right?"

"Yes," I replied.

"So why isn't Officer Brown—"

"Charles." I waved my hand toward the big man behind us.

"Fine, Charles. As I was saying, if Rex was in such bad condition, then why isn't Charles worried? Does he seem worried to you?"

I glanced back at him. "No," I muttered, drawing my eyebrows together.

"Why is that, do you think?" Rowan asked.

"Because he knows something about Rex's condition," I replied. "I also believe him when he says he doesn't know where Rex is . . ."

"But what about Rex being shot and in the hospital? Do you believe him about that?"

"Yes," I said. "You should have seen his face."

"Okay, alright," Rowan said.

"He could be dying," I whispered, "and I wouldn't be there." More tears fell, these silent.

"Let's not go there," Rowan said. "Think about it. Everyone knows you're investigating Melonie's murder. Maybe they're using your husband's injury as an excuse for Officer Muscles back there not to let you out of his sight. So that you can't interfere with the case."

I wiped my tears and glanced back at Charles, hope rising in my chest. "He does seem pretty calm. But that might be for my benefit. Men don't always show their worry. Either way, I need to get off the island and find Rex. I have to know he's okay." More tears ran down my cheeks. "He's shot and in the hospital. Maybe the phone tree idea will work. Then, we can get everyone to help me off the island. Didn't David say if his pills were taken in the wrong dose, it could knock someone out? One of the seniors has to have that same prescription. Carol could get me some, and I could crush them up and put them in Charles's drink. Once he falls asleep, we can get me out."

"That's a good plan," Rowan said.

I went from sad to angry. "If Shane tells Jenn that they're using Rex's shooting as an excuse to stop me from investigating, they're going to wish they hadn't. I'll exact my revenge, and it won't be pretty."

Rowan laughed. "Also a good plan."

"I'm serious," I said, sniffing, unsure which emotion I felt—anger, sadness or determination.

"I know," Rowan said and hugged me.

"You have to understand. I'm scared for him. I love him more than life itself." I twisted the tissue in my hands. "If he comes out of this alive, I'm going to kill him myself."

"There you go," Rowan said. "Be angry. You have every right to be angry."

The anger didn't last long as fear and worry came rushing back. I couldn't stop crying. "I need a distraction,"

I said, "but not tonight." I hiccupped. "I can barely think right now."

"When we get back, let's have some tart," Rowan suggested.

"I can't eat," I said. Suddenly Mal made a beeline straight to the plumbers' office. Then she sat, and Finn sat with her.

"The plumbers?" Rowan whispered. "Interesting. A pharmacist and a plumber."

"I can't right now," I said. "I'll think about it later. Come on, Mal, let's go home." I barely got the words out, and yet when I turned around, Mal happily went with me. "I . . . I don't know what to do," I said, sniffing and twisting my handkerchief into pieces.

"When we get back to your place," Rowan said in a natural voice. "I'll cut the tart, then I'll see that you go to bed, and I'll do the dishes for you."

"You don't have to do that," I said and sniffed.

"I will anyway," she replied. "And when I get home, I'll see that the phone tree starts calling hospitals. We will find him." She patted me on the back. "Don't you worry about that."

When we got back, I took off Mal's halter. Finn didn't need one because he stayed by Rowan's side as if it were his job, while Mal liked to run ahead and point things out. Besides, Mal could easily be run over by a carriage and horses while Finn was nearly as big as a horse.

"Sit," Rowan said and pointed to a bar stool.

I grabbed another tissue. "I can't. It's been hours.

Does it take this long for a gunshot wound? Or are they keeping things from me?" I sent Charles another dirty look.

"I'm sure he's all right, or someone would have told you differently." She glanced at Charles, who remained stoic at the back door.

I got out my phone and texted Rex. *Please be okay, my love. Please be okay. My heart is breaking, and I want to be with you. I will find a way to be with you. Answer so that I know you are all right. Please answer.*

I waited what felt like forever. "No answer." I showed her the phone. "He always answers."

"Don't worry," she said reassuringly. "They often take away your phone when you have surgery. He'll see it when he comes out."

"But it's so late." This time there was no distraction that could keep my fear away. Tears kept flowing. My nose kept running. I grabbed another tissue. "It's been hours since Charles told me he was in surgery. Shouldn't he be out by now?"

Rowan turned to Charles. "You have that com in your ear. Have you heard anything? Is he out? Will he text her?"

"I haven't heard," he said. "But I can find out here in a little bit."

"You mean, when I'm in bed and you're waiting outside my room to ensure I don't run." I rubbed my forehead. "Where would I go, anyway? Even Sophie can't help me. There's no way to put in a flight plan if you don't know where you're going." I turned and pushed Charles hard in the chest. "How could you? How could you not check for me? How could you treat me like a prisoner when my husband's out there alone somewhere, shot and hurting?" Charles took hold of me and then enfolded me into a bear hug while I sobbed into his uniform. I was so tired and scared that Rex might be dying somewhere, that all of Rowan's ideas and rationale just disappeared and here Charles was being strong for me. He rubbed my back. "No matter what," he said, "we'll make sure you're all right."

"Come on," Rowan said. "Let's eat some tart. Dessert always makes things better." She took dessert plates out of the cupboard, then gently pulled me over and pushed me onto a stool, then gave us each a tart. "I don't see how dessert is going to make any of this better," I said. But then she cut off a bit of the tart and practically shoved it in my mouth. It was the best thing I'd had in a long time. The butter had melted into everything, causing the flaky outside to drip lightly.

I caught strawberry juice on my chin and licked my finger. "Good," I said. "Rex would have loved it." Tears started again. This time Rowan held me, and I cried some more. Finally, she gently took my forearms and looked me in the eyes. "I've got to go," she said. "But text me if you need anything."

"I will," I said and gave her another hug. "Thanks for everything."

"Of course," she said. "I hate that they've confined you while your husband needs you," she said out loud with a look straight at Charles. He stood there finishing his tart, impervious to what went on around him.

I gave her another hug, then Rowan and Finn left. The house smelled of pastry, but as good as it was, it wasn't enough for dinner. So, I swallowed my emotions and reheated a bowl of the soup she'd left, then set it on the bar for Charles along with some bread and butter. He ate it, all the while keeping an eye on me. I ignored him and curled up on the couch with one of Rex's shirts, then cried my heart out until I fell asleep.

I woke up two hours later and texted Rex again. He didn't text back, which told me he was either still in surgery and recovery or something really bad had happened. In my deepest of hearts, I hoped he was okay, and they simply hadn't given him his phone back.

I went to my bedroom to get away from Charles, then paced back and forth there, wishing Charles had just taken me to Rex instead of watching over me. It was frustrating, heartbreaking, and completely like Rex. When he got home, he was going to get a piece of my mind. I kept thinking about it. How dare he order Charles to ensure I didn't try to find him?

I sat down on my bed and texted Jenn.

What's up? she texted in return.

I told her what was going on, and she called. "Are you okay?"

I started crying for real at the sound of her voice. It'd been hours. Why couldn't I stop? I had to get ahold of myself.

"I'll take that as a no," Jenn said. "Is there anything I can do? Bring something to eat? Come over and be with you?"

"No," I replied, my voice wavering. "It's late, and you have two babies to worry about."

"You mean one and a half."

I blew out a shaky breath. "Yes, one and a half. I was just talking to Rex about maybe starting a family, and now this. I don't know what to do." All of that was true. It was hard for me to lie to Jenn. She could spot it the moment it came out of my mouth. "I just . . . I need to find him," I said. "Could you see if Shane knows where Rex is? Charles has me a prisoner in my own home. I can't do it. I simply can't do it. Can you see if Shane might know where he is? Charles says he doesn't know where Rex is, but he's so calm, I don't know if I can believe him. I'm sure Shane knows. It would make me feel better if I at least knew where he is." I lowered my voice to a whisper. "It would also make it easier to escape and go to him."

"I get it. If Shane was somewhere in a hospital with a gunshot wound, I would move heaven and earth to find him, get to him, and hold his hand."

"Why can't the men in my life let me do that?" I said more tears streaming. Stupid tears. I was feeling trapped. That's it. I was trapped.

"Once I find out, do you want me to come and create a distraction so you can get away?"

"Please," I replied.

"Done," she said. I knew that she would come, and that would make me feel better. Rowan was nice, but Jenn was the sister of my heart and my person.

"Don't worry, I'm on it!" she said.

"Thanks," I replied.

Next up was Sophie. I texted her about what was going on. It took her longer to get back to me, but I figured she was with her fiancé, and it was hard for her to get away. I knew there was nothing she could do for me if I didn't know where I was going. She would have to schedule a flight plan. No directions, no flight plans.

A look at the clock said it was late for me, very late, but still early for others. I dried my tears and started plotting my revenge. I would solve this murder, then find my husband. I started by taking a long, hot bath, making sure to soak the wood around the clawfoot tub. I might have even unscrewed the drain as best I could with only what I had in the bathroom. I pulled out some of the caulk and plumber's tape, then I let the water soften the wood a bit more before I got out carefully. Wrapped in a large bath towel and another towel around my hair, I walked past Charles, who sat in a chair between my bedroom and the bath. "Good night," I said, my face tearstained and my eyes swollen. I still couldn't decide if I was mad or sad.

Once in my room, I put on some pajamas, texted Rex again, and then texted Frances.

Allie, are you okay? she asked. *You never text this time of night.*

No, I said, then texted her the entire story of Rex being shot and in an unknown hospital and how he wouldn't answer my texts.

Oh, you poor thing, she wrote. *Is there anything I can do? Do you need food?*

No, I replied. *Rowan made me soup and a strawberry tart. I also have a bathtub leak, but could you let Mr.*

Devaney know I'm going to just call a plumber? I trust his skills, but I need to—

Allie, what are you cooking up? And with Rex shot?

I have to do something, I replied. *Until I get a text or learn where to go to be with him, I have to do something. Trust me. No one wants a fudge demonstration with a fudge maker crying her eyes out and wiping her nose.*

Fine, Frances texted. *But Douglas and I will keep an eye on you, because I know you're not telling Charles any of this.*

Thank you, was all I texted back.

Keep in touch if you hear anything, she texted.

I will.

Now all I had to do was convince Charles not to listen when I talked to Teddy.

Chapter 40

I cried through most of the night, my thoughts twisting from, *He's in a coma, and I can't see him*, to, *He's not hurt. How could he do something so awful to me?* I finally got up early and made coffee. Charles had spent an uncomfortable night on the couch.

"I've made coffee," I said. "There's also some downstairs."

"Thanks," he said when I poured him a cup.

"What do you like in it?" I asked.

"Cream and sugar," he replied. I had both and gave them to him.

Then I made bacon and eggs and toast. It was good to have a protein breakfast when you're around sugar all day. We ate in silence, and I was fine with that. When I was done, I stood to put the dishes in the sink, but he took them from me.

"I've got it," he said.

I looked at him. He didn't look much better than I did. His uniform was wrinkled except for his top shirt, which he'd taken off and laid on the top of my chair—the chair Mella currently sat on top of, with the shirt underneath her, like cats do. Charles's hair stuck up, and he needed a shave. I was dressed already and prepared to go downstairs and make as much fudge as I could without breaking out in tears again.

I drank my coffee. "Mal has to go out." I sighed. "You have to go home and at least change. Who's going to replace you?"

"Davis," he said, then finished his coffee, putting the cup in the sink.

"I left a message for the plumber. My bathtub is leaking."

"I'll let her know," he replied. He put his shirt and shoes on, upsetting Mella, who sniffed and walked off with disdain while I grabbed a jacket and put Mal in her halter.

The sun hadn't risen yet, and it was chilly enough to see my breath when we both left the apartment. I wasn't going to ask Charles how he was. In part, I was as mad at him as I was at Rex. While I stood waiting for Mal to do her business, I asked in a wobbly voice, "Any word on Rex? I've been texting, but he hasn't texted back. Surely he's out of surgery by now. Unless there were complications. They would tell you if there were complications, wouldn't they? Also, why are they telling you stuff and not me?" I was trying hard to keep my tears at bay. It wasn't working very well.

"First off, he's out of surgery, but they kept him overnight," Charles said.

"What! He's out of surgery, and you didn't tell me?" I punched him hard, but he didn't move. "How could you not tell me? Is he in recovery? Why hasn't he answered my texts? Is he in a coma? I have to go see him. You understand, right?"

"You can't." Charles took a deep breath and let it out. "He's going back to work."

"Back to work!" I exclaimed. "No way—no! Not without me seeing if he's okay first."

"Secondly," Charles said, trying to calm my outburst with hand gestures, "he's undercover." Charles was speaking so quietly that I had to get close to hear him. "He can't answer your texts no matter how much you want him to. He's using a burner phone."

"I hate it. I hate it all. I hate you. I hate not knowing. I hate not being able to talk to him. I hate that he was shot. I hate everything!" Mal looked up at me. "No, baby," I said. "I don't hate you."

Charles took my tantrum in silence. When I got back home, I unleashed Mal, then let Mella out for the day. Giving Charles my evilest look, I grabbed a clean baker's cap and coat, then headed downstairs just in time for Officer Davis to walk in and switch off with Charles. I tried not to snarl at her. Instead, I went into the fudge shop and began to make some simple fudges. My thoughts were too twisted and my mood too upset to do anything more. They say your emotions come through in your fudge. If they were right, then the three batches I made before Roxanne showed up must have turned out awful.

She grabbed an apron and asked me what was going on. I told her, and she asked me, "What are you doing making fudge? You should have called me."

"I needed something to do," I replied.

"Well, not this," Roxanne said and took the stirring paddle out of my hand. "You know better. You could have seriously burned yourself. Hang up your cap and coat. You're not coming anywhere near the fudge shop today."

"But—"

"Nope," she said. "You can't do any demonstrations in this shape, and I can handle everything else. Besides, I have an idea for a new type of fudge. I thought I'd try it on your day off, but I think I'll try it today."

"Fine," I said, crossing my arms, doing my best not to let the tears flow. I knew there was no arguing with her because she was right.

"Fine," she replied. "Now, go on. Get out of here." She shooed me off, and I left feeling as anxious as ever.

I hung up my coat and hat in the back hall like she'd asked. Then I made coffee and put out rolls, Danish, yogurt, milk, juice, and water. It wasn't a full breakfast, but it was something.

For the most part, I ignored Officer Davis. She played on her phone while I checked guests out until Frances came in at 8 a.m.

"How are you doing?" she asked. "Never mind, your face shows everything." Frances *tsk*ed. "Put a wet washcloth in the freezer, then once it's stiff, put a towel around it and place it on your eyes. It'll help with the swelling."

"Thank you," I said, my voice still quivering.

It was noon when Teddy entered the McMurphy right on time. He gave Officer Davis an odd look. "Why is she here?" he practically whispered as he nodded toward the woman scrolling on her phone.

"My husband, Rex, was shot yesterday, but I'm not allowed to go see him. No one knows where he is, and he's on some kind of project that doesn't allow me to contact him. The police are afraid I'll run, trying to find him, so I have a babysitter." I sighed. "She's been here since eight a.m., and she's practically bored out of her mind. Why don't you start up the stairs to my apartment? I'll let her go to lunch and then meet you up there to let you in."

"Can you do that?" he wondered with wide eyes.

"I'm sure I can, look at her. Does she look like she wants to be here?"

"No," he said. "Okay, I'll head up."

"Perfect." As soon as he was out of sight, I went to Officer Davis. "Why don't you go get some lunch. I'm going to take a nap. I promise I won't leave. Frances can keep an eye on me. Besides, there's nowhere to go since I don't know where Rex is." Tears ran down my cheeks, and I knew my eyes would soon puff up even more.

She looked me up and down suspiciously. "I want to talk to your manager."

"I'm the owner, which means Frances works for me, but she will keep an eye on me." I was a little put off by the officer's attitude. But she was relatively new, and how would she have known?

I walked her over to Frances's reception desk.

"Allie says I can go to lunch, and that she won't run.

She claims she's going to take a nap and that you'll keep an eye on her."

Frances looked from me to Officer Davis and back. "I'll keep an eye on her and keep her pup by my side. She won't go anywhere without her dog."

"Okay," Officer Davis said. "If you're sure."

Frances looked at me again. "I'm sure."

"Then I'll be right back," Officer Davis replied. "Since I'm out, does anyone want any pizza?"

"No, thanks," Frances and I said at the same time.

"But you should ask Roxanne." I pointed toward the fudge shop.

"Got it," the officer said, then knocked on the fudge shop door, had a slight conversation with Roxanne, and said she'd be back soon.

"What are you up to?" Frances asked.

"I have a hunch," I said and sniffed. "And I'm going to see if it's true."

"You're still sleuthing while Rex is in the hospital with a gunshot wound." I felt her disappointment.

"What else am I supposed to do?" I asked, sounding as desperate as I felt. "I can't go to him. He won't answer my texts, and I have twenty-four-hour surveillance that is driving me crazy."

Frances sighed. "Be careful."

"How can I get hurt with a police officer with me all the time?"

"When it comes to you, Allie, there's no telling."

Lemon-Blueberry Blondie Bars

Ingredients

¾ cup of butter
3 tablespoons of white chocolate chips
1 cup of packed brown sugar
2 tablespoons of fresh lemon juice
1 teaspoon of lemon zest
¼ teaspoon of salt
2 eggs
1 teaspoon of vanilla
2 cups of all-purpose flour
1 cup of blueberries

Directions

Preheat oven to 350°F.

Line 13x9-inch pan with parchment paper. In a microwave-safe bowl, melt butter and chocolate chips until smooth. Stir every 30 seconds. Pour into large bowl and whisk in brown sugar, lemon juice, lemon zest, and salt. Add eggs one at a time. Whisk until incorporated. Add vanilla. Slowly add flour ½ cup at a time, making sure to scrape the bottom and sides to ensure no dry mix is left. Fold in blueberries. Pour into pan.

Bake for 35 to 40 minutes. Cool and cut into 2-inch squares.

Enjoy!

Chapter 41

I hurried up the stairs, where Teddy waited for me at the door to my apartment. Mal raced up with me, happy to play whatever game I was playing, but when she saw Teddy, she was not happy, confirming my suspicions. I opened up the apartment and let him in, leaving the door unlocked just in case.

"The bathroom is over here," I said as we walked back. "I went to take a bath last night to calm myself down after the news . . ."

"Sorry. I shouldn't have said anything." He patted my arm awkwardly, and Mal moved between us.

Teddy looked at her. "I don't know what's wrong. Animals usually like me." He glanced over his shoulder as I opened the bathroom door.

"What happened to Officer Davis?"

"She went to lunch," I said. "But not until I swore I wasn't going to go anywhere."

"It doesn't make any sense to have you under surveillance like that," he said as he walked into the bathroom, then got down and inspected the leak. "This doesn't look that bad," he said. "It shouldn't take but a minute."

"I'm glad," I said. "Mr. Devaney was too busy today, and I was worried."

"How long has this been happening?" he asked.

"It started last night," I replied.

"It's good you caught it. It could have gotten much worse." He got down on his knees with a flashlight and looked for the bit of pipe I had dismantled. "Here it is," he said. "Odd, though. It looks like the plumbing tape on the joint has been torn. Anyway, it'll be an easy fix." He reached inside his tool bag.

"Can I ask you a personal question?"

He turned and looked at me. His eyebrows furrowed. "What is it?"

"Do you have a girlfriend?"

That took him off guard.

I pressed him. "Rowan Giles has this friend who she thinks might be perfect for you."

He practically growled himself and went back to looking for the leak. "I'm not on the market," he said. "I had a girlfriend, and she ditched me for another guy. After I did everything she asked me to—to you know, cards, flowers, dinners."

"Murder," I added.

He hit his head on the lip of the tub. "Ow! Why did you say that? Why would you even think that?"

"Instinct." I leaned against the doorknob in case I had to run quickly. But Teddy just sat down in the puddle of water still there from the leak and started to cry.

"I never thought it would go that far. It was supposed to be a prank. My girlfriend gave me the pill and thought it would be funny if I slipped it into Melonie's water bottle. She knew Melonie took her lunch break around that time, so I took everything but the washer to Stan. Grabbed the water bottle while she wasn't looking. Put the drug in and shook it up. Then I rushed back inside, put the water bottle back in place, and left for the next job. Just a bit of fun." He gulped back a sob. "But when I left to go to the next job I saw her, my girlfriend. She was all over this other guy. They were laughing at me and what I'd done. It hit me that all she'd wanted from me was to get me to play the prank. I raced out feeling stupid. I don't get it. He was a short guy with, like, no muscle to him."

My heartbeat picked up. "Did you see his face?"

"No, his back was turned to me. He wore those stupid golf clothes, all pink and checkered, with white gloves and a stupid pink-checkered hat. Stupid hat." Teddy took a deep breath and looked up at me. "I was going to turn myself in. Really, I was. But then I heard that Melonie had been murdered. I didn't know what to do." He looked at me, pleading for me to understand. "I . . . I just went to the other job and pretended it hadn't happened. What else could I do? How could I prove *I* didn't kill her?"

Tears ran down his face, and he pushed his hair back with a trembling hand. "I guess I'm off to jail now."

"I guess you are," Charles said behind me, making me jump. My heart raced, and the spit in my mouth went down wrong. I started coughing. Charles pulled Teddy up from the floor and cuffed him, giving me the evil eye as he did it.

"You want to know the worst part?" Teddy asked.

"As I ran away from the scene, she kissed that guy. I heard her say, 'We did it. You're free.'"

"Free from what?" I asked.

Teddy shrugged. "Free from me, I guess. I mean all she had to do was say the usual—'it's not you, it's me.'"

Charles gave me a look that I could only interpret as expected disappointment. Why were cops so good at that?

I sat down on the couch, and my fur babies sat with me, Mella on my lap and Mal next to me. I absently petted them both, my mind reeling. Who was the femme fatale? And who was the man with her? And most of all, what were they now free from? All I had were questions with no answers. I felt bad for Teddy in a way. He didn't know how to keep a beautiful woman except to do exactly what she wanted. But he only drugged her. That means someone else killed her. Who and why? I would never be able to figure it out now. I was positive that Charles would never let me out of his sight again.

I took out my phone and called Rex. He didn't pick up, and I expected as much. But I talked anyway. "Rex, my love, I don't know where you are or how badly hurt you are. No one will tell me anything. I hate it. You know I would move heaven and earth to get to your side. It's killing me, not knowing. The fact that I can't see you. That I can't be with you. That I can't know how you are. Charles has me on a twenty-four-hour watch, for what? He gave some lame excuse that he had orders not to let me leave. Not to let me search for you. I hate it. I hate all of it. When I see you again, I'm going to make Charles wish he hadn't been born."

"Ahem." Charles cleared his throat. His right eyebrow lifted in an expression I had come to learn as one part humor and the other part disbelief.

"I love you." I finished the message and hit SEND, then put my phone away.

I glared at Charles as he took a seat on the chair across from the sofa. He looked huge in the little chair, but I didn't care.

"You know, you got Officer Davis in a lot of trouble. She'll be lucky to get desk duty until Lasko gets back."

There was a knock on the door frame. Charles had left the door open. It was Mr. Devaney. "I'm going to have a look at your bathroom leak."

"I think he fixed it already," I said quickly, embarrassed by my little trick.

"I think I should take a look anyway." Once Mr. Devaney got an idea in his head, it was hard to dissuade him.

"I asked Douglas to come up." Charles studied me as if he knew I had set up that whole little sting—which I had. I felt the heat rise in my cheeks.

"Teddy was confused," I said. "Isn't that what really mattered?"

"You want Laird to come down here and throw you in jail before you ever get to see Rex again?" Mr. Devaney asked as he went into the bathroom.

The thought had somehow evaded me. I looked at Charles. "But I didn't interfere. I did need plumbing work, and all I did was ask Teddy if he had a girlfriend because my friend knew someone who might be interested. The rest he did himself."

"Uh-huh," was all he replied.

"I fixed the plumber's tape that had been pushed aside to make a leak," Mr. Devaney said, then glanced at me with an accusing look as he walked out.

With Mella in my lap, I would have called cat paralysis and sat there on my tablet going through my list again, but I was hungry, and I knew Mal would want a walk.

"Look," Charles said as we both stood, and I moved to the kitchen. "We know about the drugs in her system. We were very close to getting Teddy," he began.

"He didn't kill her," I said.

"That's beside the point," Charles took a stool at the bar while I got out lunch fixings. "You have to let us do our job. Now, I'm going to tell Laird that I'm the one Teddy confessed to, but he's going to be suspicious. A lot of people saw me walk him out of here."

"I'm going to make a sandwich, and I have some coleslaw left over from Douds. If you want anything, help yourself."

"Allie, listen to me, what you're playing with is very dangerous."

"You mean the coleslaw? Because I can assure you—"

"I mean this murder, and you know it," he interrupted. "We knew the possibility of two killers was very strong, and Teddy confirmed it. Now you need to let us do our job and find out whom his girlfriend talked to and what the motive was."

I got out some lunch meat and cheese, then some condiments, lettuce, and tomato along with the coleslaw. "Do you want to know what I think the motive is?"

"No, I do not," he said pointedly. "I can't have you tainting the case. As far as we know, Teddy shot her with the nail gun, killing her, and she had enough GHB in her system to make a grown man pass out."

"You heard what Teddy said his girlfriend said to the guy, right?" I fixed him a huge sandwich. "Coleslaw or no coleslaw?"

"Coleslaw," he said. "Leave it alone, Allie. We don't even know if there was actually a woman involved. Laird will fire me and arrest you, and above all, as soon as he gets out of the hospital, Rex will have my head. I can't talk about or even hint about any of that, not even for you."

"What about Rowan?" I asked, trying to distract him. "She seems perfect for you. She lives off the island. She's smart *and* gorgeous. What's not to like? Plus, I saw you looking at her—"

"Allie, this isn't about my love life," he said.

"No?" I asked, then slid him his plate.

"No," he replied, "and don't think food is going to make any difference."

"I think you're wrong," I said. "Food *always* makes a difference."

Chapter 42

Who could the femme fatale be? I wondered. Rowan could. She was tall and beautiful, and she had been at the crime scene. But that didn't make sense. She had been nothing but helpful and caring. Besides, Mal approved of her. Who else?

My thoughts went straight to Valentine Maas. She was a leggy dark brunette with green eyes who wore clingy dresses, and she admitted she was there at the time. I wished I'd been able to talk to her, but that option was gone now. Still, I wondered what Valentine might have had against Melonie. Plus, a nail gun was an odd way to kill someone. How would she have known about that? And how would she have known where to place it on Melonie's body to do the maximum damage quickly?

I texted Liz. *What do you know about Valentine Maas?*

Not much. Why? Also, have you heard from Rex? Are you okay? Do you know where he is?

No, they won't tell me where he is, so I can't even get Sophie to fly me out of here. I haven't heard from Rex, and I've texted and left voice messages, I replied. *The last I heard, he was out of surgery and going back to work! And no, I'm not okay. I'm not sleeping, and I don't want to eat. Charles had lunch, but I only took a bite, and it tasted like dirt.*

Well, you're doing a good job of holding it all together, she texted.

I can't stop crying, I replied. *Roxanne still won't let me make fudge, so I must look pretty bad. I'm not sleeping.*

And yet you got Teddy Schmidt to confess to drugging Melonie. Can I interview you later?

Sure, but I don't think Teddy actually killed her—he only drugged her, and Teddy said it was supposed to be a prank. Put a pill in Melonie's water bottle, and she would pass out. Wouldn't it be funny? His new girlfriend told him to do it. She even gave him the pill. To him, she was the most beautiful woman he'd ever met, and he'd do anything to keep her.

And you think it was Valentine Maas, Liz deduced.

Have you met her? I asked. *She looks like she should be in a made-for-TV movie.*

I met her, Liz typed back. *And you're right. I'll see what I can find out. She doesn't seem the type to do this, but who knows.*

I can't figure out a motive, I texted.

Let's see if I can.

Thanks.

Let me know if there's anything else I can do, she texted.

All of this is off the record until it's done, right?

What I want to know is how you're doing this right under Charles's nose.

I have practice with the police.

Ah, that's right, you do. Three bubbles came up, letting me know she was thinking. *Let me know if you hear from Rex.*

I will.

And Allie . . .

Yes?

Take care of yourself.

I will, I texted, then sat there with my phone trying to figure out what to do next. There was something bothering me about Teddy's description of the man his girlfriend had been with. Suddenly the phone rang. The screen said *Rex*, and my heart leapt. "Rex!" I answered. "Where are you? Are you okay? I tried to come to you, but they wouldn't let me—"

"Mrs. Manning." A strange man at the other end of the phone interrupted me, and electricity ran down my spine.

"Yes?" I could barely breathe, let alone speak.

"This is Chief Andrews," he said.

I swallowed. "Yes?" It was a whisper.

"I want to let you know that Officer Manning—your husband—is okay and safe."

"Oh, my goodness, oh, my goodness, oh, my goodness. Can I go to him? I need to see him. Where is he?"

"I understand that you need to see him," he said. "But you can't. We've patched him up, and he's back out on the case."

"No, no, no, no," I said, finally able to breathe. "You can't do that to him—or to me!" I shouted.

"Listen—" he began.

"No, *you* listen," I interrupted. "You bring my husband home safely, or I will come to your office and you're not going to like what happens next. And is that a threat to an officer of the law? Yes! Is someone going to arrest me? Probably—but it won't be you. I'm done with these games—with the threats by Officer Laird, with the twenty-four-seven police watch, and now this."

"Mrs. Manning. I know—"

"You have no idea," I spat out. "You bring my husband home!" I hit END CALL.

Charles looked at me carefully. "I'm guessing that was the chief. He wouldn't call unless Rex was okay. He's okay, Allie." He paused. "Do you need anything?"

I stood and paced, Mal following my every step. "What I need is to punch something," I said.

"Come on," Charles said.

"What?"

"Come with me." He pointed to the door.

"Why? So can you take me to jail?"

"Not to jail," he said. "But to the police station. You have to trust me on this."

"I don't trust anyone at this time. You'll be lucky I don't punch you."

"I'm sure you will. But come with me, and I can help."

"Fine." I grabbed my keys, followed him out my back door, and locked my fur babies safely inside.

The walk to the police station did nothing to lessen my anger.

"Here," Charles said and opened a door on the opposite side of the reception area. Inside was a very small gym. It had mirrors and weights, one treadmill, and most importantly, a punching bag and gloves. Charles showed me how to put the gloves on properly and how to punch. Then he held the bag and let me whale on it. I punched because I couldn't see Rex. The feel of the bag on my fists, the vibration up my arm and my shoulder, standing wide-legged and engaging my core felt almost good. I was ready to punch until every ounce of anger was out of me. So, I punched. I punched because I didn't know how he was or where he was shot. I imagined punching the chief in the face. I even punched Charles in my mind's eye. It helped that he held the bag. I punched and I punched until I couldn't punch anymore. My arm muscles were done, my core was done, and I'd run out of things that made me want to punch something.

"Done?" he asked.

"I think so," I said. "Maybe."

I took off the gloves and unwrapped my hands. I was sweaty, but I felt better.

"Next time you might need a change of clothes," he said. "But I thought maybe you'd tell me off if I'd told you to grab them."

"'Next time'? There had better not be a next time."

"Anytime you need to punch something, you're welcome to use the facility."

I pulled my soaking wet polo and jeans away from my skin and conceded. "Next time." With my husband as a cop, there *would* be a next time. I took a deep breath and let it out. “He never had to do this before, and I hate it.”

“It’s good to know you think I’m right about something.”

We walked back. My sweat had me cooled off quickly by the lake breeze. I glanced at the pharmacy window and drew my eyebrows together in confusion. “What would Officer Laird be doing talking to Officer Davis this time of night? They look pretty chummy. Do you think they’re secret lovers?”

Charles sighed. “Allie, they’re probably discussing the case.”

“With their lips?” I pointed to the couple in the alley as we walked by. I’d have missed it, but they were standing in the light of the pharmacy alley. “It might be their love life, but isn’t he her boss? That’s not good. Besides, Rex frowns on public displays of affection while in uniform. Shouldn’t they?”

“As long as it’s not public, then the uniform doesn’t matter, does it?” he said with a twinkle in his eye.

“Nope,” I said with a smile. “Not if nobody can see you.”

Charles glanced down the alley. “I’ll have a talk with her later and make sure she isn’t being coerced. Besides, it wasn’t professional of her to leave you alone before I got back.”

“To be fair, I did talk her into leaving for lunch,” I said.

“To be fair,” he replied. “Her job was to wait for me to give her a break. And she might be a pretty woman, but it doesn't mean she can be seen, what did you call it?"

"Chummy," I repeated.

"Chummy while on duty," he finished. "Chummy means she's not paying attention to the things she should be paying attention to."

He had a point there. But an idea hit me that made me frown. "Teddy said his girlfriend was celebrating with a short, thin guy. You don't think—"

"Don't even go there," Charles warned me. This time, everything about him was serious. I swallowed hard. This time, I listened.

Chapter 43

When we got back, I went into the bathroom and started the shower. I knew something was wrong about our murder theories. Someone had to have helped Teddy. He wouldn't know anything about date-rape pills. Still, I was conflicted because Charles wasn't wrong. My meddling could hurt Rex's reputation. I couldn't do that to the man I loved.

But I didn't trust Officer Laird. The least I could do was try to help without anyone knowing about it. With the shower running, I sat on the stool and texted Carol.

What's up? Carol asked.

Do you know if Valentine knows, um, knew Melonie? I texted.

Why? Carol texted back.

I have an idea, I texted. *But I need to figure out connections, anything.*

Hang on, I'll ask Laura. She's right here. After a few minutes, the three dots started again, stopped, then started.

I sighed. Then the answer came. *They were on the varsity cheer squad together.*

That's a great clue. Thank you. I took a quick shower, dried my hair, and left the bathroom.

Why would Valentine want Melonie dead? Motives: money, love, revenge, and anger.

Dressed, I went into the kitchen. "Charles, would you like something to eat?" I asked, then took out spaghetti noodles, ground beef and ground sausage, and sauce. "I make a mean meatball and garlic bread." I could hear his stomach growl from where he sat on the couch.

"You don't have to keep feeding me," he said.

"I'll take that as a yes," I replied. While I worked, I thought the smells would be a good distraction. "Do you know if Melonie had money?" It was a simple question that had him turning toward me with suspicion on his face.

"Her financial information is available to Officer Laird."

"Well, I didn't think so," I said as I browned the meatballs. "She was working a job with long hours and had a free apartment above. Before that, she lived with Rex for a while. Then she left and was suddenly back. I figured she ran out of money."

He didn't answer, which meant the answer was yes as far as I was concerned. "Teddy told me he didn't know who the guy was who was with his girlfriend. Do you think that's true?"

"No comment," Charles said.

"He gave you a description, didn't he?" I put the meatballs in the sauce and covered the pot. "See, here's the thing. I never saw Melonie with another man. Although her first husband who was rumored to have beaten her pretty badly. Maybe that's why she wanted to stay next to Rex. Then I figured she had very little money, but now that I think about it, she would get new dresses and go out to eat a lot."

"Allie," he said. "Leave it alone."

"Or maybe Melonie stole her husband." I tapped my chin. "But in that case, why kill her? Why not break up, get a divorce, and take him for everything he's got?"

"Allie." He sighed. "You're not going to get me to talk about the case." He picked up the paper and read it. "I told you this is a very dangerous case."

"I know. I'm just talking to myself," I said. "I love puzzles, and this is a good one. I think that most women wouldn't think about a nail gun. That tends to be a man's kind of thing, but women do think about poison. But this one wasn't poison, was it? That tells me there's most likely a man behind all of this."

Charles lowered the paper and studied me. "Allie, since we're stuck with each other for the foreseeable future, please give up this guessing game. I'm not going to tell you anything. I'm not even going to talk in my sleep. Leave it alone."

"Fine."

"Fine."

We ate dinner in silence. Then I fed my pets while Charles did the dishes. "Listen, I don't mean to be short with you," he said. "I can't say anything. Your life is at stake here. And I know Rex never told you anything about a case."

"True," I said. "But I always had the freedom to

ask questions, and now I can barely even talk to my friends."

"Who do you want to talk to that you can't text or message?" he asked.

"Texting is one thing. Seeing them in person is another. Plus, I can't see Rex. How do I know the chief is telling the truth?" My voice cracked. "The least you could do is let me see my friends."

"Who do you want to see?" he asked.

"Liz and maybe Jenn," I said. "We could meet together at Jenn's house. That way you could talk to Shane, and we could talk about her babies."

"Fine, I don't see why not, as long as you promise not to run."

"I don't know why you're so obsessed with my running. Like you keep saying, there's absolutely nowhere to go except maybe the police chief's office. And I doubt he would tell me anything more about Rex than you will." I blew out a long, sighing breath. "Come on, Mal, let's go for our bedtime walk." At the word *walk*, Mal jumped up on my leg, her little, stumpy tail wagging like crazy. I put on her halter and my own sweatshirt and headed down the stairs with Charles in tow.

Mella came up the stairs as we moved down. I looked at her paws and frowned. Mella looked like she'd just walked through something reddish-brown, so I picked her up. "Charles," I said and showed him her paws. "I think Mella discovered someone who's badly hurt."

Charles muttered something under his breath. "Stay here."

"I can't," I said. "Mal needs to go out."

"Let me check the alley first." He took out his gun. Then he made his way down the alley before telling me I could take Mal down the stairs to do her business but that was all. Since I didn't want Mella to go in and drag blood—potential dead-victim blood—all over my carpet, I held her, and she purred as if she'd caught a bird and laid it on the porch. "Good girl," I told her as I hitched her on my hip. I could see Mella's trail of footprints. Mal had her nose to the ground and pulled me toward where the footprints had begun. When we went around the corner, I saw Charles's flashlight shining on what appeared to be a tipped-over mannequin. But I knew it was a dead body. I couldn't see her face, but her hair and body were familiar. It was Valentine Maas.

Chapter 44

This time Charles called it in. I had to keep Mal away from the crime scene and at the same time keep Mella from licking her paws until Shane could remove any evidence—something my kitty didn't like. The purring stopped, and the wriggling started. It felt like forever before Shane got there. In the meantime, I studied the scene while Charles was busy. We were so close to the police station that both Officer Davis and Officer Laird were there quickly.

"Davis, put up a crime-scene barrier. Mrs. Manning, you need to get out of my crime scene."

I noted how angry and annoyed he was with me for standing near the wall holding Mella and keeping Mal by my side.

"She can't leave yet," Charles explained. "Her cat is the one who alerted me to the crime. There's blood and evidence on the cat's feet and a trail of evidence up to Allie's apartment. We'll need someone to keep the crowd away from that, as well, until CS Christenson gets here."

Officer Laird gave me the evil eye. "Stay out of the way, and find someone to get rid of that dog."

"Mal won't move from my side," I said.

"Get the dog out of my crime scene," he ordered.

"She'll do it," Charles said, then nodded to me. I frowned but took my phone out of my pocket, which wasn't easy with a struggling cat. I was going to have some nice scratches. Maybe Shane should swab them, too, as long as it didn't get me in trouble.

"I realize you have some sort of relationship going on here, Brown, but she's a person of interest simply by being here and her cat allegedly walking across the evidence."

"I've been with her for the last forty-eight hours, sir," Charles said.

"I don't care," Officer Laid said. "She still looks guilty, and I'm going to take her in. I'll have Davis question her." He looked at me. "Don't pull that lawyer trick on us. We'll throw you behind bars before you can say *lawyer*."

"*Lawyer*," I said, to prove a point. We both knew he couldn't throw me in jail, no matter how much he wanted to.

He sneered at me and muttered something under his breath. Mal grumbled at him. I hadn't heard her growl so many times since Officer Laird got here. I had learned never to trust a person Mal didn't like, and there weren't that many. Maybe it was because Rex was gone. Or maybe she didn't like Officer Laird because she knew I didn't like him for what he'd done to me and for his feud with Rex.

I didn't say another word. I couldn't let them use anything against me. Charles didn't even look at me, and I didn't blame him. I texted Rowan, since she was the closest person, and Finn could keep Mal company.

"What are you doing?" Laird said, accusingly.

I adjusted Mella and showed him my phone. Rowan answered that she'd be right there, and she was.

Laird had a dissatisfied look on his face, but he said nothing and turned back to the scene.

When Rowan got there, Finn was by her side, and she stared at the scene until Officer Davis came over. I reached through the crime-scene tape far enough that Rowan could take Mal's leash.

"Finn and I'll take good care of her. Won't you, Finn?" Finn wagged his tail and licked Mal's face. But before they disappeared down the alley, both dogs sniffed Officer Davis and growled.

"Get away," she said and frowned at Rowan. "Get those dogs away from me, or we'll throw you in jail for real this time. Keep them away from my crime scene. You've probably already mucked it up."

I was angry that I couldn't stop them from putting Rowan in jail. I called Jay and he promised to be there as soon as he could. It was late in the evening, and I was sure he was lounging around his home. He might have even had a beer or two. But that didn't matter. What I needed was representation and the confidence to keep my mouth shut.

That was tough for me. While I stood there with my back to the wall, I noticed something, and I think I was the only one to have seen it. I looked around in the chaos and didn't see anyone else who might have noticed.

But Officer Davis gave Officer Laird a nod and a satisfied grin. He returned the grin, but only for a brief second, then became gruff again. I studied Mella's feet so they wouldn't see me. I was in the shadows and all but forgotten in the chaos. That's when I saw it. Officer Laird had dark spots on the legs of his uniform high enough that the paper crime scene booties couldn't cover. Finally, Shane arrived.

He put down his kit and swiped his glasses to clean them, then spotted me first. "Why do you always seem to be in the middle of things, even when you have an escort?" he asked playfully. I held Mella up. He used his flashlight. "Ah, I see. I'll swab these and let you take her home. She's not going to like it when you give her a bath." He pulled the swabs out of his pocket and did just that. "Looks like she walked right over the victim." That's when he noticed the cat's paw prints going down the alley. "Too bad cats can't talk."

"You never know," I whispered. "Mella may have some of the killer's DNA on her."

Shane chuckled. "Knowing you and your fur babies, it wouldn't surprise me at all."

"Listen," I said as softly as possible. "When you can, look at Officer Laird's pants. And keep an eye on Officer Davis and Officer Laird. Something ugly is going on, and they seem pretty happy about it."

"Are you talking over there?" Officer Laird said sharply.

I shook my head and gave Shane a look.

He looked at me thoughtfully. "One more swab." He spoke louder. "There you go. Now, take this cat home and give it a bath."

I nodded.

Laird called out a few orders, then saw me moving toward the crime-scene tape. "Where do you think you're going?"

I stopped.

"I have what I need," Shane said. "I told her she could go home and give her cat a bath."

Officer Laird looked around, but all the police officers he had at his disposal were busy. "Go straight home. I find out you didn't and—"

"Lawyer," I said.

"You're really going to need that lawyer."

I ducked under the crime-scene tape and headed down the alley. Lucky for me, Liz was at the other end of the alley, moving swiftly and surely toward the crime scene. As soon as I got out of sight of the police, I ducked behind my dumpster. As Liz got closer, I motioned to her. She slipped into the shadows beside me.

"What's going on?" she whispered and glanced around the dumpster. "Are you okay?"

"Yes, Mella led us to Valentine Mass's body around the corner at the end of the alley. She's been murdered."

"I heard," she said. "I was on my way to write an article."

"I might have an exclusive for you," I whispered. "I'm going upstairs to bathe Mella. Go around to the front and meet me in my apartment. I have a theory."

"I'm always up for one of your theories," Liz said

with a grin. "You go up first in case anyone is looking, then I'll continue to the crime scene and try to ask some questions. I'm sure he'll blow me off. At that point, I'll go round to the front door and come on up."

"Perfect," I said, then walked casually up the stairs and into my apartment. Officer Davis frowned as she tipped her head around the corner to watch me. I closed and locked the door behind me. The windows were already locked. Giving Mella any type of bath was a shot in the dark. Some days she didn't mind, and others she fought like a demon. Thankfully, this time she didn't mind, mostly because I concentrated on her feet. When I was done, I put a heated towel around her.

There was a soft knock, and I put Mella on the top of her cat tree. She might forgive me in a couple of days. Then I checked who it was and let Liz in.

"So, what's the theory?" she asked.

"Just now, when they didn't think I saw, Officer Davis and Officer Laird share a look of satisfaction. We know that Teddy gave Melonie the GHB as a prank to please his girlfriend. We also know he saw her laughing and hugging a short man in golf clothes with a hat. The clothes didn't hide the fact that he was thin with little muscle tone. I'm betting Teddy's girlfriend was Valentine—who showed up dead just now."

"Okay, I'll play along," Liz said. "You think Valentine asked Teddy to knock Melonie out."

"Yes," I said. "But who do you think asked Valentine to get Teddy to pull this prank?"

I watched her put all the puzzle pieces together. "You think it's Officer Laird?"

"Yes," I said.

"But Officer Laird wasn't even assigned to the island until later. And why didn't Teddy recognize him at the police station and tell someone?"

"My guess is that Charles and Officer Davis were the only ones he saw . . . even after he was locked up," I replied.

"Okay, that makes sense. If Valentine was his new girl and he saw her with Laird at the crime scene, they had to be sure that he didn't see Laird afterward."

"Also, David is seeing Naomie Urban."

"How do you know that?" Liz asked.

"Carol and the book club told me. At first I thought that it might be how Teddy and Valentine got ahold of the GHB. While David and Naomie were on a date, they could have broken into the vet office and stolen a couple of pills."

"Wouldn't Naomie have noticed?"

"If you had so many large animals to care for, would you have time to check your inventory every day?"

"Surely she keeps her drugs locked up," Liz said.

"If you were a plumber, you might be able to sneak a key out, tell them you need a part and will be right back. Make a copy, then put the key back and finish the job. Shortly after Melonie was murdered, Valentine must have realized that she'd been set up as much as Teddy."

"What do you mean?"

"Laura said that Valentine started to tell her something weird had happened at the photo shoot. But before she could say what it was, the murder was discovered, and as the crowd formed, Laura called the book club, and she and Valentine joined them. I haven't seen Valentine since."

"You think she's been hiding from Officer Laird?" Liz drew her eyebrows together. "Why didn't she leave the island?"

"Then he could get her for fleeing the scene. She couldn't tell anyone else. Not only was she being framed, but Laird would throw whomever she told in jail."

"Okay, but if he was in the back with Valentine, and they have witnesses to prove it, then who killed Melonie?"

"Yesterday I saw Officer Laird and Officer Davis making out in the alley."

"Hmm, Officer Davis arrived first, and Officer Laird supposedly came after the murder. And who could have gone in and left through the front door of the shop without anyone—even you—thinking anything about it?" Liz said.

"Officer Davis," we both said at once.

"It would have been easy for her to hide the nail gun and then go back and remove it. No one would think anything was odd about a police officer going back to a crime scene."

"Makes complete sense. But why?" Liz pondered. "Have they worked together before? Maybe Melonie knew about their relationship and was blackmailing them. Or maybe she caught them doing something they shouldn't have been doing."

"So, they killed her," I muttered. "I don't think

knowing about their relationship would have been enough to kill her. It must have been because she caught them doing something illegal. We just need to prove it."

"What about Valentine? Why murder her?"

"That's what bothered me," I said. "Teddy said Valentine was celebrating with a man, who we think was Laird. But when he left her to disappear until he supposedly arrived to take over for Charles, Valentine must have seen him talking to Officer Davis and put two and two together. She seemed shocked when I came out the back door that day to confirm Melonie was dead. She barely said a word when Carol introduced her."

"She was killed because she knew too much. Think about it, if she did it for Officer Laird, then she would have been able to blackmail him."

"They used Valentine to convince Teddy to do their dirty work, then planned to frame them both for murder."

"It's brilliant, actually," I said. "Let's say Officer Laird and Officer Davis masterminded the whole thing. They'd make sure they weren't ever suspects. Laird seduces Valentine, who, in turn, seduces Teddy and convinces him to give Melonie the drug, and then they frame them both for murder."

"Why Teddy, though?" Liz asked.

"He would be the one most likely to be manipulated by a beautiful woman. He's not married, not dating, and not the brightest."

"Why didn't they kill him, too?" Liz asked, her eyebrows pushed together.

"Charles and I caught him before they could kill him and make it look like a suicide."

"I should go to the photo shop and see if I can find anything that links Melonie to either Officer Laird or Officer Davis," Liz said "It had to be blackmail. Melonie was always able to have designer clothes and eat out, even though she only earned a photo shop manager's salary."

"You're right, blackmail makes the most sense," I said. "Melonie knew something, but she was worried it could get her killed, so she stayed near Rex."

"She had to have told them she had proof," Liz said.

"But they must have figured out that she *didn't* have proof. That might be why she had the flowers sent from the unknown 'Oscar.' They were letting her know that she wouldn't get any more of their money," I said.

"So, how do we convince everyone that two police officers are behind the killings?" Liz asked.

"When I was at the scene before Mella was swabbed, I noticed what looked like blood spatter on Officer Laird's uniform. We must have found Valentine's body before he had the chance to change," I said thoughtfully.

"And Officer Davis is already here substituting for Megan," Liz said.

"I bet Laird's the one who convinced the chief that Rex would be the best officer to investigate something away from Mackinac, simply to keep him from getting suspicious," I said. "It's brilliant, really. After all, who suspects the police? But I think they got carried away. One murder might be easy to cover up. But not two."

"If they killed Valentine, Teddy has to be next. With

him in jail, the only way to kill him without looking suspicious is to make it look like suicide," Liz deduced.

"Someone has to get to the jail and alert someone in the department," I said.

"Not you," Liz said. "Is there anyone else you can trust?"

I thought for a moment.

"Rowan," we both said at the same time.

"We'll tell her our theory, and she'll be happy to go. Besides, she's pup sitting Mal. A good reason for me to go to her room," I said.

We took one flight down but before we turned down the hall to Rowan's door, we ran face-to-face into Officer Davis. She had her gun drawn on us. "Where do you two think you're going?"

Chapter 45

I took a sideways step so that more of my body came between Liz and the gun. "Seriously, a gun, Officer Davis? Don't you think that's a little much to keep me from trying to find Rex? Especially since the chief already called me to tell me he was okay?"

"We were only going to get her dog from Rowan Giles," Liz said, her eyebrows drawn together as if confused.

"You know, the woman with the Great Dane?" I asked. "The one who helped by taking Mal away from the crime scene like Officer Laird wanted?"

"Wait, weren't you helping with the crime scene?" Liz asked. "Now, that would be an interesting headline: 'Valentine Maas dead, Officer Davis threatens citizens with a gun'."

"I was ordered here to keep an eye on Allie," she replied. "Once again, I've found her sneaking out of the McMurphy. It will be easy to frame you for Valentine's murder. After all, you found her body first."

"What about Liz?" I asked. "How are you going to explain shooting her?"

"Both of you—upstairs," Officer Davis ordered.

I acted surprised. "But that doesn't make any sense."

"Liz McElroy, you helped Mrs. Manning evade her police order, and that's called aiding and abetting. We had a fight. It was self-defense. Now, go." She pointed the gun upstairs again.

"Okay," I said. "I understand telling me to go upstairs. But I need to get my dog. It's not far down this hall and will only take a minute." I took two steps toward Rowan's guest room.

"Stop! Don't take another step. You've been talking way too much. I saw how you looked at Bruce. I saw you talking to each other in the alley," Officer Davis said.

"'Bruce'?" I acted confused.

"Officer Laird!" She grew more and more agitated.

"How did I look at him? I was concerned about Valentine. Why would looking at the officer in charge of the crime scene be odd?"

"I'm not buying it," Davis said. "You two know way too much."

"About what?" I asked. If she was going to kill us, I wanted to know how close I was to the truth.

"It's not your business to know what," Officer Davis said.

"It seems it would be our business if we're going to die for it," Liz pointed out. "Besides, do you really believe you'll get away with killing us? Won't that draw attention? I mean, Melonie, Valentine, and if we're right, Teddy, and now us. It's a little much, isn't it?"

"We've got a boat," she said. "We'll be out of here

and across the border to Canada before anyone even discovers you."

"Clever," Liz said, as a gun followed by a man in jeans and a flannel shirt stealthily moved around the corner of the staircase behind her. It was Rex.

I tried not to react, but I gasped, and Officer Davis turned, her gun in her hand. At the same time, Rowan stuck her head out to see what was going on, and both dogs pushed past her, then went running down the hallway and tackling Officer Davis before she could get a shot off. Her gun went sweeping across the hall as she kicked and bucked, trying to get Finn off of her. Rowan used her foot to sweep the gun even farther away from Officer Davis.

"Give it up, Davis," Rex said. Finn held her down by standing on her back, and Mal held her by the collar. "Put your hands behind your head, and stay very still."

For a moment, Officer Davis did as she was told. But when Finn stepped off her body to give Rex room, Officer Davis threw Mal off her, then got up to make a run for it. Both dogs blocked her way. "Get away, you mutts!" she cried.

Rowan ran, picked up the gun, and then took a shot, hitting Officer Davis right through the knee, keeping her from running or fighting. Officer Davis fell, holding her knee and wailing." You shot me!" Both dogs bared their teeth.

"And I'd do it again," Rowan said. "Don't you ever call Finn a mutt!"

This time Officer Davis did as she was told and put her hands behind her back. Rex cuffed her.

"I'm losing blood," she cried.

"I'll get a rag from the utility closet." I ran down a flight of stairs, grabbed a clean rag from the closet, and took it back upstairs, but Charles was already taking her away. Guests had come out of their rooms at the sound of the gunshot. Rowan let them know everything was alright. Meanwhile, Liz was on the phone with Charlene to get someone to check on Teddy.

With everyone else busy, I jumped on Rex and wrapped my body around him, letting the rag drop to the ground. I kissed his face all over, then heard a slight gasp and saw the pain on his face. Worried, I let go of him.

"You're hurt," I said. I touched his chest under his clavicle where a bandage was wrapped and his arm was in a sling, then I smacked him on his good arm as happy tears flowed. "How dare you? How dare you not let me be there during your surgery and recovery? How dare you not let me hold your hand? Not let me know if and when you were alright! How dare you not let me know where you were, and then keep Charles with me twenty-four hours a day to ensure I couldn't get to you? Yet you wanted to move heaven and earth to find Melonie's killer!"

"Allie—" he began.

"Oh, no—nope. You can't sweet-talk your way out of this."

"I was working on following Laird's tracks," Rex said. "After I was shot, Charles was assigned to protect you, not keep you locked up. We had to make it look like Laird's idea."

"What about Officer Davis? Was she protecting me that day, too?" I asked, trying to stay mad.

"Charles kept up the charade. We needed to keep her preoccupied for a few hours, and you were downstairs with Frances. We knew Melonie was blackmailing Laird and Davis over the murder of Oscar Wells."

"Charlene tells me they've already called the EMTs," Liz said and held up her phone. "Teddy's going to be well enough to take him to the district jail."

"Here." Rowan handed Rex the gun. "You might want this."

"And you are?" Rex seemed a bit confused.

"Rowan Giles," she said. "Remember? I was at the crime scene . . . camera . . . talk a lot when I'm nervous . . . Great Dane." She pointed at Finn, who sat beside her, tongue lolling, happy with a job well done.

"Oh, right," Rex said. "Thanks for your help, but there's no need to worry. We got to Teddy shortly after he was hanged and left to die. But we couldn't get to Valentine fast enough."

"You knew that Officer Laird had convinced Valentine to give Teddy the GHB to knock Melonie out?" I asked. "You knew about Officer Davis? And yet you left me alone with them?" I smacked him again.

"Ouch." He rubbed his good arm as best he could. "Charles had it all under control."

"And your 'new' assignment?" My emotions were once again a jumbled mess.

"I was assigned to the Oscar Wells case. He caught Laird and Davis stealing drugs out of the evidence room and selling them on the street. So, they killed him. Melonie witnessed the whole thing. That's why she came back to the island. But then she got greedy and tried to blackmail them."

"So, they killed her, too," Liz said. "Why the nail to the heart? If she'd been found soon enough, she could have survived."

"They wanted to make it look like a lover's revenge. They knew she didn't stand a chance here on the island. The EMTs would have done all they could, but it would have taken too long for the life flight off the island."

"What I want to know," Rowan said, "is, where did Teddy or Valentine get the drug? From a vet? From the pharmacy? How did they get it without anyone knowing?"

"Oh, my gosh," I said as it hit me. "It had to be from Officer Laird. Think about it—there must have been some of it in an evidence room. I bet he brought it in from his usual station and gave it to Valentine to give to Teddy."

"That means neither David nor Naomie were involved in Melonie's murder," Rowan said.

"So why did Mal insist on going to the pharmacy, then the riding stables, and finally to the police station?" I asked, confused. "She's usually so helpful in solving crimes."

"I'm pretty sure you know why," Rex said, with an infuriating twinkle in his eyes.

I scowled at him.

"What do they represent?" he asked.

"The pharmacy is where you get drugs . . . the stables where you house horses . . . and then, of course, the police station," I muttered. "Drug, horse, police. Drug, horse, police. Drug . . . Are you telling me Mal was trying to tell me all along that the GHB came from the police station?" I looked down at Mal, who looked at me as if I was a small child who had finally gotten it. "Oh, Mal." I picked her up and hugged her, then looked at Rex. "I thought she meant that David and Ed were involved, and that I should tell the police." I looked at Mal. "I'm sorry, sweetie, but that was a tough puzzle for me to solve." She put her head on my shoulder, as if to say, *It's okay*.

We all chuckled.

"Beside Melonie and Valentine," I said, "everyone else is safe?"

"Yes," Rex said.

"And Shane found the blood I spotted on Officer Laird's uniform?"

"He did," Rex said. "Nice catch."

I frowned as I realized something. "If Officer Laird and Officer Davis were here, then how did you get shot?"

"They hired a hit man to take out Oscar Wells. I was part of the team that brought him to justice."

"By getting shot and not coming home," I muttered. Then I gave Rex the side-eye. "You're not getting out of this so easy, and neither is Charles."

"Yes, ma'am," he said. I smacked his good arm again. "Don't call me 'ma'am'."

"If you don't mind my asking," Rowan said, "how did Melonie know they murdered this Oscar guy?"

"Laird and Davis were taking money from the local businesses. When Oscar refused to pay, they hired a hit man to kill him, sending a message to the other shops in that neighborhood. It was pay up or die. What they didn't know was that Melonie was there when the hit man killed Oscar. She hid in the kitchen. A few days later, she saw Officer Laird talking to the killer and handing him what looked like an envelope full of money. After that, Melonie ran back to the island and then tried to blackmail them. They started looking for her. When Officer Davis came up here to work, she recognized Melonie right away. That's when the second part of the plan was hatched. Laird seduced Valentine, knowing she had ties to the island."

"When she realized she would be framed for murder," I said, "she called the station to turn herself in, and hoped she could use her testimony to negotiate a lighter sentence."

"So, they killed her," Rowan finished. "Wow, this has to be the craziest vacation ever." Rowan gave me a hug. "Thanks for trusting me to help." Then she hugged Liz and shook Rex's good hand. "It was nice to meet you all. Finn and I will be going back home early tomorrow morning. I have to figure out what to do now that I realize I can't afford a business of my own yet. At least not here."

"I'd better go, too," Liz said. "That's a big story to write if I want to get it out in the next edition."

"Wait, Liz," I said. "I forgot to ask, how's Angus doing?"

"After a few days in the hospital, he's home and his old, grumpy self," she replied with a smile. "In fact, he was the one who told me I'd better help with the investigation, or he'd put me on desk duty."

I laughed. "Sounds like Angus." I gave her another hug.

"By the way, Charles, thanks for watching over my wife," Rex said and shook his hand.

Charles nodded toward me. "I don't know how you can keep from telling her things about the case. She's stubborn like a dog with a bone. Hardest thing about the whole assignment."

"It's not easy," Rex admitted, "but I love her."

Charles laughed. "My bet is that one of these days, she's going to wear you down."

"I doubt that," I replied. "He's as stubborn as I am."

"All true," Rex admitted with a grin.

Rex and I went home, where he sat on the couch as the pets carefully welcomed him back. I retrieved an iced tea for him and a lemonade for me. "I figured you're on pain pills."

"As always, you're right," he said. I kissed him and snuggled up next to him. "It's good to have you home, you idiot. You're not off the hook yet, but it's still good."

He kissed me again, and soon everything felt right.

Acknowledgments

Special thanks to Michaela Hamilton and the marvelous crew at Kensington Books. You make my books so much better. And to Paige Wheeler and her staff, for helping to keep this series going.

And, of course, for The Island Bookstore and all the wonderful people on Mackinac Island, for letting me take liberties with facts and helping me bring this series to life.

Did you enjoy meeting Rowan Giles and her
Great Dane, Finn, in this book?
Great news for cozy mystery fans!
Rowan and Finn are about
to star in their own spin-off series.
Inspired by Allie McMurphy
(and sometimes calling on her for sleuthing advice),
Rowan sets up her pet photography business
in the nearby town of Charlevoix—only to find herself
investigating a murder.

Keep reading to enjoy the first chapter of
White Lies and Cherry Pies,
a Pets & Pastries mystery . . . coming soon
from Kensington Publishing Corp.

Chapter 1

"Rowan Elenor Giles, get down here!"

I'd forgotten what it was like to live in my family's house in Charlevoix, Michigan. Chaos with a strange bit of charm filled the rooms. I also hated the fact that I was twenty-seven, sharing a bedroom with my thirteen-year-old niece, Chloe. Rolling my eyes, I wished I had stayed in my expensive, glorified closet of an apartment in New York City. It might have been only three hundred square feet, but it was all mine.

I couldn't deny that Charlevoix was home. I loved that it was a small town with a population of around 2,400, and a quarter of those were family or friends of family. The Giles clan had had a big presence in the town for the last hundred years. My great-grandpa built the house north of Round Lake, and every generation added onto it until it was a sprawling mess, like my family.

"Who's that?" I heard Chloe's friend ask as they video chatted.

Chloe, who was stretched out on her bed with her head toward the foot, her strawberry blond hair draped over the end, replied, "Just my loser aunt who can't get a job anywhere but Meijer." My sweet Great Dane, Finn, snuggled up against her. The traitor.

"And I'm stuck with a niece who doesn't know how to pick her stuff off the floor and put it away," I said, sounding more like mom than I should. Why couldn't I be the cool aunt? Maybe because I'd lived alone too long and was no longer used to stepping over clothing, shoes, and books when I walked. Especially at night. I put my laptop down and stood before maneuvering out of the room.

"Whatever."

"Auntie Rowan!" my ten-year-old nephew and Chloe's brother, Oliver, shouted up the stairs.

"I'm coming," I yelled back. Some habits never leave you. Finn got up and stretched, taking up all the empty space in the room without a care for the obstacles on the floor, before following me down. Finn was not only a Great Dane, but a rare lilac one. His blue-gray fur and dark gray spots drew almost as much attention as his size did. "Deserter," I mumbled at him. He seemed to grin at me.

Ah, Finn. The police had rescued him from an unauthorized breeder. The shelter staff assured me he was an eight-month-old mixed breed, who would only grow to fifty pounds. I fell in love at first sight, adopted him, and brought him straight home with me. He was just a small pup then. I had no idea he was a hundred percent Great Dane or how big he would get. It was similar to those times when your eyes were bigger than your stomach and then you realized you ate too much.

I trained him well, though. He's a very smart boy, but when he reached slightly over a year old, I knew we both couldn't occupy the same space at the same time in my tiny apartment. Since I wasn't giving him up, and my dreams for living in New York had not panned out, I knew it was time to come home. The best part about Finn, besides the fact that he's never met a stranger, was that because he lived with me in New York, the chaos of my family didn't even faze him.

"She's coming," Oliver shouted.

Oh, for goodness' sake. Today was one of my two days off from my job at Meijer Grocery's baking center. I should at least be able to message my friends when I want.

I came down the stairs to two of my brothers, their combined five sons, and a handful of children watching some kind of sports game on TV. I wasn't into any kind of sports. Although I played volleyball in high school, I wasn't really good at it. Being tall wasn't enough. That kind of stuff takes coordination.

"What?" I yelled to be heard over the television and the three kids playing tag through the living room. I strolled through the big open kitchen, which had 1980s green-and-white vinyl tiles, oak cabinets, and green Formica countertops trimmed in oak.

My Aunt Kathryn poked her head out of the laundry/mud room off the back door. "There you are. You may be able to store your clothes in your dryer in New York, but here we pull them out and take them to our rooms and fold them as quickly as possible. More people than you use the washer and dryer. And get that dog out of the kitchen. You know we don't let animals in there."

"What about Paddy?" I countered. "He goes wherever he wants." Paddy was the family pet or, better yet, enforcer. He'd shown up one day and let himself in and that was that. A large orange tabby cat with huge murder mittens, the cutest round cheeks, small ears, and a nose that had black dots on the end, Paddy responded to his name right away as if he'd always been called that.

"He's a cat," she replied. As if that made a difference. Finn could easily reach the top of the refrigerator, but so could Paddy.

Aunt Kathryn is what we would call "large and in charge." She was always running around ensuring everything in the house was being taken care of by the people who should be taking care of it. Tall like nearly everyone in my family, Aunt Kathryn was very pretty. Her hair was auburn like mine, only hers was straight and hung like shining flames down her back. Like Gramma Brid, she had two pure white streaks framing her face. Her skin was porcelain white, accented by smile lines around her eyes and mouth and worry lines across her forehead. In her early forties, she had a figure to die for, and she dressed it well.

Today, she wore a soft blouse tucked into fitted jeans. She rarely wore makeup, but she didn't need to. I saw the way men looked at her with that stunned look on their face. Although, even with a warm smile, she was rarely asked out. I figured that was because of the family. Ever since Mom died, it was as if Aunt Kathryn were trying to replace her, and Dad let her. It didn't matter that she was the baby of his family and younger than my older brother, Colin. Dad said Colin had other fish to fry besides taking care of our motley crew.

"Got it," I answered her. Arguing was no use, even though my timer was set to get my clothes the moment they were dry, and she'd clearly opened the dryer before the time was up. My old apartment didn't even have a washer or dryer, but I kept that to myself. I pulled my nearly dry clothes into my basket and headed into the kitchen.

"Auntie Rowan, want to see my picture?"

"Auntie Rowan, play a game with me."

"Auntie Rowan, Mama says I have hair like yours and if I don't take care of it, it will be as messy as yours."

"Auntie Rowan, can I play with Finn?"

"Auntie Rowan—"

"Tag, you're it."

"Everyone out of the kitchen," my Aunt Sharon ordered, clapping her hands. The children giggled and went running out.

I put my basket on the kitchen island, sat on one of the stools, and sighed. "I feel like I've been in a hit-and-run." Seeing that nothing exciting was going on, Finn left, following the kids.

"You're simply not used to it anymore." Aunt Sharon pulled out a mug and poured me a cup of coffee. The cream, sugar, and flavored syrups sat in the middle of the island.

Aunt Sharon was the spitting image of her mom, Gramma Brid. They had the same light red hair, except hers had turned into the yellow blond some redheads developed as they grew older. She kept it shoulder-length. Her brown eyes were a touch rounder and her nose softer, but only if you looked very closely.

I added a spoonful of sugar and poured the cream out of a thermal carafe. "The worst part is," I said, "I'm not sure I know the little ones' names."

Aunt Sharon hid her smile as she sipped her coffee. "It's okay, you've been gone for eight years. We have quite a few children and grandchildren eight and under. That's what happens when you don't come home regularly."

I winced. "Mom's gone. Dad's always busy. Even though he's retired, he's still going here and there, helping someone build something. The rest of my brothers and sisters are older than me. They've got kids and even grandkids of their own. When I was in New York, I had to work nearly all the holidays because I was—er—am single. If the gourmet bakery I worked for hadn't closed, I would still be working there. Now I'm here, working in a grocery store of all places." I took a sip of my coffee, trying not to feel like a failure.

She patted my hand. "Give yourself a break. You've been through a lot."

"I'll try," I said ruefully with my elbows on the island beside my clothes basket, where my things were probably wrinkling. "Also, I love you guys, but I'm too old to be sharing a room with Chloe." I took another drink of my cream-and-sugar-based coffee. "Until I can find a job that pays decently and uses my skill set, it looks like I'm stuck here." I sighed. "You never know," I recited, not sounding at all like I meant it. It was a family slogan. One I wasn't into. I raised my mug to my mouth and noticed Aunt Sharon smiling at me with a twinkle in her eye. "What?" I asked, knowing that twinkle usually meant mischief.

"Nothing," she replied and sipped her coffee.

At that moment, my phone pinged with a text. It was my Gramma Brid.

Sweetie, I'm having tea with my girlfriends this afternoon. Could you be a dear and make your Napoleon cake? You're so good with puff pastry and vanilla pastry crème, and my little kitchen is not equipped to do it.

I took a deep breath and let it out. Who needs a day off anyway?

I'd be happy to, I texted. *When do you need it?*

By 3 p.m., she answered. *Thank you, dear.*

Of course, I replied. Looking at the clock, I realized it was going to be a tight timeline. But then I am a professional. I glanced at Aunt Sharon, whose smile widened. "Will you have time to keep everyone out of the kitchen? Gramma Brid needs me to bring a cake for her tea by three." I narrowed my eyes. "But you knew that, didn't you?"

Aunt Sharon shrugged, and finished her coffee while I glared. "Sure," she said. "Now scoot. Get those clothes put away. You're going to need time to get that cake done right. I know you wouldn't want Gramma to be disappointed."

A few hours later, Finn by my side, I carried a cake stand filled with a loaf-shaped confection made with thin, puff pastry and thick vanilla crème layers in between, all garnished with strawberries. I'd been so busy since I got home that I hadn't gone to see Gramma Brid. I knew she was going to give me a hard time when I got there, but she always did, and it made me smile. Her senior living place wasn't far from the house. I'd asked her once why she moved there. She was still spry and could outsmart and outwalk most people half her age. She'd laughed and told me she went there for the peace.

Now I understood what she meant.

When we got inside, I gave the receptionist a short wave and kept walking. Finn seemed eager to find out who we were visiting. In New York, Finn figured out that a new building full of doors always meant making new friends. When I stopped at Gramma's door, he sat and waited with anticipation. I knocked on the door.

"I'll be right there," she called. When she opened the door, she gave me a big smile. "There you are. Come on in." I kissed her papery cheek. "You can put that on the counter, dear. Who's this beautiful baby?" Gramma barely needed to bend over to scratch Finn under his chin and behind his ears. My boy was in seventh heaven.

"That's Finn. I rescued him when he was only a tiny pup," I said. "I had no idea he was going to get this big."

"Of course he's going to get big, silly." Gramma shook her head at me but never took her eyes off Finn. "He's clearly a Great Dane and a rare one at that. Aren't you, my handsome lad?"

Finn grinned and sighed. Gramma was the new love of his life. I rolled my eyes. "He was a rescue, Gramma," I explained. "They thought he was a mix, and he was eight to ten months old. They told me that he most likely would weigh fifty pounds."

"How could someone be so wrong about such an obvious thing?" Gramma asked, finally looking at me.

I shrugged. "They were dealing with a lot of pups at the time. I'm sure it was someone's best guess."

"Humph," she said, glancing at the cake and then back at me. "Okay, well the cake is all I need," she said before I could say hi to the three other ladies who sat at Gramma's table playing cards, no tea in sight. "You can go." She practically pushed me out. "But we'd love to keep Finn here to visit. You'll have to come back anyway to pick up your cake plate."

Finn was already stretched out on the floor in a patch of sun. As I was halfway out the door, I leaned in and waved at Gramma's best friend, Lela McCabe. They might be best friends, but Lela and Gramma Brid couldn't be more different. Gramma's hair was still light red, with the same white streaks as Aunt Sharon. She wore braids wrapped around her head. Today, she wore a sapphire blue shirt and slacks to accent her brown eyes. Meanwhile, Mrs. McCabe was small and delicate, with short silver hair and spring green eyes she played up with a jewel-toned purple A-line dress and matching purple tights. They made me feel like a slob in my old jeans coated in flour and powdered sugar and my dark blue T-shirt.

She waved back, then looked at her cards without so much as a hi or a hug.

"Um, okay," I said.

"Good, we'll call you when you can come pick up

Finn." With that, Gramma shoved me out and closed the door behind me. I heard laughter and Finn's woof. Confused, I went home to finish my conversation with my friends.

Three hours later I picked up Finn, who was filled with cookies and who knows what else. No wonder he was reluctant to leave. Gramma opened the door long enough to hand me the cake plate, then let Finn out with a scratch behind his ear. "Thanks, dear," she said, and turned her cheek for a kiss before closing the door in my face.

Something was definitely brewing, and I didn't think it was coffee.

The next morning, blurry-eyed from Chloe talking to her friend until 2 a.m., I got an early text from an unknown number.

Congratulations! We are pleased to inform you that you have been selected for an interview. Be at The Last Resort at Round Lake by noon. Bring your own baker's coat, hat, and equipment.

Whoever named the senior living place had a sick sense of humor. But people here in Charlevoix loved it. Just like they loved the mushroom houses, a collection of whimsical, fairy-tale-like structures that resembled hobbit homes, designed by local builder Earl Young in the 1920s. Not only did he design them, but after growing up fascinated by the boulders and rocks of Lake Michigan, he personally dredged out the stones used for the homes.

Shaking my head of my sleepy thoughts, I glanced at the clock. It was nearly nine. I stumbled downstairs to find Finn taking up most of the couch with his head in Oliver's lap as the kid watched an episode of a true crime show.

Aunt Kathryn and Aunt Sharon chatted at the breakfast table, but went silent the moment I entered. I grabbed a cup of coffee and added cream and sugar, then took a chair next to Aunt Sharon. "What are we talking about?"

"Did you get a text?" Aunt Kathryn asked.

"Yeah," I replied. They exchanged glances. "It looks like you already know about it," I said suspiciously.

"Gramma applied for you," Aunt Sharon said.

"It's a chance of a lifetime—well, here in Charlevoix," Aunt Kathryn said. "A gourmet pop-up supper club is starting up and they need a pastry chef. You're the perfect candidate. Now, why don't you take a shower, put on whatever clothes you bake in, and get ready to go."

"Okay," I said, my muddled brain barely catching on. "A supper club? Here?"

"Yes, and they need a pastry chef. You're perfect for the job. Now, go! You don't want to be late."

"It's only 9:30," I protested.

"It's better to be early than late," Aunt Sharon said, shooing me out of the kitchen with her hands.

"Mallory, get out of the cat food," Aunt Kathryn yelled at one of the little red-headed girls. I studied her. She was the one whose mother said she had my hair. And she did. Okay, Mallory. One name down. More yet to figure out.

Whatever the family was up to, it couldn't be that bad. At least I could wear my chef's coat and hat, not my Meijer's uniform and hairnet. Sensing I might be going somewhere fun, Finn jumped up and went with me, which was fine. The interview, or whatever, was at Gramma's place. When we went in, I let Finn go while I headed to the kitchen. I knew where he'd go. All doggies remember where the treats are. I figured he'd scratch at Gramma's door, and she'd let him in.

I stopped short in the kitchen, my gaze taking it all in as a shock of adrenaline went through me. Three other women in their coats and hats were already there and talking with the chef. I took a quick glance at my phone and was confused. I was ten minutes early.

"Put your hat on before you come into my kitchen," barked the chef. I yanked on my hat and then put on my coat. The master of the kitchen was a tall, nice-looking guy with light brown skin, piercing pale green eyes, and brown hair that held streaks of gold in it. He also looked very mad. "You're late."

"I'm ten minutes early," I said.

"You're fifteen minutes late," he stated.

"The text said—"

"Did anyone else have an issue with showing up on time?" he asked, keeping his gaze on me.

"No, Chef," they all said in unison.

That's when I saw the bleached blond hair under her cap, the blue gaze, and the smirk on Angelica Carlyle's face. I knew instantly what had happened. I don't know how she did it, but my old enemy had switched the time on my interview text. I narrowed my eyes at her. Oh, I'd get her back.

Angelica Carlyle was the one person I had hoped I'd never see again. The woman was a monster. Seriously. My brother Mike—who's my twin for three weeks each year because I was born before his first birthday—had been in love with her. They dated for three years, and the family knew she was trouble. We all knew there was no use telling Mike that or he'd do something he'd regret later, like marry her.

The summer before I left for New York, Mike asked Angelica to marry him. She laughed. Literally laughed at him as if he were incredibly stupid. She proceeded to tell him that his diamond engagement ring was pathetic, and she would never marry a lowly accountant. Then she twisted the dagger she'd put through his heart. She told him that she was only dating him because she was bored. She'd found someone new nearly a year before but still dated Mike for the sake of entertainment. Then she walked off.

The next day, I was helping my brother Devon with his boat when I saw her stroll off a yacht, giggling up at an older man. Seeing red, I stormed up to them and planted my fist right into her so-called pretty little nose. It felt good to see her eyes filled with shock and pain and her nose gushing red.

"That's for Mike," I said. Then I looked straight at her date. "Be careful with this one. She likes to play with men's hearts." I walked off.

"You shouldn't have done that," Devon said when I got back to his boat. "But I'm glad you did."

"She deserved it," I replied. Then we went about our work, ignoring the crying and carrying on down the dock. A quick glance told me the gentleman had his hand on her elbow leading her, but his expression was grim. He nodded to me as they went by, and I nodded back.

I guess that was the end of her fun with the older guy. She tried to press charges against me, but all her witnesses claimed not to have seen a thing. My cousin George, the officer in charge that day, told her that with no proof, she didn't have a case. Being related to half the people in town could sometimes be a blessing.

When I went off to New York culinary school, she told anyone who would listen that I'd never finish and would come back with my tail between my legs.

When I didn't, she decided to go to the Chicago culinary school. I have no idea why and frankly didn't care, no matter how many congratulatory ads her father put in the local paper.

My cousins said she was working for a buffet-style restaurant in Grand Rapids, a prospect that I have to admit made me very happy. But as soon as the bakery closed, and I came home to Charlevoix, she was back, too. She stopped by the Meijer's baking section at least once a day to gloat. I would simply grin and ask her if she wanted to finish this outside. She would put her nose up in the air and tell anyone who listened that I should have been charged with assault and battery. But she never met me outside.

I grew up with brothers. She didn't.

The other two contestants were Sara Morrison,

who worked with me at Meijer, and Lillian Fulton, who worked part-time at Stanek's Bakery.

"Are you paying attention?" Chef demanded.

"Yes, Chef," I replied.

"For those of you who are late." He glared at me, "I'm Chef Jeremy Brant. I studied at Le Cordon Bleu. I'm hiring a part-time to possibly full-time pastry chef for my supper club business. We will be a farm-to-table operation featuring fruits and vegetables in season that will be prepared to perfection. Am I making myself clear?"

"Yes, Chef," we all said together.

He gave us a short tour of the senior living facility's main kitchen. It had stainless steel everywhere and smelled a bit like a school cafeteria. The prep area was one long island with pots, pans, and other cookware and bakeware on shelves underneath. The mixers, food processors, and other necessary equipment sat on shelves hung on the wall.

Food racks covered a wall-to-wall, open-shelved pantry. One side wall contained an industrial dishwasher and a large stainless-steel sink with a vegetable side sink and a pot faucet. Behind the prep table were two double ovens and two refrigerators. Gleaming white tiles covered the floor. I was glad I wore my no-mark tennis shoes.

"You will be stationed side by side," Chef Jeremy said. "Carlyle on this end, Morrison beside her, then Fulton, and last, Ms. Late. Here are the rules: Each one in turn chooses what they need from the pantry to make their best dessert. The supplies are limited, so choose carefully. Once the first chef returns to their station with her ingredients, the clock starts. You'll have an hour and a half to make your desserts. Carlyle, you're up first." He pulled a stopwatch out of his pocket and said, "Go!"

Thanks to Angelica, I was going to go last and be stuck with whatever ingredients were left. I'd have less time to work in. What she didn't know was that I came from a big family and I never knew what was in the pantry. Dessert was always catered around that. Timing was something I learned over and over again in school.

"Morrison, go!"

Angelica came back with a very full basket, laughing at me. I merely grinned back. Uncertainty flashed in her eyes.

"Fulton, go!"

Finally, it was my turn. The only items left on the shelf were a small pumpkin and a bar of baking chocolate. Angelica coughed "Good luck" into her palm. I grabbed both ingredients, knowing immediately what I was going to do. Thank goodness the chocolate bar was one of the best varieties. A glance at the clock told me I had just over an hour. I decided on a pumpkin chocolate mousse, which didn't need dairy or eggs.

Working quickly, I peeled and chopped the pumpkin, then steamed it in the microwave until it was very tender. Meanwhile, I melted the chocolate until smooth.

Forty minutes left.

I placed both the pumpkin and the chocolate into a food processor and blitzed them until the concoction was smooth. Then, I poured it into eight white ramekins and chilled them in the freezer. Normally I would use the refrigerator, but there wasn't enough time for my creations to set and be plated. The hard part was to keep an eye on them, so that they'd set quickly but not freeze. I roasted the pumpkin seeds in the oven, then added some coarse salt that I found on the counter.

"Ten minutes left," Chef called. I melted the remaining chocolate and decorated dessert plates with chocolate scrolls and put them in the refrigerator to harden. The mousse was set and ready with six minutes to go.

"I've been done for five minutes now," Angelica said as she walked by to see what I was doing.

Nothing bothered me. I'd heard worse at school. Blocking her out, I pulled the plates and ramekins filled with mousse out of the fridge. I finished each dish with wavy chocolate piping on top and roasted pumpkin seeds in a small fan shape on the side.

"Time's up!"

We all put our hands up. I looked down the line. Angelica had made individual Black Forest trifles, with chocolate cake, chocolate pudding, cherry jam, and whipped cream, layered in wine glasses. Nice, considering she had her choice of ingredients and the longest amount of time.

Sara Morrison made gingerbread with a lemon sauce, and Lillian Fulton made apple crisp. Each dish contained fewer ingredients and was simpler to prepare as they went down the line until they got to mine. The simplest of all. Chef stopped in front of each baker and asked why she made what she made. When he stopped at me, he raised an eyebrow.

"Two ingredients?"

"Yes, Chef," I said. Holding back a *duh*. "This pumpkin chocolate mousse combines everyone's favorite, chocolate, with fresh, in-season pumpkin."

He forked up a bite, picked up a pumpkin seed, and tasted it. Without changing his expression, he turned away. "You've all done a nice job," he said.

Nice usually meant okay. I sighed.

"It's clear each of you did your best considering the challenge, but two stood out. Morrison and Fulton, I'm sorry, but you haven't made it to the final round."

After the other two packed up and left, Chef turned to Angelica and me. "I want to see your best elevated work. Twenty servings of something with fresh ingredients that will go with a main course of duck. Time is important in a kitchen. So, you have an hour."

I worked quickly and made twenty citrus cranberry hand pies filled with frozen cranberries due to time constraints, orange segments, and lemon zest. Then, I topped them with almond glaze and adorned them with dark chocolate shavings and a small edible flower. If he were any kind of chef, he'd know that the sweet-and-sour taste would pair nicely with duck.

Angelica presented a Pavlova éclair filled with sweet pastry crème with the sweet taste of candied apples, red currant, and a hint of ginger. The dessert was adorned with ivory white chocolate frosting, meringue pieces, and strawberry chocolate, all sprinkled with cocoa.

Too sweet for a duck meal, but whatever.

He tasted both, barely taking a forkful of mine. "I'm sorry, Chef Giles, but the job goes to Chef Carlyle."

"What?"

"Good luck in your future endeavors," he said.

His decision didn't make any sense. But I clamped my mouth shut. After they left the room, I shook my head, then cleaned up my space. Whatever. I didn't want the job until I saw Angelica here. I wanted to show her up. But it didn't happen. That was that. If he thought her desserts were better, then he was an idiot and would drive me crazy if we worked together.

I took four steps out of the kitchen when I heard them fighting. Who fights right after getting a job? Usually that was the grace period when you're both happy with your choice.

I walked toward the sound and found it was coming from inside a visiting room. Mrs. VanCan and Mrs. Filipek were on the opposite side of the closed door, listening. Mrs. VanCan put her fingers to her lips, and I nodded. The fight sounded pretty contentious. It seemed Chef Jeremy and Angelica were arguing about who had control of the dessert menus—a job that was always set by the chef. If properly paired, the dessert was a cherry on top of an excellent meal. Then, Angelica said something interesting.

"We both know there was no need for today's contest. I had you do it just so I could see the look on Rowan Giles's face. Now that it's official and the job's mine, you will make whatever menu I set. Or I'll have to tell that little secret of yours, won't I?"

"You know what?" he said. "If you want to spill that secret, tell it. I don't care anymore. You're not going to mess with my business. I swear if you do—"

"Is that a threat?" Angelica laughed. "Honey, nobody threatens me. I know too much."

The ladies and I looked at each other, our eyebrows raised.

When we heard footsteps coming toward the door, I hurried away. I figured Gramma would tell me anything I missed. Right now, I had to leave before Jeremy and Angelica found me in this hallway.

I walked down to Gramma's suite to get Finn, tell her what happened, and scold her to never do that again.

"It was for your own good," Gramma said. Finn got up, did a big stretch, and stood with me next to Gramma, who held her door. "You need a job that suits you better," she said. "An opportunity like this doesn't come up often in Charlevoix. At the very least I thought it would help to keep your skills sharp." She gave me a kiss. "Next time you come, you'll have to stay and tell me how you are. You haven't done that yet, young lady, and you know how lonely this old woman can be when her grandchildren don't come to visit."

"Gramma," I said with a shake of my head. "We both know you're not lonely. You have friends over nearly every time I visit." I leaned into the doorway. "Hi, Mrs. McCabe." I waved.

"Hi, dear." She waved back.

"Besides, Aunt Kathryn and Aunt Sharon tell you everything." She couldn't deny that.

"I don't care, I want to hear it from you, after you quit being upset with me."

"I'm not upset with you," I said. The older women in my family had guilt down pat. "It's simply my last day off and I have a date with a good book. See ya, Gramma." I kissed her cheek. "Come on, Finn, let's go home."

I headed out as quickly as possible, figuring I'd take the complex's patio door so I wouldn't have to go by the kitchen. The last thing I wanted was to have to walk by Angelica and Jeremy.

But I ran into Jeremy anyway. I stepped outside as he was coming in. He held a handful of fresh herbs.

"Nice try on the dessert," he said to me glibly.

"Yeah, well, it was clear you wanted Angelica from the first."

"I judged everyone fairly, Chef Giles."

"Really? How unimaginative is sweet fruit crème filling? And you barely touched my pie," I retorted. "Do you truly believe she could have done anything with a pumpkin and some chocolate? You don't have to answer that. I think we both know what would have happened. It's okay, though. I understand. With my schooling and experience, I'm overqualified for the job. I wish you and Angelica—excuse me, Chef Carlyle—a lot of luck. Come on, Finn." My dog sniffed Jeremy's feet, then hurried to my side as I walked around him to the sun patio. A walkway led to a garden of roses, chrysanthemums, and other fall flowers, as well as vegetables and fresh herbs. At the very end of it was a gate that opened to the street and my way home.

Jeremy turned on his heel. I could feel the need to

explain himself rolling off him. “Face it, her éclairs were more elevated than your pies.”

“More like her backside is more elevated than mine,” I said as I headed off the porch. Finn moved away from my side, but I didn’t pay attention. I was still boiling at the injustice that was Angelica Carlyle. “Why do men fall for her?” I muttered “It doesn’t matter. You’ll learn, like my brother did.”

“What was that?”

“I said, it’s more like her backside is more elevated than mine.” I reached the end of the patio and started down the sidewalk. “I know you noticed. All men do.”

“That is not what—”

I was so busy arguing with a man I had known only a couple hours that I didn’t see Finn and tripped over his tail. Fortunately, Jeremy caught me before I went face-first onto the pavement. “Finn, what in the world—”

That was when we both saw Angelica lying in the rose bushes.

“What?” he said, and shook his head as if trying to clear it.

I pushed myself out of his arms and wound my way through the bushes as they scratched me and my jeans. As much as I didn’t like her, I couldn’t leave her if she needed help, even though I knew she’d leave me in a heartbeat. “Angelica?” I asked. “Are you okay?”

She didn’t answer. She couldn’t answer. She lay staring up at the sky with empty eyes and a chef’s knife in her chest.

I knew she was dead.